LUCKY
No Prisoners MC Book 4

by Lilly Atlas

For everyone who is looking for a little luck.

After six months caring for her terminally ill mother, Kori is shocked to learn the identity of her father. Armed with the name of a man she's never met, Kori sets off across the country to meet the person responsible for half of her DNA: the President of the No Prisoners Las Vegas motorcycle club.

Raised as the stepdaughter of an MC member, Kori has one rule when it comes to dating: no bikers. Following that rule becomes a challenge, however, when she meets Lucky, a member of her father's club.

Lucky's perspective on the dating world is don't do it. He has a revolving door to his bedroom and no interest in a relationship. But what starts as harmless flirting quickly escalates until he can't get Kori out of his mind.

For a time, the relationship seems perfect, but Lucky is struggling with a secret that could destroy the club. How can he move against club leadership knowing that Kori will be caught in the crossfire?

LUCKY
No Prisoners MC Book 4

PROLOGUE

Las Vegas, November 2015

Three-fifty-seven a.m. Pretty fucking early. Why the hell he was awake, he had no clue. Maybe his female companion had inadvertently woken him when she crawled her sweet ass out of the bed and slunk into the night.

Lucky's head was a bit groggy, but the intoxication seemed to have worked its way out of his system. A quick cup of the sludge his MC brothers called coffee and he'd be good to ride home where he could actually get some comfortable sleep. This damn bed was like sleeping on a pile of rocks, and sharp nails.

Now where the hell had his cut landed?

He found it dangling from the foot of the bed. Once dressed, he made his way down the dark hallway toward the main area of the clubhouse. The building was a seven thousand square foot single story old shoe factory that had been converted for their needs years ago. The front of the building served as the heart of the clubhouse. The space was wide open, with a massive bar, pool table, dart boards, and a number of plush, albeit questionably sanitary, couches. That's where they partied, hung out, and generally caused a ruckus.

A long hallway led to the back of the building where offices and spare rooms were located as well as the giant meeting room,

1

or chapel, where the club conducted its business. Lucky loved his second home, even if sleeping there was a less than restful experience.

He trod as quietly as his booted feet would allow so as not to wake anyone else who'd spent the night. As he neared the bar, loud, angry voices broke the silence of the early morning.

"How did this happen? Tell me how the fuck this happened!" Rebel's smoke-roughened yell made Lucky wince. Their Vegas chapter president was not someone to piss off. Those who got on his bad side often found themselves missing a tooth or two. Just last year when their club brothers from Crystal Rock, Arizona were in town, Rebel had rearranged some punk's face for having the nerve to step on his foot and not apologize in a crowded bar.

"I don't know, Pres. Casper called me just five minutes ago. First thing I did was come to you." Savage sounded just as agitated as Rebel. Another man you didn't want to put a target on your ass. Like Lucky, he lived up to his nickname with gusto.

Lucky halted, unsure if he'd be welcome at this moment. If it seemed like they could use his help, he'd be more than happy to jump in, but something felt off about the situation. The small hairs on the back of his neck rose to attention. An issue requiring attention at four a.m. on a Saturday could only mean trouble.

Casper. Why did that name sound so familiar?

"Tell me exactly what Casper said. Word for fuckin' word. And give me a fuckin' cigarette. I left mine in my room."

Silence descended and Lucky pictured Rebel lighting up and sucking in that first soothing drag. In eight years, there had perhaps been three times he'd seen Rebel without a cigarette between his fingers and smoke billowing from his mouth. His leathery face and raspy voice bore the marks of a man who loved his smokes.

"Spit it the fuck out, Savage." Rebel sounded close to losing his cool. Surprising for a man who ruthlessly commanded respect and never seemed at a loss. Shit must be bad.

Lucky

"Casper said they're having ongoing issues with their supply from the cartel. Trust has been a problem since the Crystal Rock chapter ambushed them. Stealing the mil meant for the cartel pissed the Grimm Brothers off, big time. They liked working with Snake but hate Casper's guts."

Lucky remembered now. Grimm Brothers MC. Casper was the VP and Snake had been the president for a while. Nasty motherfuckers who caused serious trouble for two of his brothers, Striker and Jester. Snake kidnapped Striker's woman and blackmailed Jester's ol' lady with threats of killing her only brother. The Grimm Brothers were the sworn enemy of the No Prisoners Crystal Rock chapter.

"Shit." Rebel's curse was followed by a loud boom that had Lucky jolting. He tiptoed a few steps further into the hallway. He should leave. Spying on the President wasn't a smart idea, but now he itched to know the rest of the story.

"Did they get this month's shipment? Thirty percent of that product had our name on it," Rebel asked.

Wait. What? Lucky's blood ran cold. His club steered far away from the drug trade.

"Most of it. The cartel held some of it back as punishment for Casper's bad attitude." Savage paused and without actually looking at him, Lucky could imagine his cold eyes turn deadly. "Said they have no problem finding new buyers so Casper needs to get his ass in line."

Rebel let out a harsh laugh followed by a barking cough. "That scrawny asshole knows how much I depend on the cash from our heroin sales. He better get his shit together or the cartel will be the least of his worries."

Lucky swore his heart stopped beating for a few seconds, just before it kicked up into a fast gallop. Rebel and Savage were selling drugs. Who else knew? Who else was involved? How long had this been going on?

Nausea rolled through his gut like a violent storm. His sister had died of an overdose when she was just seventeen. One of the reasons he'd chosen this specific MC when looking to prospect was the fact that they were fierce in their stance against involvement in the drug trade. Too risky and too much collateral damage. Or so he'd believed.

"Maybe we should consider cutting out the middle man. Deal with the cartel ourselves." Rebel coughed. The man's lungs had to be blacker than tar.

"Not a bad idea, Pres. Things ain't the same since Jester beat Snake near to death. You think Casper finished the job? You know that greedy asshole was just biding his time until he could claw his way to the top and no one's heard from Snake in the months since."

"I need a drink. What a fuckin' mess." Rebel sighed, then the sound of liquid being poured reached Lucky's ears.

Well, now he sure as hell couldn't step out into the bar area. With the stealth of a ninja, Lucky crept back toward the room he'd crashed in. This was far too much information to process at four in the morning after a night of heavy drinking. His thoughts bubbled and swirled like molten lava in a volcano near eruption.

Now he got to choose between two shitty options.

Turn a blind eye and keep his trap closed.

Or run with what he overheard to someone who could help. Take it to the Crystal Rock chapter. Tell them his president and vice president were in direct violation of the club's strict no drugs bylaw. Be a rat.

And in the MC world, there was nothing dirtier than a rat.

CHAPTER ONE

Florida, December 2015

The cough would haunt Kori's dreams for years to come. A deep, harsh hacking followed by gasping breaths and moans of agony, only to circle back around to the full-body hacking again.

She rested her forehead on the wall outside the bedroom-turned-hospital suite in her mother's modest home and tried to block out the sound. She needed to get in there. To assist her debilitated mother to a sitting position and help her clear her lungs to whatever extent possible.

But Kori was tired. Her body was weary and her spirit was beaten down. The end was near. Or so said the oncologist. Even with a home BiPAP machine forcing oxygen into her mom's failing lungs, they couldn't keep her oxygen saturation at an acceptable level. Extreme weakness kept her in bed almost twenty-four hours a day. It was a vicious cycle.

The physician, who seemed accustomed to sharing bad news, informed Kori it wouldn't actually be cancer that killed her mom. She'd succumb to one of three things: a blood clot in her lung, an infected bed sore, or most likely, pneumonia. For the last three weeks, Kori had taken leave from work to be at her mother's constant beck and call.

No surprise that her mom's husband was nowhere to be found. As far back as Kori could remember, her mom had a thing for bikers. She'd been married to this particular MC member going on fifteen years. Fucking good-for-nothing bikers.

And fucking cigarettes. How many times through the years had she begged and pleaded with her mother to give up the habit? Far too many to count. Far too many wasted words.

Forty-seven was too young for Barb to have her lungs ravaged by the deadly disease.

With a deep sigh, Kori pushed off the wall and entered the room. Her mother lay curled on her side in the hospital bed, her body atrophied and so much smaller than it had been just six months ago. This illness came on fast and furious.

Well, maybe that wasn't entirely true. Her mom had ignored the worsening cough for years. Denial was one nasty bitch.

"Let's sit you up, Mom." Lifting her mother to a sitting position was as easy as picking up a child. Barb braced her hands on the bed behind her and Kori lessened her hold, but her mom's arms just weren't strong enough to stabilize herself and she almost collapsed backward. "Shh, it's okay, Mom. Try to relax. You know how panicking only makes it harder to breathe." She had to speak loudly to be heard over the hiss of oxygen.

After a few moments of rubbing her mom's back and uttering words of encouragement, the coughing fit passed and Barb sagged in Kori's arms, all her energy spent. It would take her hours to recover from that two-minute episode.

Kori positioned her mother on the bed so she was as comfortable as possible and adjusted the tubing so it was mostly out of the way. She took a quick peek at her mom's fingernails. A bluish tinge marked the nail beds. Her breathing sounded worse today as well. Something she hadn't thought possible yesterday.

"Mom?" When Barb's tired eyes opened, Kori sent her a smile. "I think it would be wise to get you to the hospital. Dr. Griffin is concerned about your high risk for pneumonia and by the way you sound today, I'm concerned as well. I can call an ambulance and have you there in less than thirty minutes."

Her mother shook her head. "No, baby girl," she rasped out. The oxygen mask muffled her words and she shoved it up far enough that her mouth was free. Her eyes fluttered closed. The rise and fall of her chest was rapid and deep, as though she was struggling for air. "What would be the point? Prolong my life by a few days? Not interested."

Yes! Kori swallowed the retort. That was exactly the reason to go to the hospital. She wasn't ready to lose her mom yet. Wasn't ready to lose the one person in the world who loved her.

"Mom, please." The plea had been whispered but somehow her mom heard her above the hissing of the oxygen. They'd been through this before. Barb was sick and tired of the hospital. She wanted—no, demanded—to be allowed to die at home. Kori wanted to respect her mother's wishes but was terrified by the prospect at the same time.

"Sit back down, baby girl. I need to tell you something important before…well, before I go." She patted the edge of the bed with her thin fingertips, the energy to lift her entire hand just not there.

Kori sat as gently as possible and grasped Barb's bony hand. "I'd rather you conserve your strength and rest. Put your mask back on."

"Shush, you. I might be dying, but I'm still your mother." The order was issued sharply and Kori chuckled. Leave it to Barb to be so weak she couldn't sit up but still find the ability to scold.

"Yes, ma'am."

Barb snorted. "Now this is serious, baby girl. I want to tell you about your father."

Kori's throat constricted and her tongue felt too big for her mouth. For a heartbeat, she considered swiping her mother's oxygen for her own use. Surely not enough air was getting to her brain. It was the only explanation for the auditory hallucination. Either that or months of sleepless nights spent caring for her terminally ill mother had made her mind fracture.

Never once in her twenty-seven years had Kori's mom uttered a single word about the man who fathered her. Kori had only asked once when she was about ten. The topic was shut down quickly and left Kori with the impression she should not bring it up again.

"Kori? Are you listening to me?"

"What?" She blinked and refocused on Barb's frail form. "Sorry. Yes, sorry. I was just—did you say my father?"

Barb nodded and inhaled on a whistling wheeze. "Yes, baby girl. He'll be all that's left of your blood soon. I'm not saying you need to go meet him. It's just…he's the only blood you'll have."

Her chest ached at the morose words. They were true. Denying the inevitable was no longer possible, but it still hurt like hell to hear her mom talk about dying. Kori didn't have any other family. "Why now? Why not ever before?"

Barb shrugged. "I was scared, baby girl."

"Scared? Of what? Is he dangerous?" She knew nothing of her mom's life back then. Barb steered away from talking about the past like one stayed away from a live wire resting in a puddle.

Her mom blew out a breath and gave a feeble shrug. "No more dangerous than the rest of them. But I was so young and alone. On the other side of the country. He was…well, he would have wanted me to stay there with you and I just couldn't. I needed to be near my parents, familiarity. So I left him and never said a word. I was always worried he'd find you and want to take you away from me." Her mother's voice was sad, full of memories Kori would never know.

"He's a biker?"

Barb nodded.

No surprise there. Barb definitely had a type. Kori swallowed around a painful lump in her throat. Countless questions swirled in her head. More than she could process at the moment. "Did you love him?"

Coughing trumped the deafening silence that followed her question. It felt like an hour before Barb settled enough to draw in sufficient air to speak again. "I suppose I loved him at the time. A youthful, wide-eyed, in-over-my-head kind of love."

Suddenly, it was all too much. The impending death of her mother. The newfound knowledge of a father she assumed she'd never discover any information about. She rose from the bed, panic clawing at her throat.

"When you're ready, there's a box at the bottom of my closet with a picture of your father and contact information from when I knew him. If you ever decide to locate him, that's a good place to start."

Jesus, she couldn't handle this right now. The room spun and sweat broke out across her brow. More bikers. Cigarettes and bikers. Barb's two damned weaknesses. Kori knew enough bikers to last a lifetime. The walls started to close in on her. "I need some air. I'll be back in ten minutes." She whirled and darted toward the door.

"Kori?"

Two steps from the door she froze but didn't turn.

"I'm sorry."

"It's okay, Mom. I understand." She didn't really, but there was a good chance they wouldn't have the time to make up if they fought. Kori would never be able to live with herself if she lost her mother while she was irritated with her. For now, she'd keep the peace and shove her muddled feelings aside. Later, when life wasn't so chaotic, she'd find a way to process everything and deal with her emotions. "I'm glad you told me."

A wave of fatigue crashed over Kori, so great it almost knocked her down. A few solid hours of sleep would help with that problem, but that was hard to come by. Barb slept in fits, waking Kori every few hours.

After pacing the living room for ten minutes, Kori returned to her mother's room and checked the oxygen compressor as had become habit. Barb was fast asleep, so Kori curled up on the recliner next to her mother's bed. For the past few weeks, she'd spent the majority of her days in that chair.

The next morning, Kori cracked her eyes open and winced when sunlight accosted them. The night had been surprisingly calm; Barb only woke three times needing assistance to clear her lungs.

Kori scrubbed a hand over her face and dropped the foot plate of the recliner. Barb would be up soon and she liked a cup of coffee as soon as she awoke. Kori tried to provide her with whatever small pleasures she could in her last days.

She rose from the chair and glanced down at the hospital bed. The second she laid eyes on her mother's still form, she knew. It was a feeling. An emptiness. A lack of spirit.

It was over.

"Oh, Mom." She sank down on the bed and grasped her mother's cold, limp hand as tears streamed down her face. Barb looked peaceful. Finally sheltered from the pain. Thank God it happened in her sleep instead of in a terrifying fit of coughing and suffocation. Barb dying with knowledge and fear in her eyes while she failed to draw in air had been Kori's biggest fear the past week or so. Tearing her eyes from her mother's face, she looked at the closet.

In the last minute, her entire world had flipped on its axis. Her mother's passing hadn't even registered, and yet, behind that closet door was another powerful shock to her system.

Should she look? Did she even want to look?

She sniffed and wiped tears from her damp cheeks. With a trembling hand, she grabbed the phone from its cradle and dialed the number of the previously chosen funeral home.

One life-altering crisis at a time.

CHAPTER TWO

Lucky stared at his reflection, the typical snarky light absent from his dark eyes. Where once a playful grin could be found on his face at all times, his mouth was flat, his expression dull. His hair was too shaggy, his beard too scruffy, as though he lacked the energy to care for himself.

Disgusted, Lucky turned away from the mirror and rested his ass against the sink. For the past two weeks, he'd wrestled with a decision so great it was bleeding into every aspect of his life. No longer did he find joy and fulfillment in the club that had been the entirety of his existence for almost nine years. Now, he looked at every brother and wondered if they were involved in Rebel's drug dealing venture.

The best and only option was to take what he knew to Crystal Rock. Shiv and Striker would be outraged at Rebel's blatant disregard for the club's bylaws. They'd take care of the problem and it would be out of Lucky's hands. But something held him back. He owed so much to this club. They were his family. They'd taken him in at a low point in his life, just months after his baby sister overdosed. He'd been an angry, revengeful shadow of a man hell-bent on vengeance.

Rebel had given him that chance for revenge, and the man who hooked his sister on heroin not only didn't sell drugs anymore, he didn't walk, or eat, or breathe. Thanks to this club.

And now, every day that passed was one more day Lucky allowed Rebel to engage in behavior that could harm some other young and far too trusting girl. It sickened him.

Over the past weeks, he'd collected enough evidence to present to the Crystal Rock chapter and prove Rebel and Savage's guilt without question. He wouldn't chance ruining the men's lives unless he was sure what they were up to. His president and VP were neck deep in the drug trade and raking in the dough. What he hadn't been successful in discovering was exactly how many others were involved in their dealings.

He spun, faced the mirror once again, and grabbed his razor. Time to make this asshole look more like who he was. When he'd trimmed the beard to his customary goatee, he turned on the shower and brushed his teeth while the water warmed. With one last look at the now presentable reflection in the mirror, he stepped under the spray. Warm water rained down on him, easing some of the tension from his shoulders.

His mind drifted back to what he'd been thinking of seconds ago. What he'd been thinking about nearly every moment of every day for the past two weeks. It was time. Time to take this to Crystal Rock. While a large part of him felt like a dirty rat, another part of him knew it was the right thing, and a small weight lifted from his shoulders. Informing Shiv and Striker was what was expected of him. What he owed the rest of his brothers. He wasn't the one who'd fucked over the club.

But he sure felt like the one paying for it.

If her damned hands would stop shaking, Kori could actually read the number on the scrap of paper she held and verify the address. Not that she needed to. The eight or so bikes lined up outside a giant building was enough of a clue. But if she couldn't double check the address then she was completely out of stall tactics and had no choice but to make her way inside.

She'd spent the past week and a half going back and forth on her decision to seek out her father so many times she no longer knew up from down. Did she want to meet him? Probably not, but she had to. She had too many questions, too much curiosity, too much loneliness now that her mom was gone.

A longing to connect with family had bloomed in her chest in the past week. It was time to meet the man who fathered her. Even if he was another biker.

Unlike her mom, she wasn't impressed, turned on, or even intrigued by bikers. Much of her life had been spent in their presence since her mom was a biker's ol' lady, but luckily the man had never taken much interest in Kori. Once she reached her adult years she separated herself from that part of her mother's life as much as possible. They were too rowdy, too disrespectful, too controlling for her taste.

It was something she'd never understood in her mother. The draw, the attraction to the MC lifestyle. But then Barb had been as tightlipped about her childhood as she'd been about Kori's father. Somehow her mom equated being an ol' lady to respect and value.

Kori took three steps forward then spun back and returned to her car. One more minute, then she'd walk the thirty feet from her parking spot to the clubhouse. After repeating the action two more times she chuckled to herself. Since when was she such a chicken?

"All right lady, you're making me dizzy. You gonna get that sweet ass in here or what?"

She locked eyes with a grinning man in a leather cut standing about twenty feet away. Well, *man* may have been too loose a term. The guy looked like he couldn't be more than twenty. His cut had a patch that said *prospect* over his heart. Made sense given his apparent age.

"Um, yes." She cleared her throat, pissed at the timid quality of her voice. Weakness wasn't what she wanted to portray. "Yes, I'm coming." She hurried through the parking lot toward the kid. "I need to speak with Mar—uh, Rebel." The nickname would probably yield more results than her father's given name, Mark.

"What do ya need him for?" The prospect eyed her with skepticism and blocked her path to the door.

"It's personal," she said.

He cocked his head and scratched his chin. "You knocked up, honey?"

"What?" The question threw her back a few steps.

"You knocked up? Looking to pin it on Rebel? Cuz I'd bet he always wraps it and know he won't take responsibility your fuck up."

Lovely, just lovely. Fucking bikers. "No, prospect. I'm not pregnant and the reason I'm here to see Rebel is none of your damn business." Her hands landed on her hips. She may not like bikers, but she knew them, knew how they played and knew enough to keep her head above water. They respected strength but weren't usually thrilled when a woman was the one to show it. Maybe a softer approach. She dropped the aggressive pose. "Will you please take me to him?"

The prospect's expression iced over, but then he shrugged and motioned for her to follow him through the door. Probably realized he didn't care enough to pursue it further.

Hurdle one jumped.

She trailed after him through the entrance and into the clubhouse. The moment the door slammed behind her, an odd sense of relaxation and familiarity settled over her. It wasn't necessarily a welcome feeling, although the reduction in anxiety sure was. The place looked similar to the MC clubhouse in Florida. With a large bar, pool table, and bikers hanging around, along with a number of women wearing much less clothing than she was.

The feeling shouldn't have thrown her so much. Of course the surroundings felt familiar. They *were* familiar. Like it or not, the world of bikers was her world, at least on the periphery.

"Hey," the prospect called to no one in particular. "Pres around?"

Pres? Her father was the president? Now things were getting a bit out of her league.

"Office," someone answered. "Who's the dame?"

Her eyes darted around trying to assess which man the voice rose from. No luck.

The prospect shrugged. "Beats me, Savage. She asked to talk to Pres."

Finally, she located the mysterious voice. A man stood with his back to the bar, one hand holding a drink and his opposite arm around the shoulders of a woman wearing the shortest shorts Kori had ever seen. She was running one very long-nailed hand up and down his muscular chest while smirking in Kori's direction.

Her focus left the woman and moved to the guy's face. Ruthless was the first thought that came to mind. It didn't really make sense. It was not as though the word was tattooed across his head, but his eyes were sharp, cold, and his jaw was set in a don't-fuck-with-me manner. Something, some invisible force made her turn away. Maybe it was plain and simple self-preservation, but the little voice in her head warned her she didn't want to draw his attention.

"This way." With a wave, the prospect indicated for her to follow him down a dim hallway. "Wait here," he said as he knocked on a heavy wooden door.

"Come on in." The raspiest voice Kori had ever heard sounded from behind the closed door.

"Don't move." The prospect disappeared behind the door and Kori was left alone.

She blew out a breath. Her father sat just feet away. The father she hadn't known existed until just over one week ago. Shit. She so wasn't ready for this. What the hell had she been thinking coming here? Did she expect to walk into that room and feel a sudden and instant loving connection to a man who, as of now, didn't have a clue in the world she existed?

No. This was beyond a terrible idea. "I have to get out of here," she whispered as she turned and started down the hallway. She froze in her tracks as the door opened and the prospect called out behind her.

"He'll see you, lady. But I warn you, you better not be here to pull any shit on him. He's not one to fuck with."

Her heartrate accelerated and the legs that had carried her from the car seemed to quit wanting to walk.

"Lady? He ain't got all day. Get movin'." He pushed past her and ambled down the hallway toward the main area.

Right. Move.

After a cleansing breath, she spun. The four steps to the door seemed to happen in slow motion. She watched her hand reach out and twist the door knob as though it weren't attached to her body, wasn't commanded by her mind.

There was no turning back now. Time to cinch up the big girl pants and meet her father.

With one last breath, she pushed the door open and stepped into a giant cloud of smoke. Ever since her mom's lung cancer diagnosis, Kori's had an almost violent reaction to the smell of smoke. Her stomach heaved and she waved a hand in front of her face in a vain attempt to clear a section of air and make it safe for breathing.

When her eyes adjusted to the haze, her gaze landed on the man seated in an old, beat-up leather chair behind a desk.

Her world tilted on its axis for the third time in just a week and a half.

CHAPTER THREE

The door snapped closed and Kori jumped. She was so on edge it might as well have been a cannon's roar.

"Is this some sick fucking joke?" Kori's father rose from his chair, his eyes wide and mouth hanging open.

So he noticed it too. Noticed how their eyes were the exact same shape, exact same shade of brown. And how their noses had a tiny bump in the exact same spot. Well, if Kori had any doubts as to whether Rebel was actually her father, this face-to-face blew them out of the water.

"You look…"

"I look just like you." Well except for the craggy leathery face, a multitude of tattoos, and bald head. At one point, he had probably been attractive, with muscles and a fierce bad boy look, but now, his bulk had atrophied in an over-the-hill kind of way.

"Who the fuck are you?"

Frozen legs hadn't allowed her to move from her spot in the smoke-filled office. She cleared her throat. "I'm, uh, I'm sorry to just show up here like this, but I wasn't really sure a phone call would have been sufficient. The past week has been so crazy, and I finally decided two days ago that this was a good idea. So, I booked the first flight I could."

"You gonna get to the point sometime this year?" He stabbed out the stub of his cigarette, then drew another from the pack and stuffed it between his lips. His tall, aging body still hovered over the desk.

The urge to smack the cancer stick from his face was overwhelming, but she moved to a worn chair on her side of the desk and plopped down instead. "Sorry, I'm rambling. I'm quite nervous." She chuckled and blew out a breath. "Okay, here goes. My mother is, uh was, Barbara Morrison."

Memories flickered in his deep brown eyes. Good? Bad? She couldn't discern.

"She passed away about ten days ago and…and, well, she told me you were my father." *There you go. Rip off the Band-Aid.*

"Holy shit." He sagged against the back of his chair and inhaled a long drag from his cigarette. The sight enraged her.

"She died of lung cancer, so if you wouldn't mind, could you put out the fucking cigarette?" Under normal circumstances she'd die before sniping at a relative stranger like that, but nothing about the past weeks qualified as normal.

The room grew thick with tense silence, then Rebel totally surprised her by barking out a laugh. Well, the reaction was better than she'd expected. As MC president, he was used to respect, not women cursing at him and ordering him around in a bitchy tone.

"Well if the eyes weren't enough of a clue, that smart mouth gives it away." He snuffed out the cigarette and looked at his hand as though unsure of what to do with it now that the nicotine was gone. "I'm sorry about your mother. We had some good times. I had no idea she was knocked up when she left here."

Kori relaxed some in her chair. So far so good. He didn't jump up and hug his long-lost daughter, but neither did he deny her and toss her out on her ass. But, now what? As the hush in the room grew uncomfortable, she let her eyes wander. The office was pretty sparse as far as knickknacks and personal touches went, though there were a number of framed pictures of Rebel with various bikers adorning the walls.

Four ceramic dishes full of gray ash and cigarette butts decorated the desktop. Looked like there was at least one thing he had in common with her mother. Hopefully, they wouldn't do him in the way they did her.

"So...uh..." Hearing a big tough biker sound unsure of himself was a unique experience. "So, you sticking around at all?"

"I hadn't really made any plans beyond today. I figured I'd see how this all went. I booked a hotel room for the night." Did he want to see her again? Get to know her?

"You got an ol' man to get back to? A job?"

Kori snorted. She was about to sum up her sad life with one word. "No. To either. No relationship and my job let me go after I took so much time off to take care of Mom. It was rough at the end."

Rebel nodded, his face impassive. Almost as if by reflex, he reached into the cardboard pack and drew out a cigarette. The look of disbelief on her face must have registered with him because he shoved the stick in his mouth but didn't light the thing. "What? I ain't gonna light it. Geez girl, you're in my life five minutes and already bitching at me."

The sides of Kori's mouth quirked, but she suppressed the grin. "I didn't say anything."

He grunted and withdrew the cigarette from between his lips. "Not with your voice. But you did that chick thing where you look at a poor guy and scream at him with your eyes."

A genuine laugh bubbled out of her and she was surprised to see that Rebel was laughing as well. "Stay for a while," he said. "I live by myself. Got an extra room. You won't bother me none and, who knows, maybe we'll even like each other."

Kori's jaw dropped. At a loss for words, she whipped it closed again. To say the offer was unexpected would be an understatement. She ran through the idea in her head. After her mom fell ill, Kori had given up her apartment and moved into her mother's house. Well, actually, Rusty, her ol' man's house, but the faithless asshole barely spent any time there. She'd been staying there since her mom died, knowing full well time was running out and Rusty would want the space back at some point. And with no job to return to, there really wasn't anything holding her back.

Hell, maybe she could stay here permanently. As a medical office assistant, she could find a job anywhere. The idea had merit. It was at least worth a trial run. Stay with Rebel for a bit and if things seemed promising she could relocate to Vegas permanently.

Only one problem with this grand plan. The only person she knew in Vegas was a biker. And she'd be living with him. Father or not, associating with bikers wasn't in her plans, especially now that her mom had passed. After the very loud, raucous biker funeral her stepfather's club held, she'd decided that bikers were out of her life for good.

"Girl, I didn't ask you to solve the world's hunger problem. You looking to stay? Yes or no. Simple."

"Yes." *Wait, what?* The consent was out of her mouth without any permission from her brain.

The leathery skin of his cheeks stretched as a wide grin graced his face. Warmth spread through Kori's chest. Maybe there was still hope for her in the family department.

"Go on out and have a drink at the bar. I'll be done in ten minutes and I'll introduce you to the crew." The command was given in that way of people who were used to having their orders followed.

She rose and turned for the door. "Uh, sure. I guess I could use a middle of the day drink."

Looks like she was about to make a bunch of new friends.

Biker friends.

Shit.

CHAPTER FOUR

Quite a few pairs of curious eyes were glued to Kori as she stepped back into the main area of the clubhouse. There wasn't much she hated more than feeling unsure of herself, and she hadn't felt this uncertain for as long as she could remember. Which was ridiculous. She knew damn well how to play the biker game.

So she raised her head, wiped her damp palms on her skinny jeans, and strode toward the bar. A quick glance at a giant Harley clock on the wall reminded her it was only a few minutes past three in the afternoon. Far too early for the hard stuff.

"Just a beer, please. Anything," she said to the prospect behind the bar. He practically vibrated with energy, no doubt a result of suppressing his burning desire to know who she was and why she was granted a private meeting with their president. Rebel wanted to do the introductions, so she kept her mouth shut. It was too early to know how the man would react when disobeyed. And it was his club, so his show.

The young prospect returned seconds later and plunked the beer down in front of her. "Thanks," she said as she spun on the barstool before he had a chance to fire any questions her way. It was a mistake. Now, instead of facing one nosy man, she faced a room full of inquisitive onlookers. After three sips of her beer, the probing stares and not-so-discrete whispers became almost unbearable. She kept her gaze on an empty table about five feet away and could have cried in relief when the entrance door swung open and diverted everyone's attention.

Her focus shifted to the entrance, as guilty as everyone else of curiosity, and the beer bottle nearly slipped from her fingers. Holy shit. Quite possibly the most attractive man she'd ever laid eyes on walked into the room. No. Walked was not the right word. Swaggered, strutted maybe. Paraded? Whatever it was, it reeked of cocky self-confidence. She had an instant impression of the arrogant player he'd be.

The biker was tall, well developed, wore his jeans like they'd been made for the sole purpose of hugging his muscular thighs. Thank God she couldn't see his ass. She might just weep. And he had a face that bore a striking resemblance to Colin Farrell.

Her fingers flexed against the frosty bottle in her hands, though they really itched to run through the black, soft-looking goatee that rimmed his mouth. A deep ache began between her legs. She'd never been with a man who had facial hair and she shivered at the thought of that soft hair brushing her neck or breasts. Her pussy throbbed as though calling out to him for the opportunity to give it a whirl. The chances of a dry pair of panties remaining in the room were growing dimmer with each passing second.

As he hugged and slapped backs with a few of his brothers, Kori openly stared at him. From across the room, a tiny woman with huge breasts and not much covering them sidled up to him and planted her chest against his side. He dropped a polite kiss on her cheek, but didn't pay her much attention beyond that. Not possible that the man wasn't interested in a woman like her. She was as classic a club girl as they came.

As he extricated himself from Chesty McChesterson's hold, his gaze connected with Kori's. Never before had need sucker punched her from mere eye contact. Air whooshed out of her lungs and she realized her mistake the moment he waved off his brothers and left the busty and pouting woman. She should have looked away. Now she was ensnared in a royal blue trap glittering with mischief. And there was that swagger again.

"Well, hey there," he said when he was within reach. "This has to be your first time here because I would certainly remember all that gorgeous. I'm Lucky." He picked up her unoffered hand and pressed his lips to her palm. She managed to suppress any outward signs of desire, but her insides zinged with excitement the moment his mouth met her skin. "And let's just say you are about to get very *lucky*."

Kori coughed in an attempt to smother an outburst of laughter as one eyebrow rose of its own accord. Was this guy for real? Arrogance oozed from every pore like he'd doused himself in a dollar store cologne.

She widened her eyes in what she hoped was an innocence-meets-surprised expression and let out a girlish giggle. "Does that mean what I think it means?"

He stepped closer, still holding her hand and brushed his lips across the inside of her wrist. "It sure does, baby. Sex and sin."

It took every ounce of self-control Kori possessed to tamp her reaction to Lucky's lips stroking her skin. She clenched her teeth and nearly every other muscle to stop the tremor of desire that threatened to race through her. Jesus, the man was lethal. Taking his ego down a peg would be the most fun she'd had in weeks.

"Great," she said, her voice breathy and seductive. "So you can hook me up with that guy over there? I have a feeling I'd get really *lucky* with him." She pointed toward a group of bikers drinking at a corner table, not any one of them in particular.

The overconfident smirk slid right off Lucky's face like melted butter and he dropped her hand as though it burned him. Ahh, satisfaction. She gloated in her head for about three seconds before she could no longer hold in the laughter.

Lucky crossed his arms over his impressive chest and nodded, a small chuckle escaping his flattened mouth. "Nicely played. Round one goes to you…"

"Kori," she said around laughter. "And I'm sorry, but you were asking for that."

Lucky snorted. "I think I was asking for something quite different, angel. How about you let me buy the victor a free drink?"

She held up her half-full beer. "Still working on this one, thanks."

"Well then, so there is no room for miscommunication this time, how about you let *me* take you home and make you scream for the next few hours."

The man was persistent. She had to give him that. That boastful I'm-the-shit attitude hadn't been beaten down for long. She had to admit the offer was very tempting. Losing herself in mind-blowing pleasure for a few hours would go a long way toward helping her rid the stress of her off-kilter life. But... "Sorry, I don't date bikers."

He leaned in close enough to whisper in her ear. Damn, the man smelled good. The hairs around his mouth tickled the rim of her ear. Soft, just like she'd suspected. "I'm not asking for a date."

"Okay then, I don't *do* bikers." Man, this guy didn't hold back.

"Pretty sure I can change your mind, angel."

Ugh, he was bordering on predictable now. A commotion from the other side of the room caught her attention and she peered over her shoulder. Rebel emerged from the hallway and flashed her a smile. With a flick of his head, he summoned her to him. She turned back to Lucky. "Give it your best shot, big boy. But don't be too disappointed when the only one getting lucky this afternoon is your right hand."

With that parting shot, she hopped off the barstool and made her way toward Rebel. So sue her if she put a little extra hip action in her walk. Just because she wouldn't give in to the temptation didn't mean it wasn't there. And what woman didn't like admiration from a gorgeous man?

Lucky

About halfway to Rebel, the full weight of what she'd just done settled on her shoulders. She'd thrown down the gauntlet and issued a sexy challenge to a very potent biker who probably took the dare very seriously.

A quick peek over her shoulder told her she was right. His deep blue eyes gleamed with lust and his smile was all teeth. The game was on and she immediately regretted her role in starting it.

So much for getting lucky.

CHAPTER FIVE

Women responded to Lucky with two predictable reactions. If they were spoken for, they laughed at his antics, patted his arm, and rolled their eyes while secretly being flattered by the overt flirting.

If they were single, well, they pretty much flopped to their backs, spread their legs, and invited him in. It wasn't conceit that had Lucky thinking this way, it was just how it happened every single time since he'd turned fourteen and the sexy twenty-one-year-old co-ed who lived next door decided to punish her boyfriend by sleeping with the neighborhood hooligan.

What did not happen, ever, was the scenario where a smokin' hot chick made jokes at his expense, laughed in his face, then sauntered away as though he deserved as much of her brain power as a buzzing gnat.

He chuckled under his breath, his eyes fixed to the magnetic twitch of her damn fine ass as she left him in the dust. With a subtle shift of his hips, he adjusted his stance and provided some relief for his expanding cock. He didn't really give a shit if any of his brothers noticed he hid a full-blown erection behind his denim. She was sexy and he was hard. Pretty much standard operating procedure around here.

Her white-blond hair was pulled up in a high ponytail and swayed at mid-back level in time with her hips. Lucky clenched a fist, imagining the cool feel of those long strands wrapped around his hand as he pulled her head back and nibbled her exposed neck.

Damn, that had to be the blondest hair he'd ever seen. So white-blond it practically glowed, like some kind of celestial being. Jesus, had he really called her angel all because of some hair? Yup, he had. She was no angel. She was far too biker to be angelic, with jeans so tight he couldn't figure out how she walked so smoothly. And an equally tight T-shirt that showcased her breasts with a sparkly skull across her chest. Leather boots topped off the look. Aside from the hair, she looked like she'd just hopped off his Harley, not like someone sent from heaven.

He kept his eyes trained on her as she crossed the room, ending up right next to...Rebel?

Oh, fuck me.

Had he really just hit on his president's latest toy? Thank fuck Rebel hadn't been privy to their exchange or Lucky would be scrubbing the clubhouse's bathrooms with a toothbrush for the next month. And that was if Rebel went easy on him.

"Down, boy," he muttered to his erection. "You ain't got nowhere to go now."

That wasn't exactly true. Dana, who'd been all over him the second he walked in the door, would be more than happy to take care of him. He'd slept with her two, maybe three times. It all blended together, and if he was being honest, he barely remembered her. Couldn't have been that earth shattering.

He flicked a glance at Kori, who now stood with Rebel's arm around her shoulders then tossed a look in Dana's direction. No contest. Too bad the one he wanted seemed to be taken.

"Listen up!" No one ever needed to look around for who was talking when Rebel spoke. Each man in the room abandoned what they were looking at and focused on their president.

"Want to introduce you assholes to someone. This here is Kori." He gave Kori's shoulder a squeeze and smiled down at her as if she were something precious. Lucky's erection fully deflated. "Kori is family. Literally. Turns out, I have a long-lost daughter."

What the ever-loving fuck?

His daughter? Rebel had a daughter? Lucky couldn't have been more shocked if Rebel told them all he was stepping down as president. Looks like she wasn't Rebel's woman after all. A slow smile spread across Lucky's face. She was fair game.

"She's gonna stick around town for a while and stay at my place." His mouth flattened into a serious line and his eyes narrowed as he looked around the room. "Every man in here behaves around her. She's family. My blood. I hear any of you are treating her like one of the whores," he said, completely unrepentant to be speaking that way about the women in the room, "we're gonna have problems. Big problems. Got me?"

Each man, including Lucky, nodded and mumbled their agreement.

"All right. I'm gonna take her out of here in a few and get her settled. Barbecue tomorrow evening at my house to welcome Kori. Ol' ladies are invited; whores are not. Every fuckin' one of you will be on your best behavior. Don't want to scare her off just yet." He winked down at his daughter and she gave him a small smile.

She didn't look relaxed. In fact, she looked distinctly uncomfortable and like she wasn't sure this entire plan was a good idea. The girl needed some stress relief. Lucky's specialty.

Rebel said something to Kori then she nodded and walked back in his direction. When she reached him, she gave him a shy smile, in contrast with the sassy flirting she'd employed moments ago.

"Well, looks like you get the award for the most surprising woman of the day. Can't say I saw that one coming."

A light, feminine grunt escaped her throat. "Yeah, well, me either, to be honest. It's been an interesting day. Interesting few weeks."

Lucky tilted his head. There was a story there. Of course there was a story. Long-lost daughter? That reeked of dramatic scenes and scandal. She was gorgeous, no doubt about it, and on closer inspection, she bore the look of someone who been under tremendous strain recently. Dark circles lined her eyes, faintly visible through her makeup job. Her back was straight, almost rigid, and she drummed her fingers against her thigh in what he guessed was a nervous gesture.

He opened his mouth, then snapped it shut again, the statement he'd been about to make trapped behind his teeth. Had he really almost offered her an ear if she needed to vent? Lucky didn't do the confidant role. He got lucky. He made women feel lucky, then they went their separate ways. Everyone satisfied and happy. Something about Kori's sad expression had him wanting to hear her story and offer comfort.

Thank fuck his brain kicked in before the offer was out of his mouth. "You looking for a little stress relief, darlin'?" There, that suggestion was much more his style.

She chuckled. "Like a long jog followed by a tub of chocolate brownie ice cream and a vat of wine?"

He liked her spunk. He also liked her teasing, which was another first. "No, babe. Though I was thinking energy expenditure and if you'd like, I'm all for involving some ice cream."

"I'll pass," she said. "I already told you—"

"Yeah, yeah, you don't do bikers. I get it." If the fact that he rode a piece of heavy machinery was his biggest obstacle, then he was in pretty good shape. He leaned close enough to get a whiff of something clean and citrusy. "Hate to break it to you, darlin', but you got biker in your blood."

Her eyes widened and she took a step back, breasts rising and falling with the force of her rapid breathing. Lucky was completely helpless to do anything but stare at her chest. God, he couldn't wait to get his hands and mouth on them. Maybe bury his cock between them. They weren't huge, but neither were they small. High, perky, mouthwatering.

"Ahem." Rebel stepped up beside Kori and shot Lucky a look that had made more than one prospect shit themselves. "Ready to go, baby girl?"

Whoops, busted. Well, he wasn't a prospect and he wouldn't be intimidated by Rebel's newfound daddy role. Kori was sexy as fuck and Lucky planned to have her, plain and simple. He wouldn't treat her like a whore as Rebel feared, but he wouldn't hide his interest, either. Nothing wrong with a little mutual adult satisfaction.

"Guess I'll see you around," she said to Lucky.

"Count on it, angel." There he went again with the angel business.

She smiled and nodded before trailing Rebel out of the clubhouse.

Lucky rubbed his hands together and grinned like a fool. The challenge had been issued, and it was one he gladly accepted. Damn, it felt good to focus his energy on something besides the stress of figuring out what do to about Rebel's drug dealing and betrayal.

Oh shit.

He was ninety percent sure telling Striker about Rebel was the right thing to do. Kori couldn't have shown up at a worse time. Why the fuck hadn't he thought of this sooner? She'd apparently distracted him too well. At the very least, Rebel would be booted out of the club, and at the worst, he'd be leaving in a body bag. Did this change anything? Could he still go to Striker knowing innocent Kori would potentially be hurt in the crossfire? He had to. He didn't even know the woman. She couldn't factor into his decision.

Then why did he feel like he was playing with fire so hot someone was bound to be incinerated?

CHAPTER SIX

Rebel's house wasn't fancy, but it was medium sized and Kori had a room and bathroom all to herself. Maybe while she was here she'd add a few feminine touches, spruce the place up a bit. It could certainly stand to be a bit homier. The furniture was comfortable enough but ancient and worn. Not a single picture adorned the walls. No knickknacks lay around on any tables.

Her bedroom held a simple, no-frills queen-size bed. Basically, a box spring and mattress on a metal frame. No headboard, no footboard, no colorful comforter. A dresser that could use some serious sanding and more than one coat of paint was shoved in the corner of the room. That was it. Nothing else.

Maybe she'd give the dresser a little TLC while she was around. She loved that sort of work. Refurbishing furniture, working with her hands to take something that, on initial appearance, was old and unimpressive and making it beautiful once again. It would give her something to occupy her time at least, while she decided if she wanted to apply for a job here in Vegas or venture back home. Or even go somewhere else. Really, there was nothing stopping her from starting over in a whole new area. And given the fact that she was leery about tying herself to another MC, moving somewhere she had no connections might be the wisest idea.

There hadn't been much of an opportunity to chat with Rebel over the past twenty-four hours and she was okay with that. It gave her some quiet time to buy a few things for her room, settle in, and think. And she'd thought all right. She thought about Lucky's hard chest and his shit-eating grin. She thought about his swagger and the muscles in his arms that bulged in just the way that made her want to sink her teeth into them. She thought about how his strong hands would feel cupping her breasts, pinching her nipples, parting her folds...

Basically, she'd thought herself into such an aroused state, she was forced to shove her hand in her pants and take care of the problem. She'd bitten down on the pillow to muffle any cries of pleasure the fantasy Lucky may have wrung from her while she pleasured herself in her father's house like a horny teenager with no other outlet.

Apparently, her subconscious didn't get the *no biker* message.

She shook off the memories from hours ago and tried to get in the mood for the welcome party Rebel insisted on hosting.

"Hey, I thought the boss said he didn't want to see you lifting a finger for this party." One of the three prospects who'd been running around all afternoon stood a few feet away. His colossal arms were crossed over a chest so massive it looked like a caricature drawing. Rebel had said his name was Vee, after Humvee, since he was built like one.

She rolled her eyes. "I'm just filling this cooler with beer. I think I can handle it. Plus, you guys have been working your assess off to prepare for this barbecue. No harm in me pitching in a little."

Vee snorted and yanked the beer bottles out of her hands. "Sorry, babe, not even for your hot ass am I going against a direct order from the Pres. And it is a hot ass." He winked. "So I recommend you sit it down in that chair over there. Wouldn't want anything to happen to it." ·

Kori rolled her eyes. Bikers. Different club, same in-your-face sexuality and macho bullshit. Now why couldn't she have had the same uninterested reaction to Lucky?

"You threatening to spank the president's daughter, Vee?" Lucky's mesmerizing voice floated over her shoulders and wrapped around her like a soft, warm blanket.

Had her thoughts conjured him? Her face flamed, and if she was a betting woman, she'd wager it rivaled the beet-red flush that crept up Vee's neck and invaded his face.

"Uhh, no, Luck. I was just…uhh…well, you see, Rebel said…" The poor guy sputtered and danced from one foot to the other like the ground was on fire.

It might have been mean, but she had to bite her bottom lip to keep from laughing. She shot Lucky a put-the-poor-guy-out-of-his-misery look as he drew up next to her.

Lucky didn't bother to hide his own amusement and let the laughter fly. "Get the fuck back to work, prospect, and keep your eyes off the woman." After Vee scrambled away, Lucky turned his panty-melting grin on her. "Well, that was fun. But you know what would be more fun?"

She raised an eyebrow.

"How about you let Uncle Lucky take you for a ride on my powerful—"

And back to predictable. She held up a hand. "Okay, let me stop you right there. Your club brothers are going to start arriving any minute so, no, I will not be going for a ride on your hog, or your bike, or your cock for that matter. I told you. I don't do bikers. And for the record, can it with this whole King Shit act. I'm not buying it."

With that snooty speech, she spun on her heel and marched into the house. There had to be some menial task they'd let her help with. At least until more people arrived and she could blend into the crowd.

The problem was that the man tempted her in ways she hadn't experienced in ages. Her dating life was an abysmal story summed up in one word: nonexistent. She didn't date bikers, and the many bikers she knew tended to run off any nice, tame prospective boyfriend she brought home. Just because she'd tried to steer clear of the MC her mom married into, didn't mean she'd been successful.

Lucky was everything her brain and heart tried to avoid, but everything her body wanted desperately. Sometimes life was so unfair. She was almost grateful for his obnoxious cocky attitude because, without it, she just might throw caution to the wind and break her most important dating rule.

Then she'd just be a number in a long line of foolish girls who fell under the charming spell of an experienced womanizer. Wondering why she wasn't enough to keep him for more than a night or two.

And that was the last thing she needed when everything else in her life was upside down.

What was it with that woman? She was literally the only female to call him on his bullshit and flip him ass over ankles. For twenty years, he'd been charming women out of their panties with a quip and a smile. Hell, it was why they called him Lucky for fuck's sake. He couldn't recall a time when a single woman had turned him down, let alone read him the riot act.

It was different. It was disconcerting. It was...refreshing. But the weirdest part about the whole thing was how it did nothing to squash his desire for her. Instead, it only made him more determined to have her. Sure, the challenge of it all appealed to him a bit, but it was more than just a she-rejected-me-so-I'm-gonna-show-her thing. No, he felt an actual interest in both the body and the woman who owned it.

It was a strange as fuck feeling.

He snagged a beer from the cooler, popped the top, and let the frosty liquid extinguish the fire smoldering inside of him. Now he had to figure out how to get her to agree to a date.

"That one's got an ass on her that gives a man all kinds of ideas, huh?" Savage's voice cut through Lucky's musings.

Lucky'd been uncomfortable around the man ever since he'd found out he was one half of the drug running operation. Savage had never been his favorite person to begin with, but he was the club's VP, so Lucky afforded him the respect the position demanded. Now, though, it felt forced. And he was certain Savage could sense a shift in his attitude recently.

"You gonna make a play for her?" Savage grabbed a beer of his own.

"What's it to you?" It wouldn't pay to lay his cards on the table. Savage was also a man who had his nickname for a damn good reason.

"I just might give you a run for your money on this one. She might make a good ol' lady." He smiled, but it didn't reach his eyes. Nor did it warm them. Those eyes were always cold, calculating, and way too shifty to read.

Ol' lady? Really? What the hell was Savage's game? He was already in line to take over the club whenever Rebel bowed out. That wasn't likely to happen anytime soon, however. Maybe Savage thought of her as a bit of an insurance policy. Get in cozy with the new club princess to ensure he never fell out of Rebel's favor. Not for one second did he consider Savage's intentions were pure, or as pure as a hardened biker's could be.

Whatever the reason, Lucky didn't like it. Savage had a bit of a nasty reputation when it came to women. He was too rough, too severe, too controlling. Most who slept with him weren't willing to go back for seconds, or so rumor had it. Lucky had never given much thought to those rumors. They'd never been his business before. Hell, they weren't his business now. Except for the raging hard-on he had for the woman in question.

Silence settled between the two men. Lucky was at a complete loss for what to say to his VP. All that came to mind was, "Hey, what the fuck do you think you're doing pushing drugs and working with the Grimm Brothers?" And that question would get him a serious ass beating at the very least.

After a few minutes of somewhat uncomfortable silence, they both turned their attention to the house where Rebel and Kori were emerging. His president pointed and nudged his daughter in their direction. She nodded at whatever he said and made her way toward them.

"Baby girl, have you met Savage and Lucky?" Rebel asked as they drew close.

A mischievous grin formed on her mouth. "Lucky has hit on me a few times, yes, but I haven't met Savage yet."

Lucky grimaced and Kori's eyes twinkled with mirth. The little vixen. She had to know her new found old man wouldn't necessarily appreciate a member of his club trying to worm his way into her bed.

Thankfully, Rebel laughed. "Well, you are a female, and knowing Lucky, I should have expected he put the moves on you already."

"Funny," he muttered.

"Well, Kori, this is Savage, club's VP, and my right arm." Rebel gestured toward Savage as he spoke.

Kori switched her beer to her left hand and shifted her focus to Savage. Her smile faltered a smidge as she looked up into his eyes, but she rallied and allowed him to grasp her hand. "Nice to meet you."

"You planning to stay in Vegas a while, princess?" Savage asked.

She visibly bristled when the word *princess* rolled off Savage's tongue, but Lucky seemed to be the only one who noticed.

"For a bit. Not sure how long yet. I'm still considering my options." Her voice lost some of its warmth. She looked up at her father. "We haven't really even had much of a chance to talk since I got here."

Rebel nodded. "And I'd like to change that, baby girl. Dinner tomorrow? Just the two of us?"

Her face lit up once again and Lucky couldn't help but stare. Today, her hair was down flowing past her shoulders, and if he thought she looked angelic yesterday, today she might as well be wearing a flowing white dress and a halo. She was smiling now, and he wanted to be the one to put a smile on her face, but for a very different reason.

What the fuck was happening to him?

"That sounds great, Rebel, thanks," she said, totally unaware of the internal strife Lucky was suffering.

"Good. I'm gonna introduce her around a bit. Savage, I need to talk some business with you before you leave later, so don't get too wasted."

"I'll find you in a bit," Savage answered.

With a little wave, Kori turned and strode off with Rebel. Lucky risked a glance at Savage. The man's gaze was riveted to her firm ass, an almost predatory expression on his face.

Attention from Savage was the last thing Kori needed. He'd have to keep his eye on that situation. Better yet, he needed to find a way into her bed. Once he got her there, he was certain he could keep all other men from her mind.

CHAPTER SEVEN

Kori glanced at the clock on her phone for what had to be the tenth time in the past twenty minutes. Rebel was seriously late, and her rear end was growing numb from sitting on the rough concrete stoop for the past half hour.

Lateness was something she despised. Looked like that character trait wasn't inherited from her father.

The distant rumble of motorcycle pipes vibrated through the air. "Finally," she muttered. As the reverberation grew louder, she rose to her feet and rubbed her sore bottom. Rebel didn't seem the type to take her anywhere fancy, so she'd donned a pair of jeans and a simple red Harley tank top. Shorts weren't preferable for riding on the back of a bike, which meant she'd have to suffer through the warm evening in fitted denim.

The bike came into view so she rose and strolled down the driveway. No point in making Rebel come up to her when she was just going to hop on behind him anyway. A tiny ripple of unease crawled up her spine. This would be the first time she and her father really had any quality time to bond.

What if they didn't get along? What if she discovered they didn't have any common ground? Nothing to connect over? At least she could ask questions about her mother. Find out what she was like twenty-odd years ago. That should fill up a sufficient amount of time. Plus it would quench her thirst for knowledge about her mother's past. She had so many questions she'd wanted to ask but never did due to her mom's negative reaction to her past. If she really delved into it, Kori had the feeling her mother regretted her decision to leave Rebel. It would explain why she'd never talked about it. Painful memories were tough to relive.

Sunlight glanced off the chrome in just the right angle, blinding her with the strong reflection. She nudged her sunglasses from her forehead to the bridge of her nose and waited for her father to coast to a stop.

The first thing she noticed when he slowed to a roll was the lack of a President patch on his cut. Whoever the rider was, it wasn't her father. "What happened to Rebel?" she called out over the roaring bike.

The mystery rider killed the engine and blessed silence graced the neighborhood once again. He dropped the kickstand and leaned back, pulling his helmet off. Lucky's grinning face filled her field of vision and her mouth dropped open.

Well, that was attractive. Staring at the man with an open mouth, ready to catch any stray bug that happened to be buzzing by.

Not that she cared if she came off attractive to Lucky.

"He can't make it. Something came up. He sent me instead. Hop on and let's go get some grub." His smile was so wide, it looked like he'd just won a million-dollar poker pot.

Not for one second did she believe in this bogus coincidence. "All right, nicely done. What? Did you offer to polish Rebel's bike every day for the next month to get him to let you come?"

He threw back his head and let out a genuine laugh. The sound ran down her spine and settled between her legs. Great. Just what she needed. A sexy, off limits man who turned her on with just a laugh.

"No, babe, though I gotta admit I thought about it. This really was just dumb luck. Must have something to do with my name." He winked.

Kori huffed out a sigh. Damn it. She was starving and had been looking forward to a dinner out. "Please, I've heard all about how you got your name. Listen, cowboy, you may be used to women falling at your feet, but I've told you a number of times. No dates with bikers."

"Come on. You gotta be hungry." He gave her a look that was probably as innocent as he could get. On anyone else, it would be positively sinful, but he lived a notch above the rest of the world on the sin-o-meter.

"I'm good." She spun toward the house just as her traitorous stomach let out an oh-so-appealing growl.

This time Lucky's laughter grated on her nerves.

"Okay, how about this. I promise to be a perfect gentleman. Nothing beyond some light flirting. No blatant innuendos. No unauthorized touching. No mention of sex."

Well…she really was famished and had been looking forward to getting out for a few hours. Slowly, she turned back to him. "Completely hands off?"

He nodded and a teasing glint lit his eyes. "Hands one hundred percent to myself. Unless you ask me to put them on you. Ball's in your court."

She raised an eyebrow.

A shrug lifted his shoulders. "Hey, I said I'd be a gentleman. Didn't say I was a martyr." With another semi-innocent smile, he held out a spare helmet.

Kori's empty stomach won out and she stepped closer. "Okay, fine." She grabbed the helmet. "But this is not a date. You did not win anything here. You did not wear me down. I'm just freakin' hungry."

"Yes, ma'am," Lucky said, his eyes on her as she secured the helmet. He looked damn good seated astride the powerful machine with the T-shirt under his cut stretched across his wide chest. The idea of sitting with her arms and legs wrapped around him for an unknown period of time was discomfiting. He had an effect on her body and mind that was powerful and went against her sense of self-preservation. It would be impossible to be so close to him and not react.

But she'd damn well try.

"All set," she said. She placed a hand on his rounded shoulder and forced her fingers to remain stiff instead of prodding the muscles as she so wanted to do. With a quick look to the heavens in search of common sense, she swung her leg over the bike and settled in behind Lucky.

She'd been on a bike a handful of times, but not enough to feel fully secure when the dangerous hunk of metal lurched forward. Without any other options, Kori wrapped her arms around Lucky's midsection and held on for dear life.

After about ten minutes of trying to hold on while maintaining at least an inch of distance between her front and Lucky's muscle-corded back, she gave up. Her core strength wasn't sufficient enough to maintain the position and her trunk sagged against Lucky. That's what she got for skipping planks in that yoga class at the gym.

It was a poor idea. The press of Lucky's body against hers was far too warm and solid. Far too comforting, something she'd done without for so long. When was the last time she'd found any comfort in a man's body? Even more dangerous was the arousal and magnetic pull to him.

It had been too long and that's what made it so treacherous. Had she been laid recently, had she had a man in her life, she may not have been so tempted. As it was, she had to link her hands together around his waist to keep from trailing them downward and assessing whether he was half as affected by their proximity as she was.

Thankfully the trip only lasted a few minutes more before he pulled into a dirt parking lot and stilled the bike. Even before she got a good look at the small building, the tantalizing smell of spices and cooking meat tickled her senses. Her mouth watered and she could practically taste the food.

"What is this place?" The building was tiny, nondescript, and certainly not on the Vegas strip, which was where she assumed he'd take her to try to impress her with the flash and lights of Vegas nightlife.

"This place—" Lucky let out a groan as he removed his helmet. "This is the best eating in Vegas. It's a hole in the wall, non-tourist-discovered Tex-Mex joint that makes fajitas so amazing, you could cry. Mmm, I think I may be as hungry as you are." He winked. "Not to mention, I've kept this place my little secret and haven't shared it with the club, so you won't have to hang out with bikers tonight. Well, one biker, but I've already promised to behave."

His enthusiasm was infectious and she found herself excited to check the place out. Local eating was her absolute favorite and the fact that he didn't take her to some showy, flashy establishment on the strip impressed her.

"Okay, let's do it. It smells fantastic." She hung the helmet from the handlebar as he did and climbed off the bike, falling in step next to him as they made their way to the entrance. True to his word, Lucky didn't make any suggestive comments about their ride, didn't reach for her hand, didn't sling an arm around her shoulders. He was a perfect gentleman and respected the boundaries she'd demanded.

So why the hell was she so damn disappointed?

CHAPTER EIGHT

"So tell me," Lucky said as he drew the frosty beer bottle to his lips. "Why the no biker rule? Bad experience?" Man, the ice cold, hoppy flavor was the perfect complement to the spicy salsa and salty chips.

He'd grown up coming to this restaurant. Even worked as a busboy during his misspent youth. Rosita, the matronly owner, had caught him red-handed stealing from a delivery truck. Instead of turning him in, she put him to work. He'd been treated like family ever since.

"Geez," she said as she ran a fingertip through the salt on the rim of her margarita glass. "Aren't we supposed to start with simple, get-to-know-you questions? Like, what do you do for a living? Where did you move from?" She brought her index finger to her lips and licked it clean of salt.

Jesus. If she had any idea of the massive hard-on he was hiding under the table, she'd toss that drink in his face and twitch that sexy ass right out the door.

"That would be if we were on a date, angel." He snagged a chip and sank it into the guacamole. "You made it clear this is not a date. So, I don't need to stick to any polite date small talk rules."

Her delicate snort made him chuckle. "Somehow I don't imagine you do much in the way of politeness on dates. In fact, I bet you don't even go on dates."

Well, she had him there. "Point to you," he said, lifting his beer bottle in toast to her. "But you're avoiding my question."

"Okay, cowboy, but you asked, so don't get offended."

"Takes quite a lot to offend me, babe."

The right side of her mouth lifted in a half grin. "I'll bet it does." She sighed as though resigned to the fact she couldn't stall any longer. "My mom is—well, was, I guess." She cleared her throat and shook her head as though shaking off sadness. "Anyway, for most of my childhood, she was a club...girl with a club near Tallahassee, in Florida. The Red Devils. Ever heard of them?"

Lucky shook his head. There were hundreds of clubs across the country, most weren't outlaw, but he didn't know every single club. And for now, he wasn't sure if she was referring to an outlaw club. "One percenters?" he asked.

She nodded and he believed her. Just the fact that she knew the expression, that one percent of motorcycle clubs were outlaw, was enough to let him know she knew her way around an MC.

"Anyway, I grew up around the club and eventually, when I was about ten, she became an ol' lady. Was married to the same guy until she passed. The same lying, cheating, scumbag that fucked anything with tits. The younger the better." Her voice was full of bitterness as she shook her head. "And it wasn't just him, it was just the culture of the club. No one was faithful. No one gave a shit that the women were treated like garbage. I want no part of that shit. Hence, no bikers."

He'd love to shoot down her claim, but she was pretty dead on with the culture of most clubs. Sex was easy to come by. Women looking to party flocked to the clubs and to say they were free with their bodies was an understatement. Temptation was rampant. Access was comically easy.

That wasn't to say Lucky didn't know plenty of brothers in committed monogamous relationships, but he knew quite a few who weren't loyal to their ol' ladies either. "We aren't all like that."

She cocked her head and raised an eyebrow. "We? You saying you're big into monogamy, *Lucky*?"

The way she said his name grated on him. Like she was mocking him and his reputation. Unfortunately, her willingness to challenge him and not just say what he wanted to hear for the sake of pleasing him appealed to him in a way he didn't expect. "No. I'm not saying that. Not at all. Which is why no woman I'm with is ever under the impression that they are in for anything more than a mutually good time. However, I know myself well enough to know that if I did, in fact, make that kind of commitment, I'd be loyal to it. Miserable, but loyal." He winked.

"Hmm." She studied him for a moment and he could tell he'd surprised her with his honest answer.

And it was honest. He had no interest in being a one-woman man, however, he also had no interest in hurting anyone. He loved women. What was the point in making one feel worthless? Men who entered serious relationships under false pretenses didn't impress him. He was blunt and upfront about what he wanted. One or two nights of fun, then done. Kept things clean and easy.

He met her serious gaze across the table and the air hovering between them crackled and popped with electricity. For the first time in his thirty-four years, Lucky wondered what it would be like to spend more than a few torrid nights with one woman. How would it feel to wake up to a familiar face each morning? A face that topped off an incredibly sexy body. A face that also belonged to a sharp, interesting, witty woman. Might be kinda nice.

Thankfully, he was saved from his out of character, runaway thoughts by the pop and sizzle of piping hot fajitas. "*Hola*, Lucky. It has been too long." Rosita placed Kori's fish tacos in front of her before setting his mouthwatering plate on the table. "I do not want to keep you from your pretty lady, but I wanted to say hello."

"Hi, Rosita. This here is Kori." He rose and gave Rosita a kiss on her wrinkled cheek.

Kori greeted the older woman and Rosita chatted with them for a few minutes before leaving them to their meals. They fell into easy conversation between bites and before he knew it, they were each sipping a second drink, and plates were being cleared. He found himself enjoying the evening more than any he'd had in quite some time.

A comfortable silence fell between them as they listened to the upbeat Latin music and polished off their drinks. Kori's attention was on the rapidly filling dance floor and the laughing couples who twirled and salsa danced their way around the room.

She really was gorgeous, but not in the in-your-face way Lucky was used to. She didn't dress with the sole purpose of attracting a man's eye, didn't eye his dick and drop not-so-subtle hints as to her goal for the evening. Nope. She wore a simple red tank top that hugged her full breasts and clung to her curves but kept her cleavage concealed. She enjoyed her food in a way that said she wasn't trying to impress him with her dainty appetite, and she flat out told him sex of any kind was off the table.

Her eyes sparkled and her foot tapped to the rhythm of the music as she observed the dancers. She probably had no idea, but her body swayed in time with the beat as well. This was one woman who wanted out on that dance floor. Well, it just so happened he could hold his own out there. Rosita made sure of that in the years he'd worked for her. It was the perfect excuse to have her in his arms while maintaining the rules he'd set for the evening.

He could dance with her and keep his hands in appropriate, nonsexual places.

Hopefully.

Lucky held a hand out and cleared his throat. "Okay, I can't watch you dance in your chair by yourself any longer. Let's get out there and show 'em how it's done."

Kori turned her head and stared down at his hand like it was a trap. Her lips pursed and she looked like she wanted to say yes, but held herself back.

"Please. I've been a good boy. Just a few dances, nothing more."

She lifted her gaze, and excitement burned in her eyes. If he wasn't mistaken, there was a distinctive gleam of lust as well.

Well, damn it. She was supposed to the sensible of the two. How the hell was he supposed to keep his hands in the safe zone knowing her actual wants didn't match up with what she said?

CHAPTER NINE

Kori's tongue wouldn't form the word *yes*. And even if it would, her mouth wouldn't open to allow the assent out. On the flipside, the words *no thanks* didn't grace her lips either. Instead, she stared at his outstretched hand and willed herself to make a decision.

The right decision.

The smart decision.

Lucky *had* stuck to every promise he made her. He'd been a complete gentleman, a great conversationalist, and a fun dinner companion. He also looked good enough to be the dessert that capped off her amazing meal.

Who was she kidding? This had nothing to do with her general rule of not dating bikers, and everything to do with the fact that she was wildly attracted to a man who flat out told her he never stuck around for more than a night or two.

Hello, disappointment.

Kori knew herself too well to think she could sleep with Lucky a time or two and be done with it. Maybe if he'd just been the cocky, womanizer she met a few days ago, but nope. He had to go and be sweet, and attentive, and easy to talk to. Qualities that appealed to her emotions as much as his muscles appealed to her libido.

"Do you even know how to dance?" Where the hell had those words come from? They sounded dangerously close to flirty consent.

A mesmerizing smile transformed his face. When he was genuinely amused, not the I'm-trying-to-charm-you-out-of-your-pants smile that he so often flashed, but a real smile of happiness, the left side of his mouth rose just a hair higher than the right. It gave him a carefree, almost boyish look and she couldn't help but return the grin.

"Ahh, you'll have to find that one out for yourself."

"Okay." *What?* No, that wasn't the word that her brain had sent to her mouth. "Just a few dances. And this is not a green light for anything else, mister. Understood?"

"*Si, senorita,*" he said as he snatched her hand and pulled her toward the dance floor. He moved fast, as though he was afraid she'd change her mind in the ten-foot trip.

With practiced efficiency, he spun her and drew her into a perfect salsa hold. Her eyes widened and she stared up at him.

"Guess I do know what I'm doing."

Kori couldn't help but laugh. His crooked smile and teasing were infectious. She knew the basic steps, plus a few extra moves, but was no expert herself. However, with a good lead, as he seemed to be, she shouldn't have any trouble keeping up.

He spun her again and she ended in the same position she started in. In a salsa hold, close to him, but not touching. True to his word, he kept his pelvis and torso on his side of the line. It wasn't long before she was relaxing into his hold and following his competent lead. The next thing she knew, she had her head thrown back and excited laughter was bubbling up from her as he twirled her in a complicated pattern.

Their hips swayed, a few platonic inches separating them, and while it should have placated her need for space, all she could think about was how it would feel if she closed the distance between them. His firm chest was the kind a girl would love to press against as he held her close. Was he turned on? Did this closeness affect him as it did her?

The thought of him erect and wanting her, just inches away had moisture pooling between her thighs. It was as though an unseen force was pulling her pelvis closer to his. She resisted it with everything she had, but the reasons for doing so were becoming muddled in her head.

The music changed and a slow, sultry pulse meant for lovers filled the restaurant. Lucky drew her flush against his body and she stiffened. Holy shit it felt good. Brain scrambling good.

"Fuck. I'm sorry," he said. "I wasn't thinking." The serious look that stared down at her verified his words. "The song just… demanded it." He shrugged, his lower body moving against hers.

"It's okay," she said, her voice low, raspy, almost unrecognizable. "You're right. It's how the music should be danced to." She allowed herself to relax against him and truly process the sensation of him against her.

Her breasts pressed against the hard planes of his chest. As they swayed to the music, his upper body moved against hers and her nipples beaded to tightened points. The answer to her earlier question was a resounding yes. The man was turned on. Hard. Very hard, and nestled into the softness of her stomach as though she'd been made for this very reason, to cushion his steely length.

The problem was, that left her throbbing center, too low to grind against him. An insane thought crossed her mind and she almost shifted, straddling one of his legs so she could apply pressure to her core and find some kind of relief.

Her gaze met Lucky's and she couldn't tear herself away from the intensity staring back at her. Somehow, he read her mind, and as their hips rolled and moved to the music, he shifted, inserting one thick thigh between her legs. Then, the hand on her back drifted downward and came to rest a millimeter above her ass, anchoring her to him.

He kept to his word, hands in appropriate places, and had she any brain cells not focused on lust, she would have laughed at the irony of it. Hands dutifully in the safe zone while she practically rode his thigh.

She had no idea how many songs they stayed that way for, gazes locked, bodies gently grinding to the sensual Latin beat. With each second that passed, a bit more of Kori's resolve crumbled. Her body's demands overrode her brain's sensible wishes and she pressed even closer to Lucky.

His erection ground into her stomach at the same time her clit rubbed over his thigh and she was helpless to stop the small moan from slipping out.

"Christ, Kori," Lucky whispered in her ear. "Do you have any fucking idea what you are doing to me, babe? I'm trying to follow the rules, but you're making it damn near impossible. There's only so much I can take."

He spoke through gritted teeth, as though in pain. Would it really be so harmful? Breaking her no biker rule for one night. Would it even be fully breaking the rule? She told Lucky she didn't do bikers, but it really meant she didn't date bikers. Because she didn't *do* anyone. Not without a few dates and at least the possibility of a semi long term relationship.

Perhaps it was the pleasant hum of two margaritas coursing through her bloodstream, but her determination weakened. She'd been given all the information upfront. There would be no dating. There wouldn't necessarily be a second…encounter either. She was an adult. She could have a one night stand and survive to tell the tale. And if her instinct was right, it would be quite a tale to tell.

Fuck it.

She opened her mouth and the words just flew out. "Take me home, Lucky."

Lucky's entire body grew nearly as rigid as his cock. He was dangerously close to shooting off just from the way her soft stomach cupped his straining erection and the heat of her pussy against his leg. All he could think about was gripping her ass tight with both hands and rocking her on his thigh until she flew apart. Christ, he wanted to watch her come. Over and over.

"Take—" He cleared his gravelly throat. "Take you home to Rebel's?"

"No, Lucky." She shook her head as she spoke. "Take me home to your place."

There was a God. Almost. He needed to be sure that she was one hundred percent certain of what would happen the second they walked through his door before he let himself feel triumphant. "Kori, you know what's going to happen once we get there, right? It will be fuckin' amazing. More amazing than I think either of us can imagine, but you know, right? If you walk into my home, there's only one way this night will end."

She drew her lower lip between her teeth and he groaned. If he didn't know better, he'd swear everything she was doing was a calculated move to drive him insane. But it wasn't. Kori was just naturally sexy as fuck. "I know. And I want it."

"I'm a biker. It's in every cell in my body."

"I know that too."

There it was. Verbal confirmation. He tried to swallow, but his throat was thick and made the action near impossible.

Just one more test.

By now, they'd completely stopped moving with the music and Lucky cupped the back of Kori's head. His plan had been to shoot for slow seduction, but the sight of her lips parting as she realized his objective blasted his good intentions to hell. He captured her mouth in a soul-searing kiss that rocked him to his core.

The air heated as his brain registered the softness of her lips. There was no hesitation on her part. She met him head on and battled him for control of the kiss. He stroked his tongue against hers and had to forcibly remind himself they were in public.

Another two seconds and he'd be tearing at her clothes like a madman, other diners be damned.

With his last shred of sanity, Lucky tore his mouth away from hers. Kori's puckered nipples pressed against her tank top and rose and fell with the heaving force of her breathing.

Yeah, she wanted this. Maybe as much as he did. They were in for an explosive night.

He disentangled their bodies and grabbed her hand.

"Let's get the fuck out of here," he said as he tugged her toward the door.

CHAPTER TEN

By the time they reached Lucky's high-rise apartment building Kori's nerves hit the same level as her lust. The combination of two margaritas, dancing with Lucky, and the kiss to end all kisses fried the circuits in her brain, but with each passing minute, she was coming back into herself.

There was a good chance this was a mistake. A pleasurable mistake, but a mistake nonetheless.

"I can practically hear you talking yourself out of this."

"What? Huh?" Kori blinked. Lucky stood beside the bike, helmet off and hands on his hips.

Shit. How long had she been sitting there staring off into space like an idiot? "No...um...I, ah, I was just lost in thought. No big deal."

"You change your mind?"

She looked at him, really looked at him. No trace of the smooth-talking womanizer remained. In his place was a man whose eyes burned with lust. His body was taut, probably from holding himself in check, and there wasn't any trickery or practiced lines coming from him.

She wanted him, plain and simple. The hum in her blood once again became more lust than anxiety.

He scratched through the hair on his chin as he waited for her answer. That goatee had tickled her chin and she'd grown weak in the knees when she imagined the soft strands of hair brushing along her breasts.

"No. I definitely did not change my mind." It took her a few times due to slightly trembling fingers, but Kori removed the helmet and hopped off the bike. Lucky threaded their fingers together and guided her toward the building.

Keys in hand, he turned and faced her. "Last chance," he whispered, his mouth so close, his breath wafted across her lips.

Instead of giving him words, which he might question, she gripped the leather panels of his cut and yanked his mouth to hers. Just as with their first kiss, this one spiraled out of control in seconds, only this time there was a clear winner in the war for domination.

Still holding one of her hands, Lucky spun them and nudged her until her back hit the warm glass of the apartment building entrance. He found her other hand and held both of her wrists against the glass, immobilizing her and preventing her ability to touch him. The hard press of him against her mimicked how it would feel to have him driving her into a mattress and her heartrate sped to a gallop.

He tilted his head, deepening the kiss and Kori was lost. Kissing him was ten times more intoxicating than the tequila in the margaritas.

Just as she was about to beg him to touch her, a whoop of laughter cut through the fog of lust. It was followed immediately by a few obscene catcalls. Lucky tore his mouth away and yelled, "Fuck off," over his shoulder. "Shit, Kori. We need to get inside before I fuck you right here against the glass where every damn asshole who lives in the building could come down and watch the show."

Her head spun and she nodded. After one more quick, hard kiss on her swollen lips, Lucky unlocked the door and guided her through.

"Second floor," His voice was strained, rough. "Head on up, I'm two steps behind you."

Halfway to the first landing, she peeked over her shoulder. As promised, Lucky was exactly two steps behind her, which put his eyes at just the right level to watch her ass as she ascended. Sneaky man. No wonder he wanted her to precede him.

When they reached the second floor, he took her hand again and led her to a door with a brass 204 nailed in the center. He unlocked the door and pulled her through. Dropping his keys, phone, and wallet on a small table near the entrance, he directed her down the hallway and into a bedroom.

He hadn't bothered with the twenty-five-cent tour or even with any lights, but once in the bedroom, he switched on a small bedside lamp. It provided just enough light for them to see each other without cutting through the seductive mood with harsh illumination.

From what Kori could see, the room was well furnished but sparsely decorated. No pictures or artwork adorned the walls, but the queen-size bed was neat and everything seemed clean.

"I'm not much for decorating," Lucky said as he drew her flush against him. He placed one hand under her chin and nudged her head back.

"Well, I'm not exactly here for the décor."

"Oh no?" His lips landed on her lower throat and scorched a trail up to her ear.

The combination of heated kisses and the light tickle of his facial hair caused her knees to literally wobble, the sensitive skin of her neck somehow in direct connection to them. She lowered her head so their mouths lined up.

"What are you here for then?" His lips brushed against her mouth as he spoke.

"Hmm." She slid her arms around him and down his back until she gripped his ass with each hand. After giving him a squeeze she said, "I'm here for this." Then she licked across his closed mouth. "And I'm here for this. But mostly—" She rose on her toes and rocked the top of her mound against his erection. "Mostly I'm here for that."

His chuckle turned into a groan when she fused her mouth to his. Before she had a chance to deepen the kiss, he stepped back and she nearly stumbled forward seeking his warmth. The expression on his face was powerful, unreadable.

Shit. Had she been too aggressive? Maybe that wasn't his thing. He was a macho biker after all. Something she'd do well to remind herself frequently so she wouldn't start thinking this was anything more than it was.

"Take your shirt off." He sounded close to the edge. Like he was working hard to keep himself in check.

The thought of being the object of such focused attention was a bit unnerving. Sexy strip shows weren't exactly her thing, so Kori didn't bother to dance or try to make it something it wasn't. She drew the fitted tank over her head and dropped it to the floor.

"Bra next." His voice dropped to nearly a whisper.

Kori swallowed. It was almost painful as all the liquid dried up in her mouth. She reached back and undid her bra, letting it drop from her arms without any flourish.

"Jesus." Lucky's gaze was fixed on her chest.

The heat of his stare was like a physical caress. Kori's nipples tightened. Did he plan to touch her at some point tonight? She needed his hands on her.

A tinny clank of metal sounded, making her jump. She was hypersensitive to all sights and sounds.

Holy shit. Lucky's belt hung open and he drew his zipper down, pulled out his cock, and stroked it, without once taking his attention off her breasts.

"You're so gorgeous, Kori. I can't remember when I've been this hard."

She'd never watched a lover masturbate before, never really got the appeal. She got it now. The sight of Lucky pleasuring himself while looking at her nudity was hotter than just about anything she'd ever witnessed.

"Pants next. Panties too. Take them off at the same time."

She was wet. So wet. Soaked. Now there'd be no hiding it. She drew her jeans and panties over her hips—okay, this time around she did throw in a little wiggle for Lucky's benefit—then returned to a standing position.

"Fuck," he whispered. "Go sit on the edge of the bed. Lean back on your elbows and spread your legs. Wide. As wide as you can."

Following orders in bed wasn't typically her style, but she went with it and found herself loving it. The past six months had been so full of responsibility, heavy decisions, stress of balancing work and being a caregiver for an ailing parent. She was so tired of being the one to take charge, made choices, bear all the responsibility.

Lucky's commands took all of that away. For the next little while, she'd give in to him. Allow him to relieve her of all her worries, her obligations, her choices. All she'd do was follow his lead and reap the benefit of his experience.

She got in position, aware of Lucky's eyes on her the entire time. After she splayed her legs, he sauntered over and stood between her knees. Before she had time to do more than gape at his impressive erection, he dropped to his knees.

"Christ, Kori, you're drenched. Your thighs are fucking wet."

Heat rushed to her face and she started to close her legs.

"Uh uh, no way, babe. It's hot as fucking hell." He turned his head and licked her inner thigh, lapping up her juices.

His intentions became abundantly clear. "Um, Lucky?"

"Yeah, babe?" He trailed his tongue closer to the apex of her thighs. The silky hairs of his goatee stroked over her skin in a hundred featherlight touches that had goosebumps erupting all over her thighs.

"You don't need to ah...do...ah...that." Could she embarrass herself anymore?

Lucky rested back on his heels. One eyebrow rose so high it was practically at his hairline. "You don't want me to eat you out? You don't like it?"

Her skin was hot and flushed a combination of mortification and desire. Maybe the bed could just open up and swallow her whole. Then she could avoid this conversation. Or maybe she should have just kept her big mouth shut in the first place. "No, ah, that's not it. It's just, not my favorite."

"Not your favorite. Hmm." He pressed a kiss to her thigh. "That's too bad, because it's certainly my favorite."

"Going down on a woman is your favorite?"

"Fuck yeah. And I can already tell eating you out is going to be at the very top of my favorites list. You smell fucking amazing. And the tiny taste I already had? Delicious, baby. You'll see."

"I'll see? How will I see?"

"You gonna give me what I want?" he asked.

His declaration of how much he enjoyed it seemed sincere.

Kori's last boyfriend hated going down on her, made it seem like an arduous chore he couldn't stand. It had really affected her ability to enjoy oral sex. So, she'd stopped asking for it, and he never offered. The man before him had no idea what the hell he was doing and was way too arrogant to actually follow any direction. Again, she gave up on expecting it or asking for it. She was starting to think the experience would be vastly different with Lucky. "Yes," she said.

"I promise I'll change your mind. You'll be begging me to eat you out every day."

Every day? That had to be a figure of speech. Lucky didn't do every day. He'd made that crystal clear.

Her mind started to spin out of control with a million questions and thoughts. Just as she reminded herself that no matter what he said or what happened throughout the night, he was first and foremost a biker, he swiped his tongue through her folds, from the base of her pussy, right up to her clit.

"Oh my God." Her arms gave out and she collapsed back on the bed. Lucky chuckled and the vibrations had her stomach clenching. He pushed her legs wider, so wide the muscles stretched with a slight burn. Then he tongued her again and Kori was lost.

Yeah, there was a very good chance he was going to change her mind.

CHAPTER ELEVEN

Holy shit, the woman was fucking delicious. Lucky could have spent the entire night between her legs, feasting on her as though she was his very last meal on earth. Well, maybe not the entire night. His cock was so hard it bordered on painful and at some point, in the very near future, that would have to be addressed.

Kori's response was everything a man could hope for when pleasuring a woman. She moaned and thrashed, gripping his hair and holding him against her like she never had it so good. Like her whole world would crumble if he stopped.

No way in hell was he stopping.

Not until she screamed out her release, and maybe not even then.

Yeah right, she didn't like oral. Christ, if he didn't know better he'd think she was trying to smother him against her pussy with her strong thighs. His broad shoulders kept her legs wide open, but she squeezed him in a vise grip that clenched tighter with each whimper she emitted.

He gave her everything he had, licking, sucking, grazing his teeth over her most sensitive areas until she was a mess of pants and moans.

"More, Lucky, more. You're driving me crazy."

She had no idea what crazy was. His cock throbbed and ached with the furious need to be buried inside her. Her pussy would be tight and squeeze him to the point of insanity. He could tell by the way it clenched and spasmed around his tongue.

"Please, Lucky. I'm so close," she all but yelled at him.

He smiled. "Whatever the lady wishes."

Eager to feel her come, he sank two fingers her slick channel. As he pumped them in and out, her cries grew louder, more desperate. She'd completely abandoned herself to the pleasure and was lost in it. Lucky wrapped his lips around her clit and sucked. That sent her over the edge.

Her legs clamped down on him so hard he couldn't have extricated himself from the soft trap if he wanted to. A long, loud moan left her lips and her hips arched off the bed as she jerked through a powerful release.

He gentled his fingers, but kept them inside her, loving the hold her body had on him. Slowly, she calmed and a fine sheen of sweat coated her limp form as she lay sprawled on his bed.

Lucky rose and shucked his clothes before scooting her up the bed as he crawled up and over her. The smile she gave him was satisfied and just a little shy. Her lowered himself, so they were skin to skin, but kept the bulk of his weight supported on his elbows. Between them, his dick rested in the soaking wet V of her thighs.

"Well, I think it's safe to say you changed my mind. That wasn't like anything I've ever experienced and it just might have made the top of my own favorites list." There was wonder in her voice.

The feeling of conceited male pride that shot through him was something no man could resist when a woman said something like that. And this wasn't just any woman. It was Kori. Gorgeous, smart, funny, and a bit wary Kori.

He kissed her. Soft at first, but it didn't take more than three seconds for their need to bleed through and the kiss became hungry, frantic. When he ended it, her eyes were wide and she licked her lips, testing the new experience of having her own flavor on her taste buds.

The sight of that tongue had him groaning. "Told you, babe. Fucking delicious."

"Thank you," she whispered, and he knew exactly what she trying to convey. It wasn't gratitude for his mouth on her pussy or even the magnificent orgasm, but for taking an experience that hadn't been pleasant in the past and making it what it should have been. What it always should be.

"You gonna let me fuck you now?"

Her smile turned playful as she wrapped her legs around his waist and glided her wet pussy along his tortured length. "I'd have let you fuck me without all that, not that I'm complaining about the best orgasm of my life."

"Shit, babe, you're gonna feel better than anything I've ever had. Ease up a second. I need to get a condom on before I take you bare and risk knocking you up." He said those words on purpose, to shock himself. To remind himself of the fire he was playing with here. Unfortunately, instead of making him take ten steps back as it normally would, the idea of her growing and swelling with his child turned him on even more.

Fuck.

"Good thinking," she said, untangling her legs and letting him up.

He dug through his pockets until he found the strip of four condoms he'd shoved in there earlier, on a wing and prayer.

Kori seemed to have lost any shyness or reservation in the last few minutes. She lay on the bed, propped on a pillow, knees bent and legs spread, her glistening pussy on full display. The curve of her lips let him know she was well aware of her effect on him.

"You came pretty prepared for someone who should not have been expecting to get laid."

"I must just be an eternal optimist," he said as he settled back between her legs. It took a monumental amount of effort not to just ram into her, but somehow, he managed to tear a condom off the strip, rip the package open and roll it down his length. He had to do it himself. If she touched him now, he'd shoot off like a rocket, ruining all the fun. "They were all I had or I'd have stuffed my pockets to the brim."

"I'm clean, but not on the pill," she said with a shrug. "It's been a while since I needed it, so thanks for thinking of this."

"I've always gloved up, and I'm clean as well. I'd never put you at risk that way." As he spoke, he ran the tip of his erection through her folds. She gasped and raised her hips, following his movements.

She was so beautiful, laid out before him, trusting him to take care of her. That level of trust wasn't lost on him, especially since her one rule was no bikers. It was something he took seriously and he vowed she wouldn't regret this night. Or any other nights they might have, but that was something to think about later.

Right now, he needed inside her, but first...he still had yet to taste those full tits. A mistake that would be remedied in about three seconds. He lowered his head and sucked a puckered nipple into his mouth.

"Oh, yes. Suck me, Lucky." Her back arched, pushing her tit further into his mouth.

Ahh, so she liked that. He drew on her hard before switching to the other side and repeating the action. With gentle pressure, he bit down on her nipple and she cried out.

The uninhibited sound shot straight to his cock. Enough. Playtime was over. Time to get down to business.

Lucky released her nipple and grabbed her hand, wrapping her soft palm around his cock. She didn't play any games, didn't tease. They were both too needy for that. With a firm grip, she guided him to her opening.

He pushed into her in one long, slow, steady stroke. Jesus, she was blazing hot and tighter than he ever experienced. His eyes nearly crossed as inch by inch he disappeared into her. When he was seated to the hilt, with his balls resting against her round ass, their gazes locked and Lucky's entire world tilted on its axis.

It wasn't tangible. Wasn't something he could put his finger or even explain. It was a sense, a feeling his life had just changed. Contentment, belonging, possibilities, rightness…pure perfection all flowed through him. There was a connection between them that went far beyond mutual physical pleasure. It was powerful. It was intense.

It was scary as shit.

Kori must have felt it too because her eyes widened and a flash of alarm crossed her face before she lowered her eyelids. Unfamiliar and consuming emotions were easier to ignore if she cut the visual connection. It allowed her to concentrate solely on the physical and he wasn't having any of that shit.

If he was going to drown in this pool of madness, he was taking her with him.

"Don't block me out," he said. He pulled out to the tip, then flexed his hips and plunged back in, this time with much greater force.

A startled gasp left her lips and her eyes flew wide open. Blue irises, blurred with pleasure and vulnerability stared up at him.

"Eyes on me. The whole time."

The rhythm he found was fast and hard. He pummeled her with his dick, over and over, drawing harsh cries and moans from her. Each sound was music to his ears. It wasn't long before he found himself barreling toward a powerful orgasm. "You close, babe?"

Her eyes remained trained on him, but they seemed unfocused, lost in the pleasure. "Yes, so, so close."

Thirty seconds was about all he had left in him. Delaying his orgasm until his partner came was never a challenge. Not until tonight, anyway. He shifted, scooping her legs up until they rested on his shoulders. With the new position, he sank even deeper into her. In just three strokes, Kori began to tremble and her pussy clamped down on him. His name fell from her lips over and over as she came.

No way could he hold on with her body grabbing him like the tightest fist. He flew over the edge not two seconds after she did. Jesus Christ, he came hard. Harder than he could ever recall.

True to her word, Kori maintained eye contact with him throughout. Never had he stared into a woman's eyes as they came, and the experience was just as powerful as the entire encounter had been.

"I'll be back in one second," he said as he dashed off to take care of the condom. When he returned, she was sitting on the edge of the bed scanning the floor for her lost clothing. "You better not be about to tell me you're leaving."

She jumped and looked over her shoulder. "Oh, well, I don't want to wear out my welcome. You can't tell me you're a spend-the-night kinda guy." Now that the heat of the moment had passed, everything changed. Posture rigid, gaze unsure, she drew the bedsheet up and around her body, covering her nakedness.

Not happening.

Although, she had a point. He made it his business to get in, get off, and get out. Now, he wasn't an asshole, and the woman always enjoyed herself, at least once, but when it was done, it was done. Tonight, however, the idea of Kori leaving left him cold. It was completely crazy, so out of character, even his brothers wouldn't recognize him, but for tonight he didn't care. That could be tomorrow's worry.

"I wouldn't have stuck four condoms in my pocket if I only planned on using one." He laid back on the bed, snagged her by the waist and toppled her down. She landed with a squeak. While she was distracted by the fall, he yanked the sheet away from her and sucked a nipple into his mouth.

Her squeak turned into a moan and the tension drained out of her muscles.

"Let's see. I think we can use one on my kitchen counter because I'm getting hungry again. Then I'd give my left nut to have you ride my cock, so that's two. Then we can take that last

66

sucker into the shower with us while we clean up." He winked. "We'll be pretty dirty by then. What do you say, angel?"

She studied him with a serious expression. What the hell was going through her mind?

"Hmm, so that means you aren't planning on taking me from behind."

That was as good as an agreement, and for reasons unknown, his heart soared. "Next time, beautiful. Next time."

And there would be a next time. He'd make fuckin' sure of it.

CHAPTER TWELVE

Kori suppressed a giant yawn and squirmed on the barstool. Going from a two-and-a-half-year sex drought to an all-night pleasure fest left her sore in more than a few places. A nice comfy recliner was what she needed right now, not an unforgiving, wooden barstool. But that wasn't an option.

Rebel had called her cell early in the morning with a million apologies for standing her up and they rescheduled for a lunch date. The timing was perfect. She needed an excuse to get away from Lucky. The intensity of what they shared, both emotionally and physically, had her running scared.

Dinner had been spent coming to grips with the fact that she was crazy attracted to a biker and giving herself permission to indulge in one night with him. By the time they left, she'd been cool with it and prepared to break her rule.

Then, they'd gotten back to Lucky's place and everything was blown right out of the water. They connected on a level she'd been searching for her entire adult life, but had never found. Not to mention he talked of next time as though he wasn't finished with her, as though he wanted to spend time with her.

Why did he have to be a biker? A sexy, badass, alpha biker named for the ease with which he bedded women. A biker who made her laugh, made her smile, and made her come like the world was ending. A biker was the last thing she wanted or needed.

Growing up, how many women had she seen shattered by the violence, drugs, and most of all, the infidelity rampant in an MC? Far too many for her to be jumping into bed with the first biker who looked her way. She thought of her mother. Her ol' man, the asshole, couldn't keep his dick in his pants if it was minus twenty degrees and he was standing in the middle of a blizzard.

"Hey, Kori, give me five minutes then we can roll out," Rebel said.

Savage stood next to him, arms crossed over an impressive chest. But his eyes, that stared at her with an undisguised hunger, seemed to lack some human element. They were creepy, unsettling, and made her feel like prey. And not in the sexy I'm-about-to-ravage-you way.

"No problem, I'm not in any kind of rush. Whenever you're ready to go is fine by me, Rebel." Calling him Dad didn't seem right just yet.

"Thanks, baby girl."

Her heart squeezed at the nickname. As far back as she could remember, that's what her mother had called her, no matter how old she got. To hear it from Rebel's lips was disturbing, but not necessarily unpleasant. Almost like her mother was there lending her approval of Kori's choice to seek him out and spend some time in Vegas.

"Savage can keep you company while I finish taking care of some bullshit." He glanced between her and Savage and a smile curled his lips. "In fact, Savage, why don't you join us for lunch?"

Say no. Say no. She wouldn't be rude but really didn't want to spend an extended period of time in his presence. There was just something about him that set off her red flagometer. It had nothing to do with his heavily tattooed arms, neck, hands and probably many other parts she couldn't see. It had nothing to do with his grim expression, hardened face or slightly crooked nose. Nope, it was those damn cold eyes.

"I'd love to, Pres. I'll be here with your little girl when you're ready to bug out."

Rebel slapped Savage's back then strode in the direction of his office.

Her hackles rose. Little girl? Really?

"Mind if I sit here?" He indicated the empty seat next to her.

What was she supposed to say? *Yes, I do mind. Please leave?* "It's all yours."

"You look like him, you know?" He rested back against the bar, stretching his far-reaching wingspan along the wooden bar top. If she leaned back herself, she'd pretty much be in his embrace, so she didn't. Back straight, she remained close to the front of her stool.

"I thought the same thing when I met him. Same eyes and nose."

Savage nodded. "Gotta say, though, you're much better looking."

A genuine laugh bubbled out at his comparison of her attractiveness to her bald and bearded father whose face bore the marks of his unhealthy lifestyle. Maybe she'd been wrong in judging this book by its cover. "Well, thanks. I'm a bit relieved you think so."

He cupped her right shoulder then stroked his rough fingers down her arm. She jumped then grimaced when her sore lady parts bumped against the stool. Not pleasant.

"How about after lunch we come back to my room here and I let you suck my dick?"

Nope, she was dead on in her initial impression. Creep.

"Uh, yeah, I don't think so." Did he really just ask that?

"I'll make sure it's good for you, babe. You've got some great tits. Hot ass, too."

Her face flamed and her discomfort level rose to red. Mindful of her sore body parts, she slid off the stool and away from his touch. "Look, Savage. I'm kinda seeing someone." Oh Jesus, why

70

the hell had she said that? She'd basically just claimed Lucky. Not smart.

The leering smile dissolved off his face and his eyes iced over. Obviously, this was not a man used to hearing the word no from women. Not surprising since club whores were ready and willing to drop to their knees for any club member at any time.

He leaned closer. "Listen, bitch, don't think that just because you're the new club princess that you're anything special. You got a snatch and a purpose just like the rest of 'em." The look in his eye was…well, it was pretty damn savage, and whatever hunger she had a few minutes ago soured to nausea in her gut.

"Look—"

Two arms banded around her waist from behind, locking her against a hard chest. A prominent bulge pressed into her lower back and a set of fur rimmed lips landed on her neck.

Lucky.

How was it that after just one night, she knew him by touch alone? Granted, almost the entire night was spent experiencing said touch, but still. It was too much, too fast, and yet she'd never been more grateful for the interruption.

She craned her neck and smiled up at him. His face was hard, attention on Savage, but after just a second he looked down at her. Then, he kissed her. The kiss was a bit too hungry, a bit too possessive for a simple greeting. It was more of a claiming, a warning to Savage.

A bone between two snarling dogs was not what she wanted to be, and she prepared to tell both of them just that. But then Lucky pulled back and looked at her with lust-filled eyes.

"Hey, angel," he whispered.

There was no posturing, no competition, no thoughts of Savage. Just Lucky's handsome face and her rapidly beating heart.

"I have so much shit to do today, but I was useless. Figured I might as well come get a fix before I get back to work."

He genuinely sounded like he needed her to get through his morning. Her heart melted into a gooey puddle in her chest. She was swimming in some deep water and needed a life raft.

A throat cleared and she jumped and swiveled her head back around. Rebel was back and he stared at her and Lucky with one eyebrow raised and hands on his hips.

Whoops. Busted by Daddy like a fifteen-year-old. She chuckled but no one else seemed amused by the situation. Rebel's mouth flattened with displeasure, Savage looked like he could murder Lucky with his bare hands, and if the tension in Lucky was any indication, he wasn't pleased either. Crap. Rebel had told them all to keep away from her, not that it was his right to do so. She and Lucky were consenting adults. If Rebel thought he was going to parent her, he had another think coming. Still, she felt a little guilty for any trouble Lucky might get into over this.

"So, ah, ready to go, Rebel?" Best idea was probably just to blow it off so everyone could get on with their day.

"Yeah, I'm ready. You got a lot to do today, don't you, Lucky? Let's go, baby girl. You're on the back of Savage's bike."

Lucky's arms tightened around her to the point of uncomfortable. Shit. Riding on the back of an MC member's bike was a huge deal to them. She'd been on the back of Lucky's last night and the way he was acting now, there was a good chance he'd go for Savage's throat if she got within ten feet of the other man's motorcycle.

"Actually, I have some things to pick up this afternoon, and I'll need the trunk space. So, I'll just take my car and meet you at the restaurant."

Savage shook his head. "No can do, princess. You heard the boss, you're riding with me." The fuck-you-smirk on his face was aimed right at Lucky.

"Rebel, really, I need a bunch of stuff if I'm going to stay awhile and it will be a pain in the ass if I have to come back here and get my car first. I'll drive myself."

Rebel scratched a hand through his beard before nodding. "Fine. But let's move. I'm fuckin' hungry and I need a drink." He turned and strode out of the club house, Savage hot on his heels.

Kori faced Lucky but couldn't make eye contact after that unnerving scene. "I better get going."

He kissed her, hard and quick, then growled against her ear. "I'll be at Rebel's by four. I want you there, ready to explain what the fuck I walked in on."

Yikes. Goodbye fun and sexy Lucky from the previous night. Hello seriously pissed off biker Lucky.

"I'll be there. We'll talk." She wiggled out of his embrace and jogged after the men.

Two goals for the afternoon. First, survive a lunch with her new father and his leering lackey. And second, survive an interrogation by an angry biker she alternately wanted to fuck and run from. Should prove to be a day full of fun and games.

CHAPTER THIRTEEN

"So, you and Lucky, huh?" Rebel asked after two beers and a diet cola had been delivered to their table in the small, family run diner.

He didn't waste any time. Looked like they weren't going to let that elephant stomp around the room for very long.

"Well, uh, I guess so. I'm not exactly sure what it is yet, so no point in talking about it." She traced drops of condensation down her glass and kept her gaze averted. One look in her eyes and they'd know she was fibbing. They'd know last night had knocked her on her ass and she hadn't quite righted herself yet.

"Hmm." Rebel drank from his bottle then leaned back in his chair. "Not sure he's the best fit for you, baby girl."

Was he for real? Pretty much the only thing Rebel knew about her was that she was his surprise daughter. He didn't even know her birthday let alone what kind of man that was right for her. Not that she disagreed. Lucky definitely wasn't for her, but there was something up Rebel's sleeve.

"Really? Why's that?" The iced tea left a bitter taste in her mouth as she waited for an answer she didn't want to hear.

Rebel shrugged. "He's just not one of my best men. Bit of a slacker, not a great producer. I'd be over the moon if you wanted to be an ol' lady, but I can think of a few better men than Lucky."

She swallowed a rancid sip and tried to think of a response. Rebel was full of shit, she was sure of it. For some reason, he didn't want her with Lucky and seemed to be forcing Savage, who'd been quiet through the exchange, upon her.

Before she had a chance to open her mouth, Rebel spoke again. "Just saying, I think you should aim a little higher on the food chain." He cast a look at Savage and the pieces clicked into place.

Savage was being groomed to take over the club at some point. If she was his ol' lady by the time Rebel stepped down, he probably thought he'd still have some control. MC politics. And there was why she tried so hard to stay away all these years. Now, one week into this Vegas trip, she was in lust with a biker and smack in the middle of a mess. Great.

"You know what? I'd much rather use this time to get to know each other better. We can save the discussion of my love life for another day."

Rebel grunted but seemed satisfied with her request. Luckily, the perky young waitress arrived with their lunch. After placing their meals on the table, she stuck out her chest and fluttered her eyes at Savage.

He made no move to disguise the way he zeroed in on her breasts. The girl couldn't have been older than eighteen. Savage had to be twice her age. Lovely. If this was how he acted when he was trying to win her over, Kori couldn't even imagine how he'd treat an actual girlfriend.

"Anything else I can get you? *Anything* at all?" Her voice was high pitched, whiney.

Oh please. Kori mentally rolled her eyes.

"We're good, sweetheart." Savage winked before digging into his fries.

Kori's appetite had fled an hour ago, but she forced a bite of her burger. Conversation eventually turned to the get-to-know-you questions and answers that were much more comfortable. Rebel learned her birthday, where she went to school, what she did for a living, and he asked a surprising number of questions about her mother as well.

In return, she learned he never married, had no other children —that he knew of—and the club was his life. Savage remained mostly quiet through the meal throwing winks her way every time Rebel sang his praises, which ended up being quite frequently.

Savage was his right-hand man. Savage kept the club running smoothly. Savage would make an amazing president one day. Savage was respected by all club members. Pretty much the only thing Rebel didn't mention was what kind of lover Savage was. Kori could pretty much guess that one for herself.

They lingered for about two hours before Rebel needed to get back to the clubhouse. He gave Savage a few chores and both men zoomed off on their bikes in the opposite direction she planned to take.

It was two o'clock when she returned to Rebel's house. That gave her two hours of peace before she had to deal with Lucky. Rebel's liquor cabinet beckoned her and she poured herself a healthy glass of scotch. Sure, it was early, but it was a Saturday and she wasn't planning to drive anywhere for the rest of the day. Why not imbibe?

Maybe it would help calm the whirling in her mind that began the moment Lucky picked her up last night and only seemed to stop when she was on the verge of coming.

After pouring herself a drink, she sank onto Rebel's tattered couch and rested her head back. If she fell asleep, the sound of Lucky's bike would wake he before he made it halfway down the street. A nap would do her good. Give her brain time to rest stop obsessing over the past few days' events.

Of course, her dreams might have a different idea.

"Come on, Robbie, I don't have all fuckin' day." Lucky scratched the back of his neck and scanned his surroundings. They were completely alone in the alley. Not that that was any kind of surprise. The stench from the restaurant dumpster would keep anyone with an IQ above that of a worm away.

Apparently, he was pretty dumb.

Rex shifted and rubbed his track-marked arms. The man couldn't stay still for more than five seconds in a row. His beady brown eyes were just as hyperactive as the rest of him. And, man, were those eyes sunken. Heroin and whatever other chemicals the guy could shove in his veins or up his nose had kicked his trash for years and it showed in his bony, strung out appearance.

"Spill, Robbie."

A lock of greasy, mud brown hair fell in front of Robbie's eyes and he shoved it away before blowing out a breath.

"Look, Lucky, you know I'm loyal to you man, but going around and asking questions behind Rebel's back? That's just asking for a shit load of trouble."

"Aww, Robbie, I didn't realize you cared so much about my safety." Lucky had saved the other man's life a year or so back. It was a case of right place at the right time. He'd come across Robbie getting his ass beat after a drug deal gone wrong. Since then, Robbie had been a great contact to have on the streets.

Robbie snorted. "I don't. It's your club, your fuckin' ass to risk. But who the fuck is gonna look out for me when Rebel or Savage—that motherfucker's crazy. Anyway, who's gonna protect me when they find out you've been snooping around and asking shit about them?"

"The only way anyone will find out shit is if you run your damn mouth, Robbie. And if you do that, Rebel and Savage will be the least of your problems. Get me?" He loomed over the thin man, using his physical superiority to his advantage.

Robbie held up his hands up near his head. "Hey, man I ain't gonna say nothin'. And don't be like that. We're friends."

With a frustrated sigh, Lucky dug into his pocket and pulled out two twenties. "We are definitely not friends." He waved the money under Robbie's nose. "Now, what do you have for me?" The fact that thirty seconds after Lucky left, that money would be flooding through Robbie's veins made Lucky feel sick, but he needed the information any way he could get it.

The junkie's eyes lit up like a Christmas tree. Christ, was this was it was like for his sister at the end? Would she have done anything, sold her soul to anyone for a few bucks' worth of dope? It was a stupid question because he knew the answer.

It was yes. She would have done any damn thing for a hit. While Lucky's twenty-two-year-old self was overseas fighting for his country, his seventeen-year-old baby sister, Melissa, had been giving blowjobs in the back of a car in exchange for drugs.

The memories still had the power to make him physically ill.

"Hey, you listening, man?"

Shit.

Lucky shook his head to dislodge the unpleasant thoughts and focused on Robbie. "Yeah. Talk."

"Word is that Rebel and Savage want to up their game. Right now, they're small scale suppliers, but they want to be major players. Won't happen today, they have too much competition, but they're ruthless enough to get there soon."

Shit. This was exactly what Lucky was afraid of. His president was too greedy, too money hungry to be satisfied with a few extra dollars in his pocket. Once he realized how much cash he could rake in pushing that shit, it was only a matter of time before he became a ruthless contender in the ever-competitive war to be Vegas's drug kingpin.

"Okay, he wants more. No surprise there. Any idea what this might mean for my club?"

"It means he's gonna need help soon. He's selling good shit. Word is getting out and customers are lining up. Best guess? I give it five months. In five months, he's gonna be a major player and he's gonna need more manpower. Where's the easiest place to get it?"

"Fuck. The club."

Robbie nodded. "Can I have that money now?"

"Yeah." Lucky handed over the bills. "Thanks, Robbie." But the other man wasn't paying attention anymore. He stared at the money, a hungry gleam in his eye. Apparently, Lucky had been replaced by thoughts of his next fix.

Whatever. His problems had just gotten much bigger than giving a shit if Robbie ignored him. Barely resisting the urge to ram his fist into the brick wall flanking the alley, he turned and walked his bike to the street.

The day had gone to shit real fast after he left the clubhouse. Actually, it took a dive off a high cliff the moment he caught Savage staring at Kori's tits like he was imagining their taste. Fucking bastard. The club's VP was the last man Kori need in her life and Lucky would be pissed about the man's interest in her even if he wasn't interested himself.

Interested. He snorted. He was far beyond interested, bordering on obsessed.

His afternoon was spent redoing inventory at two club-owned bars because a moron of a prospect fucked it all up and the bar manager called frantic when their delivery was short. It was a giant ass pain, but he was eventually able to sort it out and get a rush order that would be delivered in an hour or so. The task took three times as long as it should have because thoughts of Kori sitting across the table from Savage while he salivated over her attacked Lucky's brain every ten seconds.

And now Robbie had pretty much guaranteed the rest of his day would be shit as well. He hit the throttle and peeled out on the street. At least worry about his club over the past half hour had taken the place of obsessing over Kori.

The No Prisoners didn't push drugs. It was in the bylaws and made them different from many other MCs. It's what had drawn Lucky. After what happened to Melissa, he couldn't stomach the thought of joining an MC that dealt drugs. And most did. The No Prisoners had a number of reasons for staying out of that business, but the two biggest were it was the easiest way to keep the cops off their backs, and the easiest way to keep members from spiraling out of control.

Would the club go for it? If Rebel came to them and said they could be rolling in it selling drugs, would it pass a vote?

It was a tough question to answer.

At one point Lucky would have said hell no, but that was before. Now, with their president and VP pulling in legitimate dough, there just may be a good number of members loyal to them who were willing to follow.

Lucky had been loyal to them. A month ago, he would have said he'd die for any one of his club brothers. Now, he was finding out there was a limit to loyalty, and he was gearing up to turn on them.

Five months. In that time, he needed to make a decision he could live with and act on it.

This knowledge he had, this secret knowledge of what Rebel and Savage were doing was slowly eating away at him. He was completely alone in this and that's not how he preferred to operate. The club was a family, and they acted as one. A close knit one. They made decisions together, they worked together, succeeded together, failed together.

Or so he'd thought.

Finding out two of those members, the two that should be the most willing to put the club's needs above their own, were fucking around behind everyone's back was like a knife in the fucking chest.

The MC had taken the place of his marine corps brothers when he left the service and filled an important role in his life. It made him queasy to think of betraying them. And even sicker to think Rebel and Savage's greed put him in this position.

And now there was Kori to think about. Innocent Kori who walked into a buzzing hornet's nest, completely unaware, with the mission of getting close to Rebel. He couldn't allow her to be caught in any crossfire and needed to factor her into any decisions he made. Number one priority had to be, and was, keeping her safe.

Rebel's small house came into view. She was outside, leaning against the door frame, a glass in her hand when he coasted up to the house. Gone were the jeans she'd worn earlier, replaced by cutoff shorts that showed off her long, smooth, toned legs. The legs that had held him against her as he pumped into her for all he was worth.

Pounds of built up tension and stress drained away in anticipation of spending time with her. Blood rushed to his cock so fast, it left him lightheaded. He needed to tear his eyes off her if he didn't want to lay down the bike and make a fool of himself.

Then he remembered Savage's ravenous expression back at the clubhouse and he was tense all over again. And spoiling for a good fight. Ramming his fist into Savage's face a few times would go a long way towards easing his demons.

But that wasn't going to happen anytime soon. Looked like he was going to have to fuck the stress out.

After he got some damn answers.

CHAPTER FOURTEEN

Kori stayed in place as Lucky trudged up the driveway. Everything about him screamed pissed off. In fact, it seemed his anger had grown in the few hours since she'd left him. This couldn't all be from what happened at the clubhouse earlier, could it? The reaction seemed overblown, out of proportion to the situation, especially considering he didn't know what the hell happened with Savage.

Actually, he looked pretty close to losing it, and as he drew near, the torture in his expression became apparent. Something else had happened. Something that had him very upset.

He hopped up on the stoop and advanced on her until he was just an inch away. With one hand on the house and one on the door, he caged her in and stared down at her. His nearness made her breasts swell and had blood zinging through her veins. If she'd had lustful thoughts about him before, now that she knew what the man could deliver, the thoughts were rampant and erotic.

Kori took a small sip from a fresh glass of scotch then held it out to him. With one gulp, he knocked it back. Her gaze was drawn to the strong lines of his throat as he swallowed. The urge to lick him there, right next to his bobbing Adam's apple, was great, but she wasn't sure where they stood at the moment.

"Rebel home?"

She shook her head. "He's hardly ever here. I guess he sleeps at the clubhouse most nights."

"You enjoy your lunch?"

Did she? Good question. Not really. It would have been much more enjoyable if it didn't feel like a setup. And if Savage looked at his food instead of her breasts. She shrugged. "It was fine."

"Fine, huh? Did you eat, or did you just sit back and stick out your tits so Savage could look his fill?" His voice was dark, angry, and...jealous?

Not that jealousy was an excuse for acting like a Neanderthal. She pushed against his muscular chest, trying to get some space. Nothing happened. It was like he didn't even notice. "Back off, Lucky."

"Not until you tell me what the fuck was going on when I got to the clubhouse earlier. Why was Savage looking at you like you were his and why was Rebel looking at me like I was dog shit he stepped in? Was that no biker rule a crock of shit? You really looking to work your way through the club one brother at a time? Cuz I'm not sure how Daddy's gonna feel about his girl being a club whore."

The lust-filled blood that had been singing in her veins turned to ice. How dare he? No man spoke to her like that and got away with it. This was why she avoided bikers like she avoided an STD.

"What the hell is it to you? You had your one night. Time to walk away." Her face was so hot, it nearly made her dizzy.

A low growl erupted from Lucky's chest and he leaned in until they were at eye level. "I asked you a question."

Again, she got the impression that his anger wasn't solely due to Savage's behavior, but something more. "So the fuck what? I don't owe you any damn answers. You know, for someone who claims to be in it for an easy one or two nights, you're sure acting like a possessive ape right now." She shoved his chest again. "Back the fuck off."

When he didn't move yet again, her anger grew to boiling. Her hands landed on his chest once more and this time she was going to get him to move. But the moment she touched him, he seemed to deflate.

His chin dropped to his chest and the air whooshed out of his lungs. "Shit. You're right. I'm sorry. I'm being a complete asshole."

Her eyes widened. How often did a man admit he was wrong? Let alone apologize? Not frequently in her experience. "Why?" Her voice was barely above a whisper.

With his focus still on the ground, he shook his head, then lifted his gaze to hers. "Savage doesn't have a great reputation with women. He's, well, he's not known for being gentle. I saw him looking at you like he wanted to do all the things that I want to do to you. It sent me through the roof."

The things he *wanted* to do to her? Not the things that he'd already done to her? Did that mean he wanted more? "This isn't a conversation for outside."

With a nod and a severe expression, he said, "Go on in."

She reached back and opened the door without looking, then threaded her fingers through his. Something was wrong and if she could provide even a small amount of comfort, then she would.

He looked at their joined hands like he was surprised by the gesture, then he gave her a squeeze and followed her into the house. She led him to the couch.

The second his ass hit the couch he reached for her and drew her up and across his lap. They were face to face, with her straddling him. His hands rested on her ass.

"What happened today, Lucky?" she asked. "You look like something is really wrong."

He shook his head and picked up a long lock of her hair, rubbing it between his fingers. "Just club shit."

"Are you okay?"

"Fine, angel. Nothing for you to worry about."

Typical biker answer. Also a lie. "Why do you keep calling me angel? I'm definitely not an angel."

With a sheepish grin, he held her hair up in front of her face.

"My hair? I don't get it?"

"It's so white it almost glows. It um…" He cleared his throat and she swore a red tinge colored his cheeks. "It reminded me of an angel. Especially last night when it was spread out around your head on my pillow."

Wow. What was she supposed to say to that?

"Is Rebel pissed at me over something?" he asked, knocking the sweet feeling right out of her.

The sigh she meant to conceal snuck out as she shook her head. Maybe some physical contact would help him keep his cool while she told him. She placed both hands on his chest, under the open panels of the cut. "Look, Savage came on to me at the clubhouse and I turned him down flat. Then he got a little vulgar. It made me a bit uncomfortable but wasn't anything I couldn't handle. That's when you walked in. Rebel seems to have it in his mind that Savage and I would be good together which probably accounts for the dirty looks. Most of my lunch was spent listening to how wonderful Savage is and what amazing stuff he does for the club."

A low growl came from deep in Lucky's gut. "Stay the fuck away from Savage, babe. Rebel is blind where he's concerned, but he can be a real asshole."

She frowned. "I have no interest in him. In fact, he makes me pretty uncomfortable. But you sound kinda hostile towards him, and not thrilled with Rebel. Is something going on with you guys?"

"Just club shit, babe. Not something I can talk about, and like I said, not something to worry about. You just concentrate on getting to know your old man and figuring out if you want to stick around. My vote is yes."

Her heart soared. "You want me to stay?"

His hands on her ass clenched and ground her against his erection. "What do you think?" he asked as he kissed her.

The man was an excellent kisser. He could teach classes on kissing. Hell, he could teach a few other classes as well. But before she lost control and jumped him, she had to know. "So, not to be that girl, but you don't do relationships and I don't date bikers, so…"

"So, this is pretty fucked then, huh?" They both chuckled and he nipped her bottom lip. "I have no fucking idea, Kori. This is uncharted territory for me, but I'll tell you what I do know. I like you. Spending time with you last night, even before the mind-blowing sex, was the most fun I've had in a long time. I've got some shit going on right now. Stuff I can't, and I'm not ready to talk about, but for the first time ever, spending time with a woman made me feel better, stronger…just fuckin' good. And that's before we even talk about that mouth, and these tits." His hands left her ass and cupped her breasts, thumbs rubbing over her tight nipples. "All I know is that I want more. More of this," he said pinching her nipples through the thin shirt and bra.

Goddamn, it felt so good. Her body softened, readying for him, and she couldn't resist the need to press against his erection.

He let out a low hiss. "And more of what's in here." One long finger tapped against the side of her head. "I want to give us a try, a chance to be something. Whatever that something ends up being."

Everything besides Lucky faded into the background as she took in his heartfelt words. Words she was one hundred percent certain he'd never said to a woman before. They weren't a line. Hell, he didn't need lines. Women fell at his feet when he walked in a room. But warning bells chimed in her head. He was a biker.

Bikers were violent. Bikers partied too hard. Bikers cheated.

What her brain screamed didn't seem to matter to her heart or her body. She wanted Lucky. Wanted to get to know him as much as he seemed to want to get to know her.

Oh, Jesus. She was going to do it.

"I don't share," she whispered.

A loud snort broke the silence of the room. "You think I do? No, angel, this will be you and me only. God help any man who tries to come between that."

"Or any woman."

"There's no other woman, Kori. None who meant a damn thing. Ever. You are the first and only that I've been genuinely interested in. Okay?"

Perhaps those words should have been a red flag in and of themselves. Who made it to their mid-thirties without having romantic feelings for someone from the opposite sex, even if it was one sided? Instead of being concerned, her traitorous heart fluttered at his words. Who wouldn't want to be the only woman Lucky cared for?

"You do realize this is crazy, right? And will probably blow up in our faces?" she asked.

His answer was the same lopsided grin he'd given her last night. The real smile. No agenda, no deception. And it reeled her in. "Okay. Let's do it."

The smile grew bigger, but his eyes still told the tale of someone struggling with a demon. Maybe there was something she could do to help ease his burdens, if only for a while.

With a wink, she shifted off his lap and settled on the floor between his legs. One of his eyebrows rose as she reached for his fly. "Got something in mind for me?"

Playing with him was so much fun. Somehow, she was comfortable enough around him already to ignore her inhibitions, be silly, and tease him. "I do."

He obliged her by lifting his ass as she worked his jeans and boxers over his hips. "What's your plan? Oh fuck," he said as she wrapped her hand around his length and pumped twice.

"Hmm, I'm pretty sure you can guess what comes next."

"I can." His voice was a rough croak. "I just want to hear you say it."

"Oh, well, in that case, I'm thinking I'll suck your cock until you come down my throat. Then you can take me to your place and return the favor. I'm pretty sure Rebel is out for the night, but it's never a guarantee."

"Less talk about my president, more cock in your mouth." Lucky winked.

She chuckled. "Such a romantic," she said as she lowered her mouth to him. Starting at the base of his shaft, she licked a long line up the underside. The hiss that greeted her was like music to her ears. There was something to be said for taking a strong, alpha man like Lucky and controlling him with one swipe of the tongue.

When she got to the head, she swirled her tongue around it and his dick jerked. "Eager little sucker, isn't he?"

"Little?"

She laughed. When had sex ever been this fun? "My apologies. Eager monster, isn't he?"

"Damn straight," Lucky said.

Enough banter. Kori opened her mouth wide and sank down on him, taking him as deep as she could. He was right, there was nothing little about his cock, and it would take her a few minutes to get used to him and take him further. Not that he seemed to mind.

"Jesus, fuck," he yelled, one hand flying up to fist in her hair.

It was a new and a bit unnerving experience. Kori had always been the one in complete control when going down on a guy. Now, with his hand holding her head, she was very aware that he was giving her the control and could snatch it back at any time.

Rather than pissed, it made her hot. She became bolder as she worked him with her mouth, sucking with alternating pressure and adding her tongue to the mix. As she grew more comfortable and relaxed, he was able to slide deeper. When he finally hit the back of her throat she swallowed and his reaction was off the charts.

A harsh shout left him and he held her head harder, taking some of that control for himself. She forced herself to stay relaxed as he thrust his hips and plunged in and out of her mouth. It was a combined effort, he didn't completely take over and fuck her mouth, but much of the pace was now his to regulate.

She grew wetter by the second and wasn't sure she'd make it to his house before she needed some relief.

"Fuck, baby, that mouth is amazing. I'm about ten seconds away. You want to pull off, or you gonna swallow me down?"

Kori gripped his hips, hard, and swirled her tongue one more time around the tip before sucking him back into the depths of his mouth. She swallowed around him once again and he lost it. Salty warmth filled her throat as he came with grunts and moans.

She held him in place until he settled, then let his softening cock slide out of her mouth. His eyes were dazed, satisfied, but the hunger was still there. It was going to be a good night. "Kori, that was unbelievable. Come up here." He patted his chest. "I'll return the favor as soon as I'm not dead."

"Take me to your apartment first. I want us to be able to lose control without worrying about being caught like I'm a teenager."

"Sure, baby. Ten minutes."

She settled against his chest and listened to the slowing beat of his heart. Now that the room was quiet, her mind reeled with questions.

Was had she gotten herself into?

Was she crazy?

Was this a giant mistake?

Time would tell. She'd go with it for now, and pray her heart wouldn't end up shattered in the process.

CHAPTER FIFTEEN

Rebel cast his gaze around the empty clubhouse—his kingdom as he privately called it—and smirked. Life as a king was pretty fuckin' sweet. It wasn't that he could do no wrong, but it was pretty damned close.

These men, these brothers of his, possessed a strong sense of loyalty that bordered on blindness. For nearly a year he and Savage had been peddling drugs and not a single member of his club was in the know. Not one. Not an inkling that something was wrong. They followed him like sheep, baa-ing and doing his bidding.

Exactly what he needed when the time came to bring more of them into his little side business which was rapidly growing into a large scale side business.

He glanced at his watch. Where the fuck was Savage? His second in command was supposed to be there fifteen minutes ago and the man was punctual to a fault.

Well, he had five minutes until Rebel—

The door swung open and Savage entered, wrestling another man through the door. The guy was bone-thin with the glazed eyes of the fully baked and he looked like he'd gone a few rounds with Savage and hadn't faired too well.

"What the fuck is this, Savage?" Rebel pulled a package of cigarettes from his pocket and lit one up. He suffered from a constant low level of agitation tamed only by the flow of nicotine in his bloodstream. As he inhaled and let the drug work its magic, he kept his gaze on the man who Savage shoved into a chair.

Despite his black eye, bloodied lip and lolling head, the man appeared to be feeling no pain. Rebel knew a good customer when he saw one. Question was, what did Savage have against the junkie.

"Not what, Pres, but who. This here is Robbie. Robbie has one purpose in life—fill his veins with heroin as often as possible. Ain't that right, Robbie?" Savage asked. There was no response so he smacked the scrawny man on the back of his head. "I asked you a question, junkie."

Still no answer, so Savage shrugged.

"Savage, we've got shit to do. We don't have time for games. Get to the point." He stared at the smoke curling from his half-smoked cigarette. In some ways, he could sympathize with the man's addiction.

"This ain't no fuckin' game, Pres. We've got a problem."

Rebel raised an eyebrow. "And that would be?" He loved Savage like a son but the man could be a fuckin' drama queen at times. "Get to the point."

"Robbie's been running his mouth on the streets. Talking about the No Prisoners selling his favorite shit."

Rebel resisted the urge to roll his eyes and sucked in more smoke. "What, did you expect all these users to keep their traps shut? Of course they're talking, Savage. That's how we get more business. What the fuck's your problem?"

Savage's expression turned cold. He did deadly intent better than anyone Rebel had met. "Robbie is a good friend of Lucky."

The cigarette hung limply between his fingers as Savage's words penetrated Rebel's consciousness. Friend of Lucky. Friend of Lucky…

His eyes met Savage's icy stare and his VP nodded, confirming his worst fears. Lucky knew. Lucky was the one club member Rebel had been certain would not under any circumstances get on board with selling drugs. His junkie whore of a little sister hadn't known when to quit and sent herself straight into the afterlife when she was still a teenager. Lucky was a rabid anti-drug crusader.

A searing pain hit his fingers. "Shit!" he yelled, dropping the offending cigarette stub and shaking out his burned finger. How long had he stood there staring at Savage?

"Shit!" he screamed louder this time. "He knows?" Rebel rushed forward and grabbed Robbie by the front of his filthy shirt. His head lolled and Rebel gave him a severe shake. "You're sure he fucking knows?"

Robbie smiled and laughed, the sound giddy, almost euphoric. "He knows. We talk about it all the time. You gonna give me some more?" He swung his gaze to Savage. "He said if I talked to you he'd give me some free samples."

"Fuck." Rebel released him and he landed in the chair with a thud. With a roar of frustration, Rebel paced the room and dug another cigarette out of his pocket. This time the sweet hit of nicotine did nothing to calm the beast rising within him.

"Get him the fuck out of here, Savage. I need to think, process." In a rush of fury, he kicked over a barstool sending shards of wood flying through the air. "Any idea how long? Has he told anyone else?"

Savage shook his head. "I don't know. He's too fucking high to remember much. I'll interrogate him properly after he comes down. I have a feeling with the proper motivation and just ten minutes without a hit he'll be spilling his guts."

Rebel nodded. "Good, that's good." He ran a hand across his scalp.

"This may not be as bad as you think, Pres," Savage said. He walked behind the bar and grabbed a bottle off the shelf. After filling two glasses he handed one off to Rebel. It would take a lot more than one drink to deal with this news.

"How so? You think there's a chance in hell Lucky won't go after us for this?" He savored the welcome burn of booze hitting his system.

"There's Kori."

Rebel stopped dead in his tracks.

Kori.

Savage was right. There was Kori. Gears started turning in his head, clunking into place and activating a plan. It hadn't been long, but Lucky appeared uncharacteristically drawn to Kori. Hell, he'd been with her for a few weeks now which in and of itself was unexpected Lucky behavior. In Rebel's experience, men who'd been around as much as Lucky tended to never date much. They went from bed hopping to wedded bliss. Or at least the illusion of marital ecstasy.

A quick shudder ran through him. Let the others attempt monogamy. Not for him, and he'd never thought for Lucky, but apparently, all it took was one good pussy to bring a man down.

The fact that the pussy in question belonged to his daughter was icing on the cake. "I can use this. We can use this," Rebel said.

Savage nodded. The evil grin he did so well curved his mouth.

"You want her, don't you?" Rebel studied his VP's face.

"I do."

"Hmm. Then I think you should have her." He tossed the smoldering butt to the floor and ground it under his booted heel.

"What do you have in mind?" Savage asked, his eyes shining with excitement and if Rebel wasn't mistaken, he was hiding a hard-on behind his jeans.

"Not sure yet. Give me a day to work it out. I'll come up with a plan to get us both what we want. You'll have Kori, and Lucky won't be a problem any longer."

"Sure thing, boss. What do you want me to do with him?" Savage nodded in the direction of Robbie who'd fallen fast asleep with his face on the table.

"Keep him in the shed. Find out what he knows. Use whatever means necessary, but keep him alive for now." He could be useful over the next few days.

"Will do," Savage said. "Come on, sleeping beauty. Up you go." With his heavy boot, Savage kicked Robbie's leg.

He came awake with a start and a grunt of pain.

"Get the fuck up." Savage yanked him to a stand and practically dragged him out the door.

Alone, Rebel withdrew his pack of smokes and lit another, ideas swirling in his brain. How exactly could he use Kori's relationship with Lucky to turn the tables in his favor? A tiny voice in the back recesses of his mind, a voice he tended to ignore, asked if he was really planning to throw his daughter to the wolves.

For once, he let the voice be heard and contemplated the question. *Was* he capable of taking his new relationship with Kori and destroying it with one swipe?

A lot of money was at stake. Money Rebel had always dreamed of but never quite managed to acquire. He'd missed the first twenty-seven years of Kori's life and neither of them seemed to suffer for it. What the hell did it matter if he never formed a relationship with her at this point? She was a fuckin' adult.

And maybe she'd surprise him and end up being more like her old man than he anticipated. Maybe she'd see the earning potential and drop Lucky like a bad habit.

Rebel smiled.

Who was he kidding, really? It was a lot of fuckin' money.

"Answer's easy," he said out loud with a chuckle. "Fuck yeah, I'm willing to use my daughter to get my way."

CHAPTER SIXTEEN

"Tell me a little about your experience as a medical receptionist, Kori." Donna, the red-haired woman who was conducting the interview couldn't have been much older than Kori and ran the office in a busy multi-physician oncology practice. After going through the experience with her mother, Kori had a desire to work, even peripherally, with cancer patients. If she could so much as brighten a few moments of their day with a smile, it would be so fulfilling.

She blew out a breath. Easy question. Actually, all the questions had been routine thus far. So why was she still so damn tense?

"Sure, Donna. For the past six years, I've been the medical receptionist for a family medicine practice back in Florida. Where I lived was a small town, but we were the only family practice in town, so it was quite busy. My main responsibilities included scheduling appointments, insurance billing and coding, and basically every office task imaginable." She smiled. The docs had been a great group to work with, and she missed them. It was unfortunate it ended as it had.

"For a while, we were a bit old fashioned. Paper charts, written scheduling and such. But within the last two years, prompted by me, we switched everything to electronic. So, while I may not know exactly what systems you use, I'm quite comfortable with electronic medical records, scheduling software as well as billing software."

With a nod, Donna scribbled notes on a pad. "May I ask why you were let go?"

Sadness swamped her at the memories. "About six months ago my mother was diagnosed with lung cancer. She'd ignored the symptoms for so long that by the time they discovered it, she was terminal and spiraled downhill quite fast. I was the only one around to take care of her, and the amount of time I had to miss from work really left them in a jam. They had no choice but to replace me."

A frown marred Donna's pretty face. "Well, first off I'm so sorry to hear about your mother. And second, that kind of thing would never have happened here. This practice is very sensitive to family issues, and we'd have hired a temp while you were out, but your job would have been safe."

Even though she held no ill feelings toward her former employer, it was nice to know she would have job security should another emergency arise.

Donna smiled. "Well, Kori, I have to tell you, you sound like exactly what we've been searching for. And I only had to interview fourteen applicants to discover you." Her laugh was a bit strained.

Kori laughed as well. "Yikes. Sounds a bit stressful."

With a roll of her eyes, Donna placed the pen and paper she'd been writing with on the desk between them. "You have no idea. We keep getting these nineteen-year-olds who've never stepped foot in an office. Normally I wouldn't mind, but we are just far too busy for me to be training a novice. Experience is a must." She shook her head. "Enough of my soap box. Let me tell you a bit more about the job and we can see if you're still interested."

She was interested, very interested. The office was clean, modern, and everyone she'd met so far was welcoming and friendly. "Great, I'd love to hear more."

"Okay, so we're a seven-physician practice, all specializing in oncology, but some of the physicians subspecialize. The office is busy, crazy busy, and the docs are persnickety about things running in a smooth and timely manner. Many of their patients are quite ill, uncomfortable, sad, stressed, in pain…you get the picture. Anyway, they don't want to add to the rough time they are going thorough with scheduling mishaps, billing errors, and a poorly managed office. I run the office and we have a receptionist who works evenings from four to eight, when the office closes, but need someone for the eight to four shift. Your duties would pretty much be the same as you're used to, but we do have a billing specialist, so you wouldn't have to do too much in that arena. Just help when she gets swamped, which happens, or fill in if she's away."

The job sounded perfect. Billing was her least favorite part, so it would be no hardship to leave that task behind. Plus, she appreciated a well-organized office. Back home they'd often teased her, saying she ran the office like a military commander.

"Well, you're not running for the door, so that's a good sign."

"Really, Donna, I think it sounds like a perfect fit for me."

"Oh thank God, me too." The words rushed out of Donna's mouth. "I have to take all of this to our staff meeting this evening, but—and I probably shouldn't tell you this yet, but I don't want someone else to snap you up—we will be making you an offer. I'll email you the paperwork tomorrow. Sound okay?"

"That sounds perfect."

"Great. Let me introduce you to Cindy. She is our billing specialist. Then I'll give you a quick tour of the place." She rose from the table and indicated the door. "After you."

An hour and many handshakes later, Kori stepped outside into the warm Vegas afternoon with a new sense of purpose. She'd really enjoyed her first three weeks in Las Vegas, relaxing, coming to terms with her mom's death, learning about her father, spending every spare second of Lucky's time with him.

But the days were spent alone and bored in Rebel's house or Lucky's apartment.

It seemed like she was in no rush to leave. So that meant it was time to get a job. And an apartment. But job first.

Lucky was turning out to be everything she'd ever hoped for in a boyfriend minus the MC status. He was attentive without being smothering, supportive, intelligent, easy to talk to, and the sex was off the charts.

There were just two problems. Something seemed to be amiss between Lucky and his club and it was becoming difficult to ignore. As the weeks went on, the tension in him was increasing. He was moody, and seemed to have the weight of the world on his shoulders. But only when it came to the club. And in particular, when it came to anything involving Rebel or Savage.

Sure, Rebel was still on a mission to hook her and Savage up, but she avoided the VP at all costs. Rebel had to get bored with the fruitless effort soon. Didn't he? She'd downplayed it and kept Rebel's efforts from Lucky as much as possible. He didn't need to know every time Savage *accidentally* showed up somewhere she was or joined in on dinner with her and Rebel. Lucky didn't need to know how Rebel talked about Savage like he as some kind of golden boy. She had less than no interest in the man and didn't give him or Rebel a single sign indicating otherwise.

Maybe Lucky had figured it out anyway and it was affecting his relationship with his pres and VP. Something about it just didn't sit right. Lucky wasn't insecure. He was strong, confident...hell, he was arrogant. And the past few days Rebel seemed to have a bug up his ass about Lucky as well. Maybe the two had a falling out neither was willing to discuss with her.

And that led her to the second issue, the internal one. Despite the fun they had, and all Lucky's good qualities, he was a biker and every now and then the little voice in her head reminded her of that and warned her to keep her heart guarded. Not that it was working.

She was falling deep and hard for the man, despite her internal misgivings.

Her phone started ringing and she dug through her purse until she located it. Lucky.

"Hey, hon," she said.

"You didn't call."

Kori rolled her eyes. "Lucky, I stepped out of the interview exactly thirty-two seconds ago. I'm not even in my car yet." As she spoke, she rummaged for her keys and clicked the car doors open.

"Wow, long interview. I'm guessing that's a good sign." The warm affection in his voice made her smile. "And sorry, I just want to make sure you're safe."

"Why wouldn't I be safe? It's the middle of the day. Anyway, the interview couldn't have gone better." Ugh, the car was stifling. She rolled down the windows as she fired up the engine and blasted the air conditioning. "They said to expect an email with an offer letter tomorrow."

"Oh, baby, that's fantastic. They'd be stupid not to hire you. We need to celebrate. I'll be done in an hour and I'll swing by Rebel's to pick you up. Sound good?"

A few drinks. Time with Lucky. Yeah, that sounded damn good. "Sounds perfect."

"See you in a bit, angel."

"Bye, Lucky."

"Oh, wait," he cut in before she hit end. "Wear something short and sexy. We'll take your car."

She'd give him sexy, all right. "*Goodbye*, Lucky."

A deep chuckle was the last thing she heard before she ended the call.

His support meant everything to her. Her mother's husband lost his shit one time when her mom said she wanted to get a job. Somehow, he saw it as a personal affront, like he wasn't man enough to provide for her when really, she just needed something else in her life. Something for herself. Something besides the club to round her out. Most of the guys she knew from the other club were that way.

Lucky was different than any biker she'd ever met. His reputation as a player wasn't any kind of secret, but for the past three weeks, he hadn't so much as glanced at another female. Now in the grand scheme of things, three weeks was a drop in the bucket. She'd be lying if she didn't admit her doubt about his ability to be faithful for any great length of time.

Women came on to him every time they were at the clubhouse and he was polite, but quite firm in his refusal. So far, everything was as advertised. Why then was there was a feeling in her gut that they were on a runaway train careening straight toward the end of a cliff?

CHAPTER SEVENTEEN

"Come on, baby. Tell me what I want to hear." Lucky pumped into her from behind with a stroke so unhurried and controlled it was bound to drive her crazy. Combined with the fact that he held her hips immobile so she couldn't alter the pace or push back into him, she had to be going out of her mind.

The scrap of leather she'd called a skirt was bunched around her waist, baring the smooth globes of her ass to him. He had instructed her to wear something sexy, and she sure took the request to heart. For a few moments, he worried they wouldn't make it to the bar without pulling over somewhere so he could fuck her silly. Somehow, he'd managed a thin thread of control. She accomplished something today and deserved to celebrate.

Three drinks later and she was whispering filthy promises in his ear while he dragged her back out to the car. His hands had been itching to stroke her ass as she bent over for him in that skirt, and the reality didn't disappoint.

"Luuucky," she whined.

There it was. "Yeah? You need something?" As she growled, he chuckled and glided one hand from her hip to her breast. With a firm touch, just how she liked it, he pinched a nipple and a long shudder ran through her.

It was a novel experience, knowing a woman well enough and long enough to learn exactly what her body craved. Kori was putty in his hands and he found that he loved knowing exactly what he had to do to make her moan, or curse, or beg for more.

"You know what I need. You're killing me. I need to come. Now!" She tried to grind her hips on him, but it was useless. He held her pelvis still, buried deep inside her, unmoving. She was effectively trapped.

Her hands clung to the top of his headboard, and she couldn't let go without face-planting to the mattress. That meant she couldn't touch herself, couldn't coax the process along.

"You can come, baby. I'll make you come until the roof blows off this place. You just have to say it. Just one little word." Using the same torturous leisurely stroke he'd entered her with, he pulled out until just the tip remained inside her warmth.

It was a dangerous game. Her pussy squeezed the head of his cock like she was trying desperately to draw him back in. His dick was practically screaming at him to slam into her, but he held back.

There was something he needed from her before he could give in to the mind-altering pleasure he found every time they fucked. It was important to keep his wits about him until she gave him what he wanted.

She groaned. "Lucky, this is coercion. It's not how you get people to do things. And it would never hold up in a court of law."

He laughed, hard, and his condom-covered dick slipped further inside her. They both gasped. "You a lawyer now, angel?" She'd gone on the pill but hadn't been on it long enough to ditch the rubbers.

He swiped a thumb across her clit. Not enough to get her off, but enough to make her crazy.

"Fuck! Lucky." She slapped the headboard. "This is so unfair."

"Come on, baby. You know you want to move in here with me. You're here every night anyway. It would be stupid to pay rent on your own place when you'll be here anyway."

He returned both hands to her hips and started up a lazy, unsatisfying rhythm.

In. Out. In. Out.

Teasing thrusts that would keep her near the edge but never let her over.

"We've only been dating three weeks." Her voice grew ragged, strained. "This is crazy. People don't move in together after just three weeks."

It was crazy. But he didn't care. She'd invaded every part of his life and embedded herself so far under his skin he couldn't remember what it was like before. And didn't want to remember. He wanted what they had to last, to grow. "Fuck people," he said. "I'm thirty-fucking-four and I've been around enough to know that I want you." He gave her one hard thrust and she cried out. "You're mine, Kori. You know it. Just admit it and move the fuck in here with me."

She didn't respond so he licked a trail from the base of her spine to her neck. The salty essence of Kori flooded his senses threatening the thin grip on his sanity.

When she shivered, he gently bit the slope of her neck. "I'm scared," she whispered, so low he almost missed it.

Ahh, so that was the resistance. An unfamiliar warmth flooded his chest. It wasn't that she didn't want to move in with him, but she had reservations. Who could blame her?

Hell, he was scared too. But his fear stemmed more from the chance of her leaving than staying. Who would have ever thought he'd be convincing a woman to live with him. Not anyone who knew him. Things changed. He was certain, to his bones, that he wanted this woman in his life. Any doubts or intrusive thoughts were overshadowed by his physical and emotional desire for her.

"I'm not going to hurt you," he whispered against her ear, drawing another shiver from her.

"You can't promise that." Her voice was small, worried.

"I can promise I won't fuck you over. Won't fuck around on you. I'll fuck you," he said and smiled when she laughed. "I'll fuck you every chance I get, but I will not betray you, Kori." They'd talked a few times about her mother's relationship with her ol' man. About Kori's fear of being cheated on and how it spurred her attempt at distancing herself from bikers. About the disrespect women involved with MCs were often treated with. He hoped he'd shown her over the past few weeks how different it would be with him. He never wanted to see anything hurt her, let alone be the one to cause her pain or heartache.

She was quiet again and he dropped his head to her shoulder. Her back was warm and dotted with perspiration. They'd been at this for a while.

Shit. It wasn't going to happen. She wasn't convinced of his ability to commit and remain faithful. For the first time in his life, he regretted his past and reputation. Maybe she was right to. Could he really commit? Just because his heart and his head were saying he could now didn't mean it would last.

No. He could do it. He wasn't sure it would last for the rest of their lives. It had only been a few weeks. But he was sure he wanted it, wanted her, for as long as he could have her.

"Okay."

"What?" Had she just agreed? Holy shit. His heart drummed and his ears buzzed with the possibility of getting what he craved. Still inside her, his cock swelled and threated to explode.

She spoke louder. "I'll move in here with you."

"Oh, thank fuck." He didn't give her an opportunity to say anything else. Sure, it made him a caveman, but the fierce sense of possession that tore through him was overwhelming. She was his, had agreed to live with him, but even that wasn't enough. He needed to brand her, wanted every cell of her body full of him. Needed the world to know who she belonged to.

With a victory roar, he pulled out and slammed back into her, fucking her with rough, powerful snaps of his hips.

"Oh my God," she cried, her bloodless knuckles clutching the headboard for all she was worth. There was no choice but to cling to it for dear life or he'd probably send her crashing through the wall.

He was in a frenzy, could think of nothing else but the clasp of her pussy around his cock as he pummeled her again and again. Whimpers flew out of her mouth with every thrust. From the way he grasped her hips as he fucked her, she'd have bruises for sure. But he didn't care. In fact, he couldn't wait to see his fingerprints on her creamy skin. Evidence of how insane he'd been for her.

Her cries grew louder and her body trembled beneath him. She was close. He slid his hands up her soft stomach until he reached her nipples. She detonated with an intense orgasm the moment he pinched them, crying his name out loud.

He followed milliseconds behind her, the orgasm stealing his ability to breathe. As his body jerked over hers, he sunk his teeth into the same spot he'd nipped just moments ago. This time though, he bit hard enough to leave a mark. It set off a potent aftershock in her and she gasped.

Now that the sweat was cooling, some of Lucky's brain power returned and a bit of guilt crept in. He'd been pretty rough with her and while he liked it raw, wild, animalistic, it wasn't every woman's thing and they hadn't discussed it prior. Not to mention the fact that it was over the top, even for him.

She grew limp and her hands started to slide down the headboard. Before she had the chance to collapse, he slid an arm under her waist and eased her down onto the bed. He turned her in his arms until he could see her face, gauge her reaction.

"Are you, uh—" He cleared his throat. "You okay?"

Her eyes were closed but she smiled. "I'm not sure. Am I still alive?"

Shame hit him hard. "Jesus, Kori, I'm sorry. That was...I was way too rough."

Her eyelids popped open, and wide blue eyes stared at him. "Huh?"

"I completely lost control. I attacked you, fucked you way too hard." The more he thought about it the worse he felt.

A satisfied smile graced her lips. "Look, Lucky, I'll admit it was...vigorous. And I'll also admit I've never been fucked like that before, anywhere near that, really. But, um..." Her face turned a charming shade of pink. "I liked it."

It was as though his heart stopped dead in his chest. "What?"

"It was hot. You owned me, completely dominated me. I couldn't do anything but take what you wanted to give me. It felt so good. Amazing."

It shouldn't be physically possible after the colossal orgasm two minutes ago, but his cock stirred. "I left bruises on you, baby. Bit you. Hard."

The blush on her cheeks deepened. "Am I a freak if I liked that too? Actually, I loved it."

Fully hard once again, he groaned. "No, baby, it doesn't make you weird. It makes you fuckin' perfect for me."

"Good," she said. "I want to be perfect for you."

He ran his hands all over her, couldn't seem to make himself stop touching her. She could have a little time to rest, but it wouldn't be long before he needed back inside her sweet heat. Never had he had it so good as he did with Kori. But it was more than just fucking.

Never in his life had he stuck around for the post-orgasm conversation, cuddling, and sleeping. Never had he called a woman at least once a day for no reason beyond hearing her voice. Never had he planned his schedule around her availability. Never had he wanted to open his eyes each morning to the same beautiful sight.

The irony of it was, the fact that she spent years trying to avoid bikers was what drew him to her. She knew his world, fit it, could handle it, but wasn't hardened like many of the women he met through the club. She maintained her softness, her femininity while still being able to challenge him. Most of the girls around the club were so intent on becoming an ol' lady they'd do and say anything to please a man. Not Kori. Kori had spunk, personality. Kori challenged him to be better. For her. Yet she did it without being bitter. And all of this was before he even delved into how she appealed to him physically. She was like a drug. He finally understood how someone could sell their soul for a fix.

In fact, there was a good chance he'd already done it. As the weeks passed, he grew angrier with Rebel and Savage for their abuse of the club, but what the hell was he doing about it? Not a goddamn thing. Now that Kori was in his life, he didn't want to rock the boat. It made him a fuckin' hypocrite. Condemning those who sold and trafficked drugs while not doing a damn thing to stop it.

Fucking Rebel.

And now he was moving the man's daughter into his apartment.

CHAPTER EIGHTEEN

Kori existed in a heavenly state somewhere between arousal and delicious lassitude. Masculine, work-roughened hands coasted up her arms, down her sweat-dotted back and over her ass, again and again, inducing a sort of hypnotic state of pleasure. Everywhere he touched, small ripples of electricity shot along her skin, prolonging her orgasmic bliss.

It took a few minutes for her brain to catch up with the fact that Lucky had stopped talking and now wore an unreadable, but not satisfied expression. An almost...lost and shattered look had entered his eyes and while it appeared he was staring at her, she was sure he wasn't actually seeing anything.

"Hey." She scraped a thumbnail over his flat masculine nipple, eliciting a jolt from him. After a few blinks, his dark gaze seemed to come back into focus. "I think I lost you for a second there. Where'd you go?"

"Sorry, baby." He pressed a kiss to her forehead. "Just thinking about some club issues."

"So all that wasn't enough to relax your mind?"

He snorted. "Babe, that was enough to melt my mind. I'm sorry." A heavy sigh escaped. "There's just a bit of troubling shit going down now and it snuck in for a moment. Nothing for you to be worried about though, okay?"

No, not okay, but she didn't say that. She'd need to learn to be okay with it. A few minutes ago she'd agreed to move in with the man. This was how MC life worked. Club business stayed within the club whether she liked it or not. Hopefully, he'd come to her in his own time if he needed a sounding board. She had to trust in that. In the meantime, there were plenty of other things she still needed to learn about him. "So, how did you get involved with the club?"

"Oh, Christ." While he spoke, he rolled to his back and propped his head on a few pillows, taking her with him. As though she weighed nothing, he positioned her across his warm chest. She settled in with her legs between his and her chin resting on her stacked palms. It gave her the perfect view of his face as he shared his story.

"We had a typical low income, shitty without being traumatizing upbringing. Mom died young; dad didn't give a rat's ass about much more than hitting the slots and poker tables. That left me plenty of unsupervised time to get into trouble."

"We?" she asked.

He played with the long strands of her hair, running his fingers from her scalp to the ends repeatedly. God, she loved how he was always touching her. It seemed so much more significant than just physical touching, like he couldn't stand a break in their connection. Whether that was in her mind or not remained to be seen, but the thought thrilled her.

"Yeah. I had a sister. Melissa. I called her Missy. She was five years younger." His voice grew sad as he spoke her name. "She called me Ty. My real name's Tyler."

Had? Called? Was? All past tense. Had something happened to Missy? Kori was dying to ask but assumed he'd get to that part of the story soon enough. No need to rush it. "I like it. It's a good name."

"Thanks." He smoothed a thumb across her lips and she snuck her tongue out for a taste. A smile curved his lips and she felt victorious. To be able to make him smile when recalling obviously painful memories was priceless.

"Anyway, I was always a little shit and fell in with a pretty rough crowd during my late teen years. Grand theft auto was our specialty. We'd jack cars for a local chop shop. They threw us a decent cut. For a kid with no money, I thought I was living the high life. I quit busing tables for Rosita and spent all my free time with a bunch of low-life car thieves." He let out a humorless chuckle. "Am I scaring you off yet?"

Because of a sordid past? That she could handle. The present was far more important. "No. From what I've seen of the No Prisoners so far, the club I knew back in FL was involved in much worse stuff than yours is here. Not too much shocks me anymore."

His face clouded for a minute. What was that about? What the hell was going on with the club? She needed to pay better attention when she was at the clubhouse. Maybe she could pick up on something without Lucky having to break any club code of silence.

"Huh, well I got cocky and tried to steal some off-the-chain Ferrari. Got popped and landed my ass in lock up. Unfortunately, I'd turned eighteen three days prior." He shrugged. "You know the story. Judge gave me a choice. Enlist in the service or prison. Easy choice. So I joined up."

"You were in the Army?" Wow. Her respect for him tripled. She held those who served in the highest regard.

"Marine Corp. Four years as a sniper."

"Holy shit."

He chuckled, the vibrations jostling her on his chest. "You ain't kidding. About killed me in the beginning. To go from drinking, smoking, lazing around to boot camp was quite the shocker. I had my ass handed to me a million times before I started to get with the program. Once I got on board, my competitive side kicked in and I wanted to be the best. That's where sniper school came in."

She smiled, imagining a young, stubborn-as-hell Lucky being reamed by a drill sergeant. "How does this lead to the club?"

He resumed playing with her hair and she almost purred like a spoiled cat. "I'm getting there. I'll skip the grisly details, but after I left home, Missy spiraled out of control. Sex, drugs, you name it, she did it. Anyway, I was twenty-two and in Afghanistan when I learned she overdosed and was in a coma. Getting sent home from deployment is nearly impossible and by the time I got here—" Bone deep remorse filled his voice and she almost told him to stop. She could guess the rest, no need to relive it. But he seemed lost in the story now.

Her heart cracked and bled for the younger Lucky. What was coming was pretty obvious, but she waited for his next words to confirm her fears.

Was there a link between his past and his present? Did this sad story have anything to do with Lucky's issues with the club now?

Dredging up memories of Missy all these years later hurt like fresh pain. Kori had opened up to him. Shared fears, past hurts. He owed her the same. Amazingly, he wanted to tell her. Wanted her to know what made him who he was today. Good and bad. "By the time I got here, she'd died."

"God, Lucky, I'm so sorry. I can't even imagine how difficult that must have been for you." She dropped a kiss on his chest. Her willingness to listen without judgment and her comforting touch were the only things that kept him going with the story. Very few people had heard it. Voicing it was just too damn painful.

And then there were the months after her death. God, he'd been a fucking mess. "Yeah, the time that followed wasn't the best of my life." Understatement of the century. "I left the Marines and went off the rails a bit. After I dealt with the asshole who'd been pimping her out and supplying her with drugs, I had nothing left to fill my days. So, I traveled around on my Harley looking for a purpose. When I was at a bar in a tiny town in Arizona, I met a few guys from the No Prisoners chapter down there."

He'd befriended Acer, a contradiction of biker and rich kid, on sight. Acer had introduced him around to some other MC members, and that weekend had been the one thing to end his slippery slope into a severe depression and self-destruction. God knows where he'd be right now if he'd never met those guys. Actually, he had a pretty good idea he'd be six feet under.

"You want to stop?" Her soft voice pulled him back to the moment. The silken strands of her hair slid through his fingers like a platinum waterfall. So beautiful.

"No, sorry, just got lost in my head. I spent a week with those guys and was hooked. Their sense of brotherhood, family, loyalty was just what I was looking for. I had all those things in the Marines and had missed them. Anyway, I came home and prospected. Rest is history."

A frown marred her pretty face. "If you hit it off so well with the Arizona guys, why didn't you stay down there?"

Fuck, he sure as hell wished he had now. He wouldn't be in this fucking mess with Rebel. Though he also wouldn't have met Kori. "This is home. This is where my sister is buried. And my mom was alive until a little over two years ago. Sometimes I think about patching over to their chapter."

Shit, he hadn't meant to let that slip. It wasn't a *sometimes* thought anymore. It was pretty much a daily thought for the past five weeks. And something that would have to be acted on soon. What a shitty time to be entering his first—and if he had his way, only—serious relationship.

"Hmm." Kori sat up, her legs straddling his torso and rubbed her hands along his chest. "Just so you know, for future reference, I'm not married to this area. I'm not dropping hints or telling you how to live your life. Just something to file away for…whenever."

Christ, she was amazing. So giving. Basically, she was telling him she'd be willing to move with him if he deemed it best. "But your father is here."

With a smile, she walked her fingers up his chest, stopping at his neck then leaned forward. His hands cupped her ass and pulled her close, grinding her clit into his stomach. Arousal sparked between them as need for her flared strong, as though he hadn't had her and come so hard he nearly passed out less than a half hour ago.

"Mmm," she moaned, reaching for a condom on the nightstand. "I know he's here. We're learning each other, forming a sort of bond. If I'm fully honest, I don't see us having a super close relationship. Just a feeling." As she spoke, she wiggled her way down his body until she was positioned over his erection. "I'm just saying I don't need to live so close to him to be happy. Arizona's not far, anyway."

Their gazes met and she fisted him in her hand. With heat in her gaze, she rolled the latex over his oversensitive flesh. When she lowered herself, encasing him in the searing wet heat of her pussy, the room blurred. "Good to know," he ground out.

Damn, she looked magnificent astride his hips with her tits swaying and hair flowing around her shoulders. Her smile was radiant as she rocked against him, the illusion of control making her bold. In reality, he could take over whenever he damn well pleased, but he let her have this because she loved riding his cock as much as he loved watching it.

This…happiness he found with Kori could be his. For the rest of his life if he played his cards right. Just one obstacle stood in their way.

Unfortunately, it was an obstacle the size of a fucking mountain and had the power to wreak more havoc that just ending their relationship.

CHAPTER NINETEEN

A grating jangle cut through her normally slow, luxurious wakeup period and jerked Kori to consciousness in an instant. "Argh, who the hell is calling me at—" She snatched the offending phone off Lucky's bedside nightstand. "Holy crap! I slept until ten thirty in the morning. Oh, it's Rebel." Was Lucky even awake to hear her irritated ramblings?

Lucky's body tensed around her at the mention of Rebel's name. Yep, wide awake. His reaction to his president was getting a bit ridiculous, really. Now he couldn't even stand to hear the man's name? Maybe, when she told Rebel she and Lucky were shackin' up, she'd feel her father out, see if there was a reason for the tension beyond his deluded idea that she should be with creepy Savage.

"Hey, Rebel."

"Morning, baby girl." His ever-gravelly voice filled her ear. "Wondering if you wanted to do lunch today."

Silence settled between them for a moment while she chose her words. Most of the time, a lunch invitation was a ploy to shove Savage down her throat and that would only incite Lucky who'd snuggled her against his hard, sleep-warmed body.

"Just the two of us." Rebel must have guessed the reason for her hesitation.

Well in that case. "Sure, I'd love to."

"Great. Meet me at the clubhouse in an hour, baby girl. Good?"

"Good, Rebel. See you in a bit." Calling him Dad still didn't sit well. Why was that? Her automatic answer was that she hadn't known him long enough, but hell, she'd known Lucky just as long and was ready to move in with him. No, it was a gut feeling. The name just didn't feel right. Nothing she could put her finger on. Maybe it had something to do with the tension between him and Lucky.

She dropped the phone on the mattress and rolled over to wish a frowning Lucky good morning. "Hey, handsome. What is on your agenda for the day?" She wrapped her arms around him and pressed her breasts to his chest. There was one sure way to distract him from whatever displeasure he was experiencing over her spending time with her father.

He kissed her and rolled her to her back, settling in the nook of her thighs. "I got a text about ten minutes ago about some destruction at a bar we own. Big bar fight last night or some bullshit like that. I need to check out the damage, deal with insurance, decide if we can remain open, yadda yadda."

"Sounds like a fun day." While he spoke, she ran her hands up and down the muscular ridges of his back. They bunched and flexed under her fingertips as his breathing increased. He was so strong, so powerful, so capable, and holding all that power in her arms, knowing she could bring this man to his knees, was as arousing as his body itself. Not in a sadistic, wanting-to-humiliate kind of way, but in an empowering, feminine, sexy kind of way.

"Oh, I'm sure it'll be a blast." He kissed her again, lingering this time, and her body flared to life. How he managed to arouse her to the point of begging every single time was beyond her. "At least I can start the day off on the right foot."

She smiled and bent her knees, bringing him in closer contact with the throbbing ache only he could satisfy. "Better get crackin' then. Time's a wastin' and I don't even have a whole hour."

"Please, woman, I'll have you coming around some part of my body in less than five minutes." He nipped her jawline with his teeth, eliciting a shudder from her.

"Yeah," she said, breathless as his small bites moved down her neck. "But you've spoiled me. I'm no longer satisfied with one."

Her mind muddled as he chuckled and ran his tongue along her collarbone.

Two orgasms, one shower, and sixty-three minutes later, Kori steered her car into the clubhouse parking lot. It was fairly deserted, but one member was changing a tire on a bike.

"Hey, Kori," the long-haired biker said as she ambled toward the door.

"Hey…" What was his name? What was his name? "Um…"

"Bull," he said.

"Right, Bull, sorry. I'm still working everyone's name out. Bull like the big angry cow?"

He chuckled. "Bull as in pit bull. My bite's worse than my bark."

That explained the tattoo on his massive bicep. A pit bull with a spiked collar, holding some sort of limp animal between its bared teeth. A rabbit, maybe? "Right. I'll be sure to keep my hand away from your mouth then, huh?"

This time his laugh was loud and boisterous. "I get what Lucky sees in you, Kori. If you're looking for your father, he's out back. There's a shed out there. I think Savage is with him."

Ugh. So much for just the two of them. "A shed?"

Bull shrugged, his attention on a lug nut as he tightened it. "God only knows why they're out there. Didn't realize that old thing was actually in use. Been here three years and it's always been locked up tight. I ain't ever seen anybody go out there until today."

Unease slithered through her gut. Knowing what she knew about outlaw MCs and their business dealings, there was a good chance she didn't want to learn what was in that shed. Plausible deniability and all that jazz. "Oh, maybe I should wait until they come back out here."

With a grunt of effort, he tightened the last nut and stood, wiping grease-stained hands on his faded jeans. "Nah, babe. Rebel told me to send ya back when I saw ya."

"Okay then. Guess I'm going out to the shed. Thanks, Bull. I'll remember your name from now on."

"No prob, babe. Catch ya later." He hiked the old tire over his shoulder and whistled as he walked it over to the bed of an old rusted pickup truck.

Sure enough, behind the clubhouse was a large shed with the door shut. Ugh, this was straight out of a movie. Mysterious shed no one thought was in use. Full of what? Trafficked humans? A dead body? Kori shivered as the unease grew into a full out screaming in her head.

Don't knock! Turn around!

She rolled her eyes and straightened her back. Time to stop reading psychological thrillers and maybe find a lighter genre. Paranoia was jumping off the pages and into her mind. "Don't be a drama queen," she whispered as she raised a fist and rapped on the wooden door.

"That you, Kori?" Rebel's ruined voice came from beyond the door.

"Yeah, it's me."

"You alone?"

And, that mattered because? The edgy feeling was back, this time complete with a stomach rolling like waves in a violent storm. "Ah, yes. No one else is with me."

The door swung open and Rebel called out. "Come on in."

It took a minute to unweight the legs that seemed to be welded to the ground, but she managed the three steps over the threshold and into the substantial shed.

Three steps. Three measly advances of her legs. Maybe four seconds, maximum, and her world flip-flopped so violently she couldn't tell up from down. If Alice felt one tenth of the fear, confusion, and shock after tumbling down that blasted rabbit hole, then Kori's heart went out to the girl.

She stood frozen like a statue, except for her eyes which darted in every direction possible trying to make sense of the scene before her. Seated in a chair only ten feet in front of her was a man whose face was so battered and bruised, she'd never be able to identify him if asked.

The first thing she registered, and that gave her a small measure of relief, was that there was no way the man could be Lucky. He was too thin, gaunt almost, with greasy hair and obvious track marks on his arms. Her rational brain reminded her she'd only left Lucky twenty minutes before, but this fucked up scene shot rational thinking to hell.

The man's swollen eyes were shut. Whether voluntarily or because of the massive edema was a difficult call. Actually, the only indications that Savage hadn't killed him was a wheezing that accompanied the shallow rise and fall of his thin chest. That, and the occasional tremor that racked his frail body.

Savage stood next to the victim, his knuckles bruised and bloodied. He'd obviously been the one to issue the brutal punishment for whatever sins this man had committed against the No Prisoners. Savage was calm, hadn't broken a sweat and looked unfazed by the violence he'd just perpetrated. In fact, if it wasn't for some poor soul's blood dripping from his still-clenched fists, he'd look like a man ready for that lunch she'd been led to believe was the reason for her presence.

Why the hell did they want her as a witness to this insanity?

There wasn't a single reassuring answer to that question.

A low hum started in her ears and the room swam before her. Breaths came in rapid, choppy bursts. Kori bent at her waist, resting her hands on her knees and tried to tamp down the hyperventilation before she passed out.

After her breathing evened, she rose to her full height, but averted her gaze from the beaten man. Unfortunately, her attention landed on stacks and stacks of packaged white powder.

Drugs.

Pounds and pounds of drugs.

Jesus, there had to be hundreds of thousands of dollars of illicit drugs in this shed. Was Lucky privy to this? There was no way in hell he condoned this or participated in it. Not after what he told her about the death of his younger sister.

Kori finally noticed Rebel standing against the right wall of the shed, his arms crossed against his chest. When their gazes met, the light bulb went off and everything became clear as the waters of the Caribbean.

Lucky knew.

And Lucky was against it.

Somehow this was...what? Punishment? A warning?

"You good now?" Rebel rasped. Gone was the affection he'd come to speak to her with, replaced with a cold, unwavering tone that gave her little hope that this was somehow a tragic misunderstanding.

"Why?" Her voice was barely a whisper. *Buck up, Kori.* Showing weakness wouldn't be smart. She injected some steel into her spine and cleared her throat. "Why are you showing me this? Why the fuck am I here?"

Rebel smiled and pushed off the wall. He sent a look to Savage who nodded and landed a wicked blow to the wrecked man's stomach. His head lolled to the side but he didn't make a sound. Was he even conscious?

"It's simple, baby girl."

The nickname that just over an hour ago reminded her of her mother and gave her hope for a future that included a father now made her stomach lurch and bile burn the bottom of her esophagus.

"You're here to save your boyfriend."

CHAPTER TWENTY

"Well, it could have been a hell of a lot worse, Mac," Lucky said to the manager he'd hired for this bar. Technically, Lucky ran all three bars, but seeing as how he couldn't be in three places at once every night, he'd hired someone for each bar. That gave him time to run the business side of things without having to babysit drunk co-eds looking for a little what-happens-in-Vegas-stays-in-Vegas action.

Mac rubbed a meaty hand over his hairless scalp. "Yeah, some broken glass, coupla trashed tables." He shrugged. "A big fuckin' mess, but nothing that will prevent us from opening tonight. Fuckin' Ivy League assholes can't handle their liquor. Or keep their women under control. Every fight is over some snooty rich pussy."

Lucky snorted. "I'll get some prospects over here to clean up the mess. I'm thinking this isn't worth reporting to the insurance company. It'd just be a giant ass pain. We've got some extra tables and chairs in storage at Spinners. Prospects will bring 'em over and we should be good to open tonight." Spinners was one of the other bars Lucy handled.

"Thanks, man." Mac held out a hand.

Lucky grasped it and slapped the man on the back. "You're doing good here, Mac. Profits are up and the place is always packed. Just what we want to see."

Lucky

Mac beamed and puffed out his chest a bit. A little bit of praise went along way when dealing with employees. Lucky had learned that lesson early on and used it frequently. It set up a culture where the guys who worked for him wanted to keep him happy and keep the compliments coming. In turn, business was prosperous.

"All right, man. I'll catch you later." Lucky stepped toward the door. "Oh, wait a sec. You see Robbie around at all lately?" On a typical day, his contact spent hours at the bar. To him, happiness was a belly full of booze and veins full of heroin.

"Nah, man. Actually, he hasn't been here in two days. Figured he was sick or something." Mac shrugged and went back to his task of lining clean glasses on shelves behind the bar.

Lucky shook his head. Sick, right. In reality, one of two situations was the likely. Either Robbie ran out of money and was cowered in an alley fighting off some serious cravings, or he'd finally overdosed.

There was a third scenario. The one he'd been fearful of yet somewhat resistant to entertain as a possibility. And that was that somehow Rebel discovered Robbie had been feeding Lucky information. Jesus, that would be bad on so many fucking levels.

He left the bar and headed out in search of his source, a feeling of dread in the pit of his stomach.

Kori swallowed and wished with everything inside her that she'd never knocked on the shed door. Actually, if she were wishing for stuff, she'd back up an hour or so and wish she'd stayed in bed with Lucky. Blissfully unaware of the awaiting horrors.

"So," Rebel said. "Here's what I need from you, baby girl. Savage needs a woman. A good woman. He'll be taking over at some point and I want him settled, happy. That woman is you."

Jesus, no. Kori shook her head as the coffee she'd drank in her car worked its way back up. *No, no, no.* This could not be happening. "I can't—"

"Sure, you can," Rebel said with a swipe of his hand, effectively ending her protest. "And you will. You don't have to get married right away, but it will happen before the year is over."

Rebel's words bounced around in her skull. This had to be a joke, some kind of sick, twisted initiation into the club, right?

The serious look on Rebel's face said no. And the lustful look on Savage's face sent chills running down her spine. She glanced at the half-dead man on the chair. "Is that what this all is?" She pointed to him. "What? You'll strap me to the chair next and beat the shit out of me if I refuse?"

Both men laughed. "Not you, sweetheart," said Savage.

Icy dread filled her veins. "Lucky?" she squeaked, barely audible, but both men caught it.

"Let's just say that Lucky found out about some business dealings he doesn't fully agree with. Robbie, here—" Rebel pointed to the lifeless bag of bones "—has been running his trap, feeding Lucky information he just doesn't need to have. I cannot afford to have this fucked up. Especially not by one of my own fucking men. So that leaves me with two options. One, Lucky ends up in this chair and I put him out of commission. Or two, you marry Savage and Lucky stays safe."

All of a sudden, the stale air in the shed rose to about two hundred degrees and Kori swayed on her feet. She could barely process what has happening. If she married Savage, Rebel would leave Lucky alone? But why would that prevent Lucky from outing Rebel and his illegal drug running. Hell, it would probably enrage Lucky into taking action. That was if he didn't just leave…

Oh my God. She backed up until she hit the closed door and slumped against it in defeat. That was it. He wanted Lucky gone. This would do it. It wasn't arrogance that told her that, but the last three weeks spent in Lucky's arms. He cared deeply for her and wouldn't be able to watch her paired off with Savage.

"Ahh, I see you're catching up, baby girl."

"You're trying to drive him away."

Savage's grin was nothing short of predatory. "That's right, love. We all know Lucky's flirted with the idea of transferring to the Crystal Rock chapter. Hell, it might have happened by now if it wasn't for you. So, he'll run off to lick his wounds in Arizona, leaving us to conduct our business."

"It won't work. He'll be mad, furious. Don't you think he'll tell his friends in Arizona? To get back at you?" A flame of anger sparked in her.

"Nope. I sure don't. Not with you here in the crossfire. I've seen the way he looks at you. Like a slobbering puppy with a new toy. That pussy of yours has certainly done something to him. Thank you for that. For a while I thought we'd have no choice but to off him."

The flame ignited into a raging inferno. "You bastard. You fucking bastard," she screamed at him. The fury burned so hot she couldn't think past the hatred for these two men. "How could you do this?"

Rebel shrugged. "Really, Kori, it's not personal. It's business. We stand to lose more money than you can imagine. Money that will be partly yours. If you step back and think about this rationally, you'll see—"

"Money? You think I want your fucking drug money? Your blood money?" She pushed off the wall, legs shaking and breathing ragged as she tried to control her temper. What she wanted to do was lunge across the room, wrap her hands around Rebel's throat and squeeze the life out of him. Unfortunately, both men had the strength advantage tenfold. "And not personal? You're my father. My fucking blood."

Tears of rage and despair filled her eyes and spilled down her cheeks. What was she supposed to do? She needed time. Time to come up with a way out of this hell. But that would never be granted.

"Oh God." She wiped the salty wetness off her face only to have it replaced by the next round of tears. "I need to think. I don't know—"

"Sorry, honey, can't take the chance that you'll run right to Lucky. Besides there really isn't anything to think about. You want him to live, correct?"

A sob broke loose and she nodded.

"Then the decision is made. Tomorrow, before the barbecue I'll announce your engagement to Savage." He stepped around her and opened the shed door. "Give me your phone. Can't have you calling your boy."

Reluctantly, she handed over the phone. What choice did she have? They'd take it from her if she didn't relinquish it and she'd lose her shit completely if Savage put his hands on her.

"Go straight to my house. I've got a prospect who is gonna follow you and babysit you until I get there so if you thought you'd run straight to Lucky, you better think again. Keep your mouth shut. Do not try to contact Lucky in any way. My prospect has orders to keep eyes on you at all times. I'll tell Lucky you're busy tonight. Get moving."

With an unbelievable amount of effort, Kori tamped down her murderous rage. Savage winked and blew her a kiss before he landed another blow on his captive. For a second, she actually envied the beaten man in the chair. His pain would be over soon whereas hers was just beginning and with no end in sight.

She forced herself to walk towards the door, ominous music playing in her head like she was a prisoner in movie walking toward their executioner. She avoided Rebel's gaze and slipped through the door.

"And Kori?" he called.

"What?" She didn't bother to face him. Catching a glimpse of his satisfied smile would most likely make her vomit or charge him with the hope of clawing his face off.

"Make it look good. Everyone needs to believe this is true love."

Lucky

She gagged and rushed off to her car before the hysterical sobs could claim her. Tomorrow she would be responsible for causing Lucky a pain no one should ever have to endure. The pain of heartbreak. The pain of betrayal.

An image of Lucky beaten and broken flashed through her mind.

Rebel was right. There really was no choice.

CHAPTER TWENTY-ONE

Lucky sipped his beer and bounced his heel while he stared at the hallway leading to Rebel's office. It had been over twenty-four hours since he'd seen or spoken to Kori, and like a junkie, he was itching for a fix. A few minutes ago, a text came through from Bull letting him know she was in Rebel's office with him.

Savage was mysteriously missing as well and Lucky had a sneaking suspicion Rebel was up to his matchmaking tricks again. The rest of the club members milled around the clubhouse while the ol' ladies set up tables of food for a barbecue.

"Hey, Lucky." A honeyed southern accent that could only belong to Bitsy tickled his ear. She was fairly new to the club and had been with a few of the brothers, but if rumors were to be believed, she viewed Lucky as her ultimate prize.

"Hey, Bits." He shifted his gaze to her as she came around and stood in front of him, trailing her hand along his arm as she sidled up.

"You look lonely over here all by yourself."

On a normal day, he'd drop some line about how he'd been waiting for her, they'd flirt a little, and within in the half hour he'd have her under him in one of the back rooms. She was his exact type after all. Blond, stacked, experienced, loose morals.

Today, however there wasn't even a stirring of desire. She looked cheap, fake, and far too obvious in her quest for a quick fuck. Nope, she wasn't Kori and he straight up didn't want anyone else. Huh, maybe he really had evolved.

Bitsy placed a small hand with long, witchlike fake nails on his knee and started to slide it up his thigh.

"Nuh uh." With a shake of his head, he tapped the beer bottle against her forearm. He didn't even want to touch her. "Hands off, Bits."

Her painted lower lip popped out in a spectacular pout that nearly had him laughing.

"Sorry, hon," he said. "This ride's closed though I'm sure there are at least ten others in here who'd take you for the ride of your life."

"We'll see," she said with a wink. "Never say never." She turned and left, her hips swaying seductively in shorts that didn't cover her entire ass. Lucky took another swig of his beer and chuckled to himself as he imagined the choice words Kori would have for the other woman.

Kori had blown him off last night. The flimsy excuse Rebel had some prospect feed him about her wanting to spend a little more time with her father hadn't fooled Lucky for one second. Best guess was that Rebel pitched a fit over their impending cohabitation and Kori spent her evening soothing daddy's ruffled feathers.

While he waited for his woman, Lucky's thoughts drifted to his fruitless search for Robbie. Three hours of his afternoon wasted yesterday searching back alleys, a few crack dens, and bars Robbie frequented. Shaking heads and shrugged shoulders at each stop. No one had seen Robbie in days. Not that strung-out junkies and used-up whores were the most reliable of sources, but still…

Lucky's gut was churning.

It was time to bring Kori into the mix. At least give her enough information to decide if she'd be willing to follow him to Arizona. She'd said as much the other night, but was it just pillow talk? Or did she mean it?

She was on to him. It was growing harder and harder to hide his hatred of Rebel and Kori was no dummy. She picked up on his cues. Telling her about Rebel's deception and drug sales went against every protective instinct in him, but if he was going to rat her old man out to Shiv and Striker then she needed a warning.

"Listen up!" Rebel always sounded like someone sick with laryngitis when he yelled. His smoke-roughed voice strained and the effort he put forth was obvious, but the booming quality he aimed for just wasn't there. No matter. When Rebel spoke, his minions listened.

Lucky lowered his bottle after tipping the cool liquid into his mouth and the beer went flat in an instant. He had to work to swallow and keep it down. Rebel and Savage stood at the mouth of the hallway with Kori sandwiched between them. Her hand was tucked into Savage's, his bruised knuckles evidence that he'd been caught up in some shit in the last day or so.

What. The. Fuck.

"Got an announcement to make before we hit it hard. Smells fuckin' good in here and I'm starved." He rubbed his stomach, a giant grin on his face.

Lucky tried his damnedest to catch Kori's gaze, but she seemed to be looking at anything and everything but him. Panic clawed at his chest.

"Just want to let you all know that my daughter will be making an honest man outta Savage before the year is up." Pride evident in his eyes, he slapped a hand on Savage's back.

Lucky blinked. He should probably be pissed, outraged, furious...one of those emotions, but the words spilling out of Rebel's trap were so unbelievable Lucky couldn't make sense of them.

Kori. And Savage.

Engaged.

At any time now, the camera crew would burst out of hiding and everyone would laugh at the look on Lucky's face. For years, he'd be hearing about what an easy mark he was and how he bought it all hook line and sinker.

Seconds ticked by with nothing but confused murmurs and inquiring glances flicked in Lucky's direction.

"Congratulations!" someone yelled and Lucky had a sneaking suspicion the slightly southern twang belonged to Bitsy.

"Thank you," Savage called back as he drew Kori into his arms, her back pressing against his front. She smiled and leaned into him.

Lucky stared at her, hard. Looking for anything. Any kind of clue that she was there under duress. Any inkling of unhappiness, fear, or mistreatment. All he saw was the shining face of a woman in love. A woman who wouldn't meet his eye.

Then it came. The anger. It rose like a storm swell, swirling his blood as it grew in intensity and threatened to take out the entire room with its strength. He slammed the beer bottle down so hard, it shattered against the bar, but the sound was swallowed amid the cheers and calls for a kiss.

Savage spun Kori around, gripped the back of her head and claimed her mouth in a ferocious kiss. This was it. This was when she'd slap his face, push him away at least. Instead, she wound her arms around his neck and gave as good as she got.

Lucky had had his ass kicked a number of times. A few of them pretty brutal beatings. He'd been stabbed once as a deviant teen. Fuck, he'd even taken a bullet in Afghanistan. But nothing, not any amount of pain he'd experienced in his life compared to the ruthless demolition of his heart. There was no gentle zigzagged crack down the middle splitting it in two. With one kiss, Kori had obliterated every cell that beat in his chest.

Lucky shoved through a group of his brothers yelling catcalls and cheering at the passionate display.

Someone tapped him on the shoulder. Bull. "Sorry, brother. I really thought she was into you. I guess there was more to all those meals she ate with Rebel and Savage."

Meals with Rebel and Savage? She hadn't mentioned it. Sure, she'd told him when she was supposed to be going out with Rebel, but had never mentioned Savage's involvement. Jesus. Had she been seeing him on the side all along while pretending the man made her uncomfortable? He grunted a response to Bull and continued to work his way through the crowd.

One quick scan of the room and he found his mark. Bitsy stood with a group of club girls, her eyes tracking his every move.

"Let's go," he said, throwing an arm across her shoulders and tugging her away from the others.

"Where we going, stud?" She batted what were probably fake eyelashes and licked her lips. Too bad his dick didn't even twitch.

"Away. Anywhere with a flat surface." He strode toward the exit with her.

"Now that's more like it." She bounced up and down next to him, her tits remaining in the exact position they'd started in. Fake. Go figure.

I don't do bikers.

Well fuck her.

CHAPTER TWENTY-TWO

Kori was two seconds away from throwing up in Savage's too-eager mouth when he ended the kiss.

"Mmm," he whispered against her ear. "Tasty."

Her stomach lurched again and she looked away, plastering what she prayed was at least a somewhat believable I'm-so-happy-I'm-engaged smile on her face. As long as the outside looked convincing it didn't matter that it felt like a slow poison was killing her inside.

Savage released her and turned, shaking hands and accepting man-hugs of congratulations from his brothers. A few comments about balls and chains accompanied by some vulgar statements about her pussy followed. With no one paying her any mind for a few seconds, she scanned the crowd for Lucky.

From the second Rebel and Savage paraded her out, Lucky's laser stare was as palpable as an actual burn. But she couldn't look at him. Couldn't bear to witness the moment he realized he'd lost her to another man. A man he'd warned her about. A man he already hated.

There he was, arm slung around another woman, headed for the exit. Her heart squeezed with a crushing pain and she sank her teeth into her lower lip to keep from screaming out how this wasn't real. How she hated Savage, hated Rebel and saw no other option to keep Lucky out of harm's way.

Rebel had taken her phone, her car keys, kept a guard outside his house in case she tried to flee, and turned off the internet in his house. She was a captive in her own father's home.

If only she had time. Time to think. Time to plot. Maybe she could have come up with an out, but Rebel hadn't granted any of that. She had time now, though. And she'd use every spare second of every day masterminding a plan to rid herself of Savage and have him and Rebel punished for their actions.

Now that she saw Lucky, there were no questions, no wondering. Only one thing was on his agenda this evening. Bang that girl until he forgot about all about Kori. After Rebel's announcement, she had no right to judge how Lucky would spend his night, but seeing him leave with a club whore, knowing exactly what would happen in just a short time, was a breath-stealing agony. And only the beginning of the torment for her.

Now she'd get a front row seat as he got over her one woman at a time. Chances were high she wouldn't survive this, not emotionally.

She had to talk to him. At least see if there was some way to apologize.

On trembling legs, she slipped through the crowd and caught up to him just as he and his companion reached the exit. Out of the corner of her eye, she caught Rebel's stare. No privacy, no chance to clue Lucky in in any way. "L-Lucky?"

He froze, the muscles in his arm grew rigid across his companion's shoulders.

"Can I—I mean, is it..." She drew in a shaky breath. "May I speak with you for a minute before you leave?" There, her voice only held a moderate wobble. Best she could do under the circumstances.

For a beat, she didn't think he'd answer, then he peered down at the woman. "Wait outside for me, doll. I'll just be a second."

"Sure, baby," the slut said in a voice dripping with promised sex. She glanced over her shoulder and winked at Kori as she wiggled her long nails in a goodbye wave.

Lucky spun slowly, his expression hard as granite, jaw ticking and eyes narrowed. The strong arms that she loved wrapped around her, arms that would never hold her again, folded across his chest. The posture said it all. He was one hundred percent closed off to her. Body and heart.

"I'm sorry." Could she sound more stupid? Like her sorrow mattered. Like it changed a damned thing. "It just…happened." While she wanted to apologize, it was imperative he believe the ruse. Lying to him made the words taste beyond bitter as they left her mouth. "I never meant to hurt you." Another lame and totally inadequate line. But what the hell was she supposed to say?

"Just happened, huh?" A small grunt of disbelief emanated from him. The tone was one she'd never heard from him. Icy. Full of hatred and disgust. "I know exactly what *just happened*, babe. I don't do bikers, my ass. You settled for a few rides on the Lucky-go-round before aiming higher on the food chain. Can't say that I blame ya. You whores are all the same. Legs spread, dollar signs flashing in your eyes. Have a nice fuckin' life, Kori." He turned and slammed through the door.

Don't cry. Do. Not. Cry.

The mental pep talk was ineffective and her eyes flooded to the point of blurred vision. There was no choice but to pull herself together. If anyone saw her blubbering in the corner she'd be up a creek. With a fortifying breath, she vowed she'd find a way to make this up to Lucky, no matter how many trashy women he paraded by her.

As unbearable as being the target of Lucky's hatred was, a small part of Kori was glad he was in the dark as to Rebel's true plan. His anger directed at her was one thing, but if Lucky found out she'd been coerced, the results would be horrifying. He'd turn that anger and revulsion inward, and that would be worse.

Somehow, she'd learn to live the knowledge that he believed she betrayed him. But she couldn't live the rest of her life knowing he blamed himself. And he would. It's who he was.

The weight of that regret on her shoulders would be more than she could bear.

***

Lucky now had two goals for the night: numb his mind with enough alcohol to make him stupid, and take what Bitsy was offering until he could no longer taste, smell, or feel Kori in every inch of his apartment. Under normal circumstances, a club whore would not find herself in his home, but he had a demon to exorcise and planned to do a thorough job of it.

Bitsy was waiting for him by his bike, one high heel propped on his rear tire. The position showcased her long, toned leg. One hip was cocked to the side with her hand resting on it and her chest seemed pushed out to an unnatural degree. Despite his ideas for the evening, there was a small chance things wouldn't go according to plan. And that chance lay between his legs. It literally laid there with no apparent desire for Bitsy. No matter. Once they got naked and hands on each other he'd get into gear.

He strode to his bike, swung a leg over and donned his helmet. Then, he grabbed Kori's helmet and started to offer it back to Bitsy. She grasped it, but his hand ignored the message from his brain and wouldn't release the protective device.

"You gonna let go, big guy?" she purred next to him.

"Um, actually," he pulled his helmet off and handed it off to her. "That one won't fit. Wear mine, I'll be good." He stuffed Kori's helmet in his saddle bag as Bitsy secure his over her bottle-blond hair. "Hop on, babe."

The second, the very instant Bitsy's enhanced breasts touched his back, he shot off the bike as though he'd hit an ejection button.

Since she'd been trying to snuggle close, her momentum propelled forward. "Hey!" she cried as her hands braced on the gas tank and narrowly prevented a face plant. "What the fuck is wrong with you?"

Good fucking question. What was wrong with him? Kori was gone, lost to him. Never before had he had a problem jumping from one chick's bed to another. But the thought of touching Bitsy, the brief feel of her against him proved that game plan wouldn't work this time.

With a sigh, he shoved a hand through his hair. "Look, Bitsy, I'm sorry, but this isn't going to happen tonight. Or ever. Just head on back in and enjoy the party. I'm gonna split."

Her face went from hopeful to spiteful in a flash. "Excuse me?" She practically spat the word at him. "Who the fuck do you think you are? You don't turn this down." She pointed to herself as she spoke.

Jesus, just what he needed. A club whore with high self-esteem. "Get the fuck off my bike, Bitsy. There are plenty of other bikers in there who'd be more than happy to fuck you. I'm not one of them."

He hadn't thought it possible, but her sneer turned uglier. "Why don't you make me, limp dick."

Was it still unacceptable to hit a woman? Unfortunately, it was, but there wasn't a hard and fast rule against scaring one. He stepped close enough to let her feel the full power of his wrath. "Make no mistake about it, Bitsy. If I have to, I will make you get off this bike, and I can promise that despite whatever you're plotting, you won't like it."

Something, maybe his expression or the calm, poisonous tone he used, got through to her. Her gooped-up eyes widened and she slid off the bike.

"Come on to me again and I'll see you're run out of here." It was over the top, yes, but he was in a shit mood and Bitsy was the only target around.

The helmet slamming into his gut was unexpected, but he let it slide. "Fuck you," she muttered as she scurried—if that was possible in what had to be five-inch heels—back to the clubhouse.

Fuck this entire night. Lucky mounted his bike and sped off toward his apartment and a cabinet full of booze that was calling his name.

Minutes after arriving home, his mistake hit him full force. The entire place had Kori's mark on it. Christ, her scent smacked him in the face as soon as he opened the door. He stomped to the kitchen, and when he saw a pile of her stuff on his table, the volcano erupted. With an enraged yell, he upended the table sending her sweatshirt, a bottle of some girly face shit, a candle in a glass jar, and a vase full of flowers he'd bought her crashing to the floor.

Shards of shattered glass shot off in every direction across the kitchen floor. His booted feet crunched over the carnage as he zeroed in on the liquor cabinet. He snatched the fullest bottle and took a long, therapeutic swallow, loving the burn of the bourbon as it slid through him.

Sleeping in the bed he'd had Kori in countless times was out of the question, so he flopped on the couch. After he'd polished off a third of the bottle, his mind fuzzed and the crushing pain in his chest dulled to an ache. The suffering would be back full force once the booze wore off, but for now, numbness was a welcome reprieve.

There were a least fifty questions he'd want answers to later. When had she had the time to develop a relationship with Savage? Were all the meals she shared with her father over the past few weeks just an excuse to spend more time with Savage? Had Rebel even joined them? Was every second Lucky spent with her a complete and total lie? How the fuck could he, a self-proclaimed womanizer, fall in so deep with one woman?

And of course, the biggie. Why? Why the fuck did she lead him to believe they had something? Why the fuck did she agree to live with him?

That was a bit of a lie. There was a bigger question. A horrifying question. Was she fucking Savage?

Questions could wait, especially the last one. For now, and for the foreseeable future, the detaching oblivion of a hard drunk was his one and only priority.

CHAPTER TWENTY-THREE

Lucky was gone. Just...gone.

No goodbye party from the club. No send off or well wishing. Hell, according to the buzz, he hadn't told anyone besides Rebel that he was leaving. Patching over to the Crystal Rock, Arizona chapter as they'd discussed. Except she'd been left behind.

It shouldn't have come as a surprise. Hell, Rebel flat out predicted Lucky wouldn't stick around. But she hadn't been prepared for the shock she'd feel when he was really gone.

His departure was a hope killer. The teeny tiny shred of hope she'd been clinging to with both hands, the chance that somehow everything would work out and she'd be rescued from a life with Savage, vanished along with Lucky.

What kept her sane in the week since Rebel turned her life upside down was a tunnel vision focus on devising a plan to speak with Lucky. Agreeing to Rebel and Savage's plan was a mistake. What she should have done was run to Lucky, spill the beans, and beg him to run away with her. They could be in a bungalow on a deserted beach in some part of the world where Rebel couldn't find them. At the time of the ultimatum, her brain had frozen with fear for Lucky's life, and she could barely remember what city she was in, let alone conjure up the brain power to develop a plan.

Rebel scared her into believing there was no corner of the earth she could hide where he couldn't find her, and over the past week she'd gone back and forth believing and not believing the truth in his words. Did he have that power? Based on his behavior this week, she was starting to believe he did.

Kori had spent the last week in hell. Rebel's single-minded drive to keep her under lock and key was proving very successful. He'd spewed some bullshit to a few prospects about her being on the radar of the club her mom married into. Put on quite the show, convincing a few club members of the danger she was in.

Now, a prospect sat outside Rebel's house when she was there. Someone from the MC drove her wherever she needed to go, and a club member wasted his day hanging out in the parking lot of the medical complex she'd started working in. All under the guise of protection.

Please, what a crock. It was straight up captivity. She was never alone. Never had an opportunity to speak to someone who might give her Lucky's cell number. Not that she knew who to trust. Was anyone else in on Rebel and Savage's plan?

Rebel was no dummy. Her mind was constantly spinning, looking for a way out of her newfound prison. He knew she'd take the first opportunity she had to get away.

Her heart was not into her new job, but at least it gave her a solid eight hours a day away from the club.

"How's it going today, Kori?" Donna slid into an empty seat behind the reception window.

"Hey, Donna." Kori forced her lips to turn up in a friendly smile. What had to be her hundredth of the day. "Things are going very well. Dr. Kovach's last patient just left, and I was going to grab some lunch."

"Sounds good. Before you run off, I just wanted to say thank you. Gosh, Kori, you've been here only three days and I swear it's like you've worked here for years. I can't tell you how amazing it is that you've picked up on everything so fast. You're a rock star."

The warmth of pride bloomed in Kori's chest. It was a welcome sensation after a week of dark depression. "Thanks for the kind words, Donna. I've loved the last few days here. Everyone couldn't be more welcoming and willing to answer my questions, dumb as they may be." All true, except keeping her head in the game had been near impossible.

"None of your questions have been even close to dumb. Trust me. You didn't ask what the left and right buttons on the mouse do, so you're lightyears above the last hire."

Laughter bubbled out. Another welcome feeling she'd not experienced since the day Lucky asked her to move in. "I can see how that would be concerning."

Donna snorted. "You have no idea. Well, I won't keep you from your lunch. Just wanted to let you know you're doing a fantastic job."

Kori logged off the computer, grabbed her purse out of the bottom desk drawer, and stood. "Thank you for saying so. I'll be back in an hour."

"See ya."

As Donna turned her back and walked toward her small office, Kori used the land line to call for a taxi. She had no identification and fifteen dollars in cash she'd pilfered from Rebel. It wouldn't get her far, but it would work for today. She rattled off the address of the building next door and disconnected the call. Three minutes. It'd be a hustle, but she should make it there just as the cab was pulling up.

The two medical office buildings were connected by an above ground walkway connecting the third floors. Her plan was risky, but the only thing she could think of to slip past her guard dog. She just needed a little time. An hour alone where she couldn't feel the club's presence breathing down her neck and could think with a clear head.

Picking up the pace, she made her way across the walkway and down a stairwell that opened up outside, near the entrance to the adjacent building. With each step she took, her heart pounded faster and her breathing accelerated. Consequences would be dire if she was caught.

Sunlight accosted her as she pushed the heavy door open and stepped outside. A brown taxi was just pulling up to the curb. Perfect timing. Across the parking lot, a No Prisoners prospect leaned against his bike, thumbing through his phone, completely oblivious to her plan.

The moment she slipped into the vehicle and closed the door, a small measure of relief evaporated some of the tension she'd been wearing like a cloak. Freedom. If only for a short while.

"Where to, ma'am?" the driver asked, a middle aged Hispanic man with a picture of a smiling family on his dash.

"Montgomery Apartment Complex, please."

"That's not far from here at all. We'll be there in five minutes."

Midday traffic was light and true to his word, he rolled up outside the building within five minutes.

"Thank you," she said as she stepped outside the car. The driver agreed to return in forty-five minutes which would get her back to the office just at the end of her hour lunch break.

The key to Lucky's apartment seared her leg through her pants pocket. She'd been aware of its presence all day, just mocking her. Sure, she could get into his building, but he wouldn't be there. Word around the clubhouse was that he'd left just about all his belongings and maintained the lease on the apartment. Could that mean he was coming back?

No. It meant he couldn't stand to be in the presence of anything she'd touched. It meant he'd abandoned all aspects of his life here in Vegas. Kori rubbed a hand over her chest. Suddenly it was a bit difficult to draw in a full breath.

She trudged up the stairs to the second floor and stood outside Lucky's door, key in hand. And then, her muscles seized. What seemed like such a good idea moments ago, now seemed more like a masochistic move. "Oh for crying out loud, just open the damn door," she muttered.

Her limbs obeyed the command and she entered the apartment. "Holy shit." Disaster was too mild a word for the state of the apartment. From the number of empty or smashed bottles strewn around, the broken coffee table, and the fist size hole in the wall, it appeared Lucky'd spent the majority of the past week bombed and taking his aggression out on his innocent possessions.

Guilt hit her like a fist to the stomach. The past few days, she'd been so absorbed, wallowing in her own misery, she hadn't given much thought to Lucky's grief, beyond the fact that he'd split.

All because of her. Because there was a very good chance that in the heat of the moment she made the wrong decision. The tears came on fast and furious, streaming down her face and landing on the floor like she was somehow anointing the wreckage.

Careful not to crunch over too much of the rubble, Kori tiptoed around chunks of glass and made her way to Lucky's bedroom. The bed was rumpled and clothes were strewn about, but nothing was broken and no bottles resided in the room. In fact, on closer inspection, the room looked exactly as it had when she'd left Lucky's home eight days ago after agreeing to move in with him.

He hadn't been in there since.

Kori wiped her nose, set the alarm on the nightstand for thirty minutes and climbed into Lucky's bed. She drew the covers over herself and imagined the cold sheets were the warmth and strength of Lucky's arms instead. The sheets smelled of him, and still held a faint aroma of sex. It was the last straw.

Huge, choking sobs tore through her, disrupting the quiet and ruining any plans for a peaceful hour. Kori gave into the sorrow, buried her head in the pillow and let the tears come.

When the alarm went off, she rolled to a sitting position. Time for tears had ended.

Now it was time to put on her big girl panties, figure out a way to avoid marrying Savage, keep Lucky and herself alive, and make Rebel and Savage pay for their actions.

No problem...

CHAPTER TWENTY-FOUR

The blaring of Lucky's phone jarred him from a whiskey-induced sleep to fully awake, if not entirely alert. "Jesus Christ," he yelled into the darkness. He reached out to grab the phone, and caught his elbow on the corner of the bedside table. "Aw, fuck me."

The glow of the phone was brighter than the sun in the dark room. "Whoever the fuck this is, do you realize you just interrupted my cock when it was about to slide into some hot pussy?"

A snort followed his angry greeting. "Yeah right. A week and a half ago you were so fucking pussy whipped, I bet you haven't laid eyes on a single snatch since you left." Truer words had never been spoken.

Lucky had been in Arizona about ten days, and he'd played the game they all expected to see. He flirted, made witty comments, and made his MC brother's wives blush, but that was as far as it went. His dick had died a painful death. Unless of course he was in his shower with visions of Kori behind his eyelids. Then he was hard enough to drive a hole through the wall and he came like he was dying each time.

"Who the fuck is this? It's midnight. Someone die?" Lucky rubbed a hand across his forehead trying to massage his brain to life.

"It's Bull, brother. And I need to talk to you. Tonight. Now."

"So talk."

"Nuh uh, not on the phone. I'm at the Starlight Motel. Some shithole a few towns over from you. Room seven."

Fully awake, Lucky sat on the edge of his bed. "Yeah, yeah, I know it. Shit. I can be there in an hour tops. This better be worth my fuckin' time, Bull." He disconnected the call. "Swear to God," he muttered. "If he's here to tell me how sorry Kori is and how she wants me back, the man's going home minus two balls."

Forty-five minutes later, Lucky killed his engine outside room seven of the shitty Starlight Motel. All the motels in this area were pretty sketchy. None of the major hotel chains had made their way to the tiny town of Crystal Rock yet. He stashed his pistol in the back of his pants and started for the room. Chances were, this was a legitimate visit, not some attempt by Rebel to shut him up. It wasn't Rebel's style.

If Rebel discovered Lucky knew about his drug enterprise, it was more likely that Lucky would wake up to a bag being tossed over his head as he was chucked in the back of a van. Rebel would beat him within two inches of his life then shoot him between the eyes. Still, it was better to be safe than sorry, hence the pistol.

And the knife in his boot.

And enough marine corps martial arts fighting experience to do some serious damage to anyone who tried to take him down.

He pounded the side of his fist against the door, ignoring the peeling flecks of paint that fell to the ground. The number seven hung by one nail and swung back and forth as the door vibrated. The entire place looked one decent wind gust from collapsing.

Bull opened the door, popped his head out, peered right and left then yanked Lucky into the room. "Anyone follow you?"

"Uh, no, Bull. Paranoid much? What the hell's going on, brother?" Dark circles rimmed bloodshot eyes and Bull's long hair resembled a snarled rat's nest on top of his head. The man looked like he hadn't slept in weeks.

"Robbie's dead."

Shit. His words stopped Lucky in his tracks. Almost by instinct, he reached behind his back and whipped his gun around, training it on Bull. The solid weight in his hand provided a comfort only a trained sniper could understand. Sure, it wasn't his rifle, that was out in his saddle bags, but he was damn accurate with a pistol as well. "Why are you bringing this shit to me?"

Bull was no idiot. His eyebrows shot to his hairline and he raised his hands in surrender. "What the fuck, man?"

"Rebel send you?" Lucky wasn't taking any chances now. Bull wouldn't be here if Robbie overdosed or was hit by a delivery truck. No, he was here because Robbie was killed. And Rebel topped the charts as Lucky's main suspect.

"Rebel? Fuck no. You think I'd be here in the middle of the night freaked out as shit if Rebel sent me?" Bull maintained his arms raised position relaxed his stance now that Lucky didn't appear to be about to put an extra hole or two in him.

"So why? Why me? Why now?" Lucky asked.

"Can you put that thing away? I know you can shoot a fleck of dust from a million miles away. You're making me nervous, brother."

"You armed?"

Bull snorted. "Of course. And after I fill you in on the whole story you'll know why. Just one gun, though."

Lucky could only imagine the shit they were both in now. "Put your weapon on the table." He inclined his head toward a tiny round table next to the aging television. "Then sit on the edge of the bed and I'll put my gun away."

Bull did as he asked without argument. When the man was seated at the edge of the bed, Lucky sat in a chair at the small table and rested his gun on the tabletop. Safety remained off, and the pistol was well within reach, but he rolled his shoulder and relaxed a fraction. "All right. Start talking."

Bull nodded and blew out a breath before lifting his head and looking Lucky right in the eye. Lucky appreciated the man's willingness to dive right in and own whatever tale he was about to tell.

"I've been banging this chick for the past few weeks. Man she is…" He held his hands out in front of his chest. "Ya know?"

Seriously? Both their lives could be in jeopardy at this very moment and Bull wanted to make sure he knew his plaything had huge tits? "The point, Bull. Get there."

"Right, sorry, bro. Anyway she…uh…well, she's a recreational user. Nothing major, just at parties and shit. But anyway, she and Robbie were tight. She came to me two days ago saying that Robbie was MIA for a few weeks and she thought Rebel offed him."

Lucky's blood ran cold at the confirmation of his worst fear. But it still didn't make sense. It wasn't time to put his cards on the table. Not until he was certain of how much Bull knew and exactly where the man's loyalties lie. He made sure his voice didn't betray his concern. "Why the hell would she jump to Rebel?"

One of Bull's eyebrows rose and he shot Lucky a you're-not-fooling-me-for-one-second look. "Okay, Lucky. We'll play it your way. Lexa told me Robbie's been spouting off about buying drugs from the No Prisoners for the past few months. Good shit apparently."

Poor Robbie. He'd promised Lucky he'd keep his mouth shut about the No Prisoners involvement. And there was the problem trusting someone who'd sell their first born for a fix. Loyalty only went as far as their stash. "Pretty serious accusation, Bull."

"Damn straight it is. Didn't believe the bitch for one second myself. Until I went back to the clubhouse after we shut down last night. Left my phone behind the bar. As I was coming out, I saw Savage and Rebel loading something up in the bed of a pickup. It was a body. No question. Figure it was too coincidental to be anyone but Robbie."

Shit, shit, shit. Could they be any more fucked? Was Rebel on to either of them?

"Look, man, I get it. You're as freaked out as I am about this shit. But the way I see it, you knew. You've known for a while and that's why you split."

"I left because of Ko—"

Bull waved him off. "Yeah, I get that shit too. You left because Kori had your dick tied in so many knots you could barely take a piss. But you'd been off before your girl even came to town. Growing more hostile toward Rebel and Savage by the day. I connected the dots, asshole.

"Here's the way I see it. You got three choices. Spill the beans, ignore it, or jump on board. There are a number of members who I think wouldn't see beyond the dollar signs and would get in bed with our two fearless leaders. Knowing what happened to your sister I find it hard to believe you'd choose that option or the ignore it option. That leaves telling someone. Striker or Shiv maybe, since confronting Rebel would be suicide."

Lucky cleared his throat. Bull was far more intelligent than he'd ever given the guy credit for. "I haven't decided what to do yet."

"Well it was probably smart to remove yourself from the situation entirely, and I'm guessing you were leaning toward talking with Shiv and Striker about it, but now you're trapped. Kori being stuck in the middle and all that."

Lucky cursed, stood from the chair, and paced in front of the door. The gun remained on the table. Bull wasn't there to fuck him up. He was in just as deep now.

"You gonna ask how she's doing?" Bull asked.

"No."

"Not so well. I've only seen her a few times, but she looked worse each time. Depressed, skinny, pale. Like she's not taking care of herself."

Really? Had he not heard the no? Lucky lunged for Bull and grabbed his friend by the collar, yanking him off the bed. "I said

I didn't want to know. She ain't happy with Savage? Well that's too fuckin' bad. She made her bed."

Bull nodded, his hands rising in surrender once again. "Yeah, she did. That don't mean it's easy to watch her spiral down. Also doesn't mean you want her chewed up and spit out by this whole mess."

No, it didn't. That's the last thing he wanted. Because while she'd ripped out and stomped on whatever form of a heart Lucky had, he couldn't bear to see her caught in the clash of what had the potential to be a civil war if he told Striker and Shiv.

But now it seemed like he had no choice. Rebel was silencing trouble. Getting rid of Robbie because he ran his mouth was a demonstration of just how seriously they took their new business venture. It was time to do something before anyone else was killed or before they destroyed the club.

"For what it's worth," Bull said. "I don't think they realize you're on to them. I don't imagine Rebel would have let you come down here and chance you talking to the leadership here if Rebel knew you were on to him."

Lucky released Bull's shirt and resumed pacing. "Sorry, brother."

"No bother. I know it's a world of shit." Bull remained standing. "But if there is a chance for our club to survive without anyone losing their head or without dragging us into the fucking drug trade, something needs to be done."

Lucky stopped walking and faced his club brother. "I will take care of this. We've got some shit going on with Acer and his old man causing trouble for us, but it should be settled pretty quick. Once that's off our plates, I'll bring this to Shiv and Striker."

"What about Kori? Rebel pushed Savage on her hard, man. She'd just lost her mom, just met her father for the first time. That's enough to mess up anyone's head. Maybe she's realizing how badly she fucked up. I'm telling you she don't look good."

An ache began between Lucky's eyes and he squeezed the bridge of his nose in a failed attempt to counter the pressure. "I don't know yet. I'll figure something out."

It took hours to convince Bull to return to Vegas and go about his normal business. The guy wanted to go off the grid until the dust settled. That would only throw up a red flag.

After many go arounds, Bull caved. They spent time getting their stories straight and making plans to discretely stay in contact.

It was early morning by the time Lucky emerged from the motel, desperately in need of a bed and a stiff drink. He stretched and scanned the parking lot.

What the hell?

If he wasn't mistaken, Fia, Acer's woman, was loading a suitcase into the trunk of a car and heading off in the opposite direction of Crystal Rock.

Lucky pulled out his phone as he fired up his bike and prepared to tail Fia out of town. Jesus. Only six a.m.

Could this day get any worse?

CHAPTER TWENTY-FIVE

The poker game wrapped up as Kori collected stray beer bottles from the poker table, the counter, the floor and what seemed like any flat surface in Savage's house. For the past four hours, she'd endured crude jokes, ass pinches, waitress duty, and Savage's wandering hands. She'd perched on his lap with a plastic smile on her face while the men got rowdier and drunker with each passing hour.

This was it. The night she would make her escape. She didn't yet know where she'd go, but had a good feeling this might be her only chance. Prior to poker, Savage had been drinking at the clubhouse and wasn't in any state to drive. Kori barely contained her shock and excitement when he tossed her his car keys and her wallet and ordered her to drive them to his apartment for the game. Thanks to his buzz, he hadn't thought to relieve her of either when they arrived.

From the moment they walked in the door, she'd been feeding him shot after shot. If he would just pass out, she'd have her chance to escape. The prospect who'd lived up her ass the past ten days had been given the night off since she was under Savage's *protection*. It was the closest to an open window she'd had since she walked out of that damned shed and she planned to take full advantage.

Kori was the only ol' lady at poker. The rest of the women in attendance were club whores, there with married and single

151

members alike. Kori's stomach had soured as three of the men playing tonight came through the door. They were married and Kori knew their wives, but was expected to keep her mouth shut and behave like the good little woman she pretended to be.

She knew this for what it was. A punishment. For the past two weeks, she'd avoided Savage's advances. Hell, she'd avoided *him* like a nasty disease. Thankfully work was so busy she'd been able to stay late a few nights for some overtime.

But time and Savage's patience were clearly running out. The thought of touching him, seeing him naked, sleeping with him kept her throwing every possible excuse his way, but she feared her luck had run out.

"There you are." Savage wobbled into the kitchen on unsteady legs.

"Just clearing away some of the mess before I take off." She'd nursed one beer for as long as she could draw it out. When the men were involved in a particularly tense hand, she escaped to the kitchen and refilled her bottle with water. Getting drunk was not something she could risk tonight with so much on the line. Her heart pounded faster and harder with each passing minute. Freedom was so close she could taste it, but she had to tread carefully. If she screwed this up, she might never get another chance to sneak away.

"Take off?" he asked as he stumbled toward her. "Where the fuck do you think you're going?" His eyes were glassy and his tongue sounded too big for his mouth, but Kori wasn't under any impression that he'd be impaired if it came to a physical altercation. He outweighed her by at least eighty pounds and towered over her.

"Oh, well it's midnight and I have to work tomorrow, you know. I'm just gonna head back to Rebel's so I can get some rest." She dropped the bottles in the trashcan then spun to grab some more.

Savage was there. Right there. In her personal space about two inches away. "Oh, um, sorry. Just trying to get the rest of the bottles."

"Leave 'em." He reached for her and she reflexively backed up.

After the past hours of his large hands roaming all over her, the idea of his touch was sickening. She hit the wall after only three steps. Shit. Her eyes darted left and right. Where was the quickest escape route?

Nowhere, apparently. He boxed her in, a hand on either side of her head as he leaned toward her. Booze-infested breath flowed from him with each exhalation. Kori clenched her teeth to keep the involuntary cough from betraying her disgust.

"You think I'm stupid?" he asked.

She swallowed hard. *Don't gag.* "Stupid? No of course not. Why would you ask that?"

"You think I can't see what you're doing here? Avoiding me? Putting me off." He pressed his front into her, the erection unmistakable against her stomach.

Kori jerked back, but there was nowhere to go and all she managed to do was smack her head against the wall. "No of course not. I just have to work and it's late."

"You're staying here." He ground his pelvis rhythmically against her.

The beer she'd drunk earlier burned at the back of her throat, seconds away from making a return visit. She raised her hands and pushed against his chest. "Back off, Savage. You're smothering me." When he didn't budge, the tiny hairs on her arms and back of her neck stood on end.

He leered down at her, a maniacal grin on his face. "Looks like you're not going anywhere right now."

She shoved again, to no avail. The man was like an immovable wall. She turned her head as his mouth descended, but he wasn't deterred and instead of taking her lips, he latched on to the side of her neck.

Kori bit back a scream. What was the point? No one was around to hear her and he'd probably get off on her distress. His tongue slithered up the side of her neck and she froze, statue-still, as though he'd somehow forget she was there if she didn't move. Her mind screamed at her to fight, to run, but her limbs wouldn't obey.

He slid his hands up her sides and when one closed over her breast, her body finally kicked into action. "Get the fuck off of me!" she cried as she fisted his hair and yanked with all her might.

"Fuck! You bitch," he yelled, but it was enough to distract him into giving her some space. She rammed her palms against his chest and this time he stumbled to the side, no doubt impaired by the copious amounts of alcohol he'd consumed. She'd take whatever advantage she could get.

She dashed toward the front door, grabbing her purse from the kitchen table as she fled.

The creepiest laughter she'd ever heard outside of a Stephen King movie followed her, much too close for comfort. When she was mere feet from the door, a rough hand grabbed the back of her shirt. As she flew backward, she managed to spin around swinging her purse like a baseball bat.

It glanced off the side of Savage's head and he blinked but kept charging. Her back hit the door and she was in much the same helpless position she'd been in just seconds before. "Savage, please, stop."

"You are my woman," he said, his speech more slurred than it had been. As more alcohol registered in his system, she just might have a chance to escape. If only it would zap his strength. "This is mine. I'm done with your bullshit." He pinned her arms against the wall at the sides of her head.

"I'm not really your woman. You have to know that. There's only one reason I'm here." This time, there was nothing frozen about her body. She thrashed and struggled. She would not be leaving here tonight a victim.

Lucky

The slap that landed against her right cheek came so fast and was so unexpected, Kori didn't have more than a blink of time to prepare for it. Fiery pain erupted from her jaw to her hairline and her head snapped to the side. For a split second, the world went fuzzy and her eyeball felt like it had ruptured out of the socket.

Stunned, she blinked and tried to bring the room back into focus.

Savage grunted. "That's better. Looks like you just might need a firm hand, huh? Now listen up, bitch. I don't give a shit why you're here. I don't give a shit if you like it or want it. You're here and your mine. Start fuckin' acting like it or I'll make your life a living hell. We clear?"

She righted her head and blinked again. His fuzzy face become sharper. Were they clear? Hysterical laughter bubbled out of her. Nothing was clear after that blow to her face.

"What the fuck is so funny, bitch?" He'd returned his slapping arm to her wrist and gave her a shake against the wall.

Suddenly everything was clear, crystal clear. Anger replaced the shock in her system. She would flee across the country. Disappear. They'd never find her. Lucky was gone so he was no longer in danger, no longer a threat to her father and Savage. She'd hide and lick her emotional wounds until she came up with a viable plan.

With a warrior's roar, she lifted her leg and ground her three-inch heel into Savage's shoeless foot. His agonized cry was music to her ears. With any luck, her heel went straight through his flesh.

"Shit!" he yelled as he hopped on the uninjured leg, cradling his damaged foot.

Without a drop of remorse, she ran forward checking him with her right hip and shoulder. The combination of intoxication and a one-legged stance did him in and he crashed to the ground, taking out a small table in the short hallway leading from the front door to the rest of the apartment.

Kori didn't bother to hang around and see if he was unconscious, dead, hurt, or alive and thirsty for blood. She snatched her purse from the floor and fled the apartment as fast as her trembling legs would allow.

As she darted down the two flights of stairs to the ground floor, she kicked off her tall shoes. Running down steps and across a parking lot in heels would slow her down more than she was willing to risk.

She made it to the car after what felt like a three-mile jog. Every second or so she'd peeked over her shoulder. So far, no sign of Savage. Jesus. What if she'd killed him? What if he hit his head as he broke the table? Would it be considered self-defense?

They were all questions she'd have time to answer later when she was away and safe. She yanked the car door open and risked one last glance at Savage's apartment. His door opened to the outside steps and he ran out screaming obscenities and chasing down the steps after her. She slammed and locked the car door, fired up her vehicle and sped out of the lot like the hounds of hell were chasing her.

When she was thirty minutes north of Vegas, she pulled into a rundown motel. Her limbs had finally stopped shaking and she was able to draw in a steady breath. She killed the ignition and dropped her head to the steering wheel.

What the hell had happened to her life? Tears burned behind her eyes, but she blinked them away. Crying could come later. Now she needed a plan. She had no personal belongings. No clothes, no shoes, no tooth brush. Going back to Rebel's to retrieve anything was out of the question. But for the first time since this nightmare began, she did have her purse complete with identification and credit cards.

For now, that was enough. Enough to get her through the night. Enough to get her far away from Vegas and all things biker.

CHAPTER TWENTY-SIX

Lucky stared at the amber liquid in the glass. What was it, his third? Fourth? Did it matter? Was it concerning that he no longer felt any different after a few drinks than he did stone cold sober? He leaned over and placed the glass next to the open bottle on the ground near his Adirondack chair. His alcohol consumption had shot through the roof since Kori left him.

What a fuckin' pussy he'd become. Here he was, once again, getting wasted and thinking about a woman who probably hadn't spared two brain cells on him since he left. Beyond pathetic.

"Okay, time's up." Acer jogged the three steps up to Lucky's back deck. "The place is nice. I was wondering if you ever planned to invite anyone out here."

Lucky had rented a house in Crystal Rock a week ago and if anyone asked, no he did not rent it with Kori in mind. He'd always wanted a house with a large porch, oversized bathtub, impressive kitchen...

Jesus, he was getting sick of himself.

"What do you mean, time's up?" Luck grabbed the bottle and offered it to Acer who waved it away.

Acer lowered himself into a second chair next to Lucky's. "I'm good, brother. What I mean is your wallowing. Hiding out. Drinking yourself to death. Whatever you want to call it. Time's up. It's done. Time to talk to someone about the reason you came to Crystal Rock. The reason you're working so hard each day at marinating your liver. The reason you haven't slept with a single woman in the month you've been here."

Lucky huffed out a harsh laugh. So much for thinking he had everyone fooled. He put up a good front. Smiles, flirts, winks, but just couldn't bring himself to touch a woman who wasn't Kori, let alone fuck one. The thought almost made him ill.

More evidence of the pussy he'd become.

"There has to be a reason you left Vegas. I'm sorry I've been so wrapped up in my own shit since you arrived that I haven't had much time to check in with you."

Leave it to Acer to realize not all was as it seemed. He was one smart motherfucker, had grown up in a world of wealth and power Lucky would never know anything about. Yet somehow, they hit it off. "How's Fia?"

"She's hanging in. Actually, she's doing pretty well. And she's sitting in her car in the driveway. Told me I had fifteen minutes to talk to you then she was coming to do the job herself."

"Well that explains why I didn't hear your bike."

"Quit stalling."

"You know, I'm not really one for a heart to heart." Reaching for the bottle again, he took a healthy drink. Screw the glass. The bottle was much more efficient.

"Shut the fuck up and talk to me before I sic Fia on your ass." Acer held a hand out for the bottle and took a drink this time when Lucky handed it over.

"Fia can come after my ass anytime she wants." Lucky laughed as Acer's middle finger went up.

"Don't think I've forgotten that you hit on my woman recently." Acer took a healthy swig then returned the bottle to Lucky.

"Please, you know I wouldn't have touched her even if she begged." Fia had been abducted and assaulted by a sadistic man less than a year ago. With Acer's help, she was moving past the trauma, but had a lot of issues with her confidence as a woman.

Lucky told her he'd gladly sleep with her if and when she'd felt ready. Of course, he hadn't meant it. One, his head was too fucked up over Kori and two, he'd never betray a brother like that. But the offer went a long way toward squashing her fears of being seen as a desirable woman again.

"I know that now that I've watched you steer clear of anything female over the last month. At the time? I wanted to pound your ass."

Laughter erupted from Lucky's gut. Damn, that felt good. This was exactly what he'd been missing in Vegas for quite some time. The brotherhood here was strong whereas it had been disintegrating in Vegas, even before he learned about the drugs. He hadn't even realized it was happening, but now that he was essentially with a new club, the differences were glaring.

He tipped his head back and stared at the clear blue sky, not a wisp of a cloud in sight. Sweat dotted his forehead and soaked his T-shirt, partly from the almost one-hundred-degree day and partly from the stress of what he knew he had to do.

"There's some shit going down in Vegas, bad shit." Even though he wasn't even touching on what was actually happening, guilt hit him like a sledge hammer. He felt dirty, like a diseased sewer rat.

Acer's back straightened. "Christ, Luck, I had no idea. Do they need help up there? Man power? Where's the threat coming from?"

Lucky shook his head and gave Acer the respect of looking him straight in the eye. "It's internal trouble. Like I said, bad shit. Stuff I should have probably taken straight to Shiv when I got here. Hell, before I got here. But, there are...complications. And then I walked into a mess here with the threat from your father. But that's resolved and I've run out of time. I need to talk to them."

"Man, you are a cryptic bastard. I get it though. They need to hear first if it's a problem within the club. Bad, you say?" The bottle was passed between the them again and Acer took a long drink.

"The worst."

"Shit."

"Couldn't have said it better myself."

Footsteps sounded around the side of the house and Fia appeared a few seconds later. "I gave you guys one extra minute." She winked. "I'm just generous like that."

As she climbed the steps, Acer held a hand out. "Thanks, baby. You're too good to us."

With a laugh, she took his hand and allowed him to pull her onto his lap. It was nice to see her looking relaxed and at happy in Acer's arms. She'd been through hell and still reacted negatively when in close quarters with most men. But not Acer, and surprisingly, not so much with Lucky. She seemed to have taken to him and trusted he'd never hurt her or breach her invisible boundaries.

Acer nuzzled her neck and whispered something in her ear that had her giggling and swatting his arm. "Behave," she whispered, then turned to Lucky. "So, Lucky, tell me her name."

She had to ask just as the liquor filled his mouth. Damn her feminine insight. He sucked in a breath and choked as the bourbon sloshed down his windpipe. "Whose...name?" he asked between coughs.

Legs crossed and back resting against Acer's chest, she cocked her head and smiled. "The woman who messed with your head. The woman you're apparently saving yourself for."

It was Acer's turn to choke this time, although the bastard wasn't drinking anything. He could suffocate on his spit for all Lucky cared.

Saving himself. Christ, if he hadn't sounded like a pussy before, he sure did now. The worst part was that Fia was entirely right. He wasn't chasing any chicks on the negative chances that he'd somehow get Kori back. What a loser.

Fia smiled a satisfied grin as though she enjoyed getting under his skin. Her glee at his expense was almost worth it after observing her have a few panic attacks and seeing her almost killed by a psycho.

"All right, nosey. There was a woman. There isn't anymore. That's all you're getting. Hope you're happy."

Her grin spread practically to her ears. "Good enough for now, my friend. But I'll be back for more later."

"One of those complications you mentioned?" Acer asked.

Lucky nodded. *The* complication.

"Shiv and Striker should both be at the clubhouse if you want to ride with us. Figure you may not want to drive after all that." Acer pointed to the bottle still in Lucky's hand.

Questions were visible in Fia's eyes, but like a good ol' lady, she didn't voice them. It would be a waste of breath. Neither Lucky or Acer would tell her what was going on. Not at this point anyway. Maybe later, if the situation became dangerous or there was a threat to the families they'd be clued in. But not now. Fia had been with Acer long enough to know how it worked.

Lucky rose from his chair. "Shit, let's go." It was now or never.

CHAPTER TWENTY-SEVEN

Kori sat in the rapidly heating car, bouncing her leg against the floorboard. Three minutes ago, she'd killed the engine in hopes that the car would become too warm to tolerate thus forcing her out. Nothing else had worked. She'd been sitting in the car for the past thirty minutes staring at the Crystal Rock chapter's clubhouse.

First, she tried an encouraging internal pep talk that fell flat. Then she scolded herself out loud. She'd even tried screaming at the top of her lungs in hopes that it would relieve tension.

No dice.

This seemed to be working though. It wouldn't be much longer before she had no choice but to leave the car. That or roast.

For the last two weeks, Kori had been hiding out in the cheapest motel she could find, two hours north of Vegas. She'd quit her job, paid cash, used a fake name and a cheesy hat and sunglasses disguise if she needed to leave her room, which she did not do often. She was petrified of being discovered. So many times over the fourteen days, she wanted to drive to Crystal Rock, but the unknowns kept her away. Would Lucky believe her? Would he toss her out on her ass if she showed up? Would her presence put either of them in danger? For all she knew, Rebel was monitoring the club, looking for her there. Hell, were the president and VP of the Crystal Rock chapter trustworthy?

The questions grew more intrusive and she eventually grew so lonely and eager to see Lucky that she was willing to take the chance. Lucky trusted those men. She would trust them too.

A knock on the window, right next to her ear caused her to yelp. Her hand slipped from the wheel and hit the horn, making her jump a second time. Jesus, she had to get a grip.

With an unsteady hand, she opened the door and looked up. And up. And up. A huge hulking form of a man loomed over her car. Everything about the giant was massive; his muscles, his long hair, his height. If it wasn't for the teasing grin on his face and the twinkle in his eye she may have slammed the door and driven straight out of the lot.

"Everything all right, miss? You sure have been sitting here for a while. Looking for someone you hooked up with recently?" the giant asked.

"What? Uh, no. I'm sorry I've been loitering. I just...um... well, it doesn't matter. I need to speak with either Shiv, or Striker, or both. It's very important." She straightened her shoulders and shored up the courage to look the large man in the face. Unfortunately for a few moments, she forgot about the purple bruising across her right cheek. The big guy noticed it and his smile flipped to a scowl.

"I'm Jester, by the way. Who did that to you? One of our guys?" He gripped her chin with a bear paw sized hand that was much gentler than she'd ever have imagined he could be and tilted her face, examining her cheek.

"Uh, no. No one from around here." She slid a hand over her cheek. So much for expensive makeup. "And I'm Kori."

He studied her for another moment before pulling her door all the way open. "Come on out, Kori. I believe both Striker and Shiv are in the chapel. They shouldn't mind an interruption. I'll walk you in."

"Thank you." She slid out of the vehicle. "Wow, I thought Vegas was hot."

Jester snorted. "Vegas, huh? You ain't seen nothing yet, girl. Come on, this way." He led the way into the clubhouse, past a wooden bar, to a set of floor-to-ceiling heavy wooden doors.

Her stomach dipped as his meaty fist rapped against the door and she had to lock her knees to keep from bolting back down the stairs.

"You okay, lady? You're looking a little green around the gills."

"Yeah I'm good."

"It's open," a man called from behind the door.

Jester popped his head in. "Hey, Pres, VP, there's a lady here to see you guys. Says it's important."

"All right, send her in, Jester," a different man answered.

"Thank you for the escort." She smiled up at Jester.

"No problem. And don't worry, they don't bite too hard." He shot her a wink then ambled toward the bar.

She stepped into the room and found two men sitting on either side of a large rectangular table. One was older, with a gray beard and long gray hair tied in a ponytail. A thick cigar that had burned down to about three inches was between his thumb and forefinger. The stogie emitted a pungent aroma that wasn't quite as offensive to her as cigarette smoke. Still, the lung cancer lecture was dancing on the tip of her tongue.

The other man was younger, probably upper thirties, with slightly mussed dark hair, an intense expression, and impressive biceps. They sure grew 'em handsome in the desert.

"What can I do for you?" the older man asked. She assumed he was Shiv.

"Um, hello..." Her voice was barely above a whisper so she cleared her throat. "Excuse me. My name is Kori and I need to speak to you about a few things, um, with regards to your club." She stood in the doorway wringing her hands like a nervous kid, but she couldn't help it. Her insides were shaking like she was a kid in front of an unhappy principal.

Striker narrowed his assessing gaze then his eyes widened with recognition. "Kori? As in Rebel's recently discovered daughter?"

"And Savage's fiancé?" Shiv added.

Well, shit. She should have assumed they'd know who she was. Rebel had been planning some big bash in her and Savage's honor. It made sense he would invite his Crystal Rock brothers. Hopefully that wouldn't put her at an immediate disadvantage. If they blindly sided with their MC brothers from Vegas she'd be screwed. And of course, she was complaining to the chapter president and VP about another president and VP. This had failure written all over it.

"Yes, that's me."

"Hmm," Shiv said. "Well come on in, grab an empty chair." The men exchanged a wary look.

She couldn't blame them, really. Her arrival was quite out of the norm.

"Question," Shiv asked as she took the empty chair next to Striker's. "Either of them know you're here?"

"Ah, no, they definitely do not. In fact, they probably don't know I've left town, and I'd appreciate if it stayed that way."

Striker looked ready to argue, but Shiv held a hand out. "Next question. This visit have anything to do with that fading bruise on your face?"

Damn it, why did she keep forgetting the freaking bruise? "No, well, it played a strong role in my leaving, but it's not why I'm here in Arizona."

"So why are you here? Striker asked, his tone full of impatience.

"Rebel and Savage are selling drugs." For the entire four-and-a-half-hour drive, Kori rehearsed exactly what she wanted to say to these men. Her prepared speech started with a statement about how she knew the club's bylaws were important and taken very seriously. Then she'd planned to go on about loyalty and brotherhood, all things that had been touted her entire life by various MC members. Then she'd end with gripping indecision over what was the right course of action to take before finally breaking down and admitting what she knew about Rebel and Savage.

At no point had she decided to vomit out the information in such a blunt manner. Apparently her subconscious had different ideas and decided cutting straight to the chase was the best way to go. If the looks on both men's faces were any indication, her subconscious may have been very wrong. What five seconds ago was a cautiously wary vibe in the room, now was icebox frigid. Shiv blew out a long stream of smoke and Kori was surprised it didn't freeze and plunge to the table.

He snubbed out the stump of a cigar in an ashtray that needed to be emptied three days ago, then leveled her with a look she'd never forget. Dark, dangerous, deadly. She was on ice so thin she didn't dare move.

"Pretty serious accusation, girlie. But I get it. Your ol' man's knocking you around. It ain't what you signed on for. Hell, I even agree it makes him an asshole. And maybe you're mad at daddy for not being there for you while you were growing up. He missed your dance recitals, your prom, the sex talk. I get it all. But..." His tone was lethal and a shiver raced down Kori's spine.

Don't fold.

"You cannot throw shit around like that. You want revenge? Fine. Slash his tires. Yank out the hair of whatever bitch he's tapping on the side. Rack up daddy's credit card. Do not fuck with the man's standing in his club. You have any idea the shit storm you're on the verge of triggering?"

Was this guy for real? This was what he thought of her? Of women? That she'd concoct this story as revenge for getting slapped? Of course it was. He was an MC president, after all. Please. She could cut the man's balls off herself for that. Her hands clenched to tight fists.

Striker hadn't so much as blinked. The muscles she'd admired minutes ago bunched with strain. Kori could literally feel waves of tension wafting in her direction. "Do you have any proof of your claims?" he asked.

Shiv's jaw dropped and he swung the piercing gaze to Striker. "Don't tell me you believe this bullshit? Get your head out of your ass, Striker."

Kori opened her mouth to speak, but Striker beat her to it. "I'm not saying I believe her." He cast a quick suspicious glance in her direction before refocusing on Shiv. "What I will say is that Jester's been bitching about Rebel lately. Since we've had all this nonsense going on with Acer's old man, Jester's been handling business with them. He's been saying for weeks that Rebel's been erratic. Missing phone meetings, disinterested in business. He's been off. That's all I'm saying."

"Shit," Shiv said as he produced another cigar seemingly from thin air.

Okay, enough was enough. "I do not have proof. No physical evidence I can hand you right now. But I've seen things, and I've heard things. I can tell you exactly where the drugs are. I can tell you exactly when I saw a man they'd beaten nearly to death. Hell, for all I know he's dead now. I can also tell you that I think the rest of the club is in the dark, but I don't know how long that will last. Rebel has plans, big plans to grow and expand this business."

Shiv still glared at her, but the complete disbelief was replaced by a small glimmer of curiosity. A willingness to listen to her. "Why come to us with this?"

"There are good people in that club. People who will either be forced to go along with Rebel's plan or be harmed. It's not right."

"That's it? You're just a good Samaritan?"

She shook her head. "No. There are other reasons. But they are my own and have no bearing on the fact that what I bring to you is the truth." Somehow, she managed to ignore the urge to run and hold his gaze without looking away. She just wasn't ready to share anything about her relationship with Lucky and how she'd been strong-armed into ending it so tragically.

Thank God, she hadn't seen him on her way into the clubhouse. She was dying to know if he was there but too chicken to ask. Once she left here, she was off to the east coast. As far from Vegas as she could get while still being in the US.

Shiv lit the new cigar. "Well isn't this a giant ass fuck." He turned to Striker. "Get Jester in here. I want to hear his thoughts."

Striker disappeared and a thick silence descended, the only sound in the room that of Shiv puffing on his cigar. Thankfully Striker was back within a minute. "Pres, Lucky's with him. Says he needs to speak to you about something that can't wait."

"Fuck me," Shiv muttered.

Lucky was here. Kori's stomach bottomed out and her spine straightened. If only she had the superpower of invisibility.

Striker returned to his seat at the table as Jester stepped into the room, Lucky hot on his heels. Of course, his head swiveled in her direction as soon as both feet were through the doorway. He stopped dead in his tracks and zeroed right in on her. Good thing his superpower wasn't laser eyes because she'd be a pile of embers in her chair.

"What the fuck is she doing here?" he asked in a cold tone she'd yet to hear from him.

The hair on her arms stood on end as shards of ice pricked her heart. The weight of four men's prying gazes rested heavily on her.

"Hey, Lucky."

CHAPTER TWENTY-EIGHT

"No," Lucky said. "Fuck no. What the hell is she doing here?" This could not be happening. Kori was here. In Crystal Rock. Was Savage with her? Was this one last screw you before they rode off into the sunset of wedded bliss? And why did she have to look so goddamn beautiful? Why was her long platinum hair up in that high ponytail he loved to grip as he pulled her head back for his mouth.

"Well, if my guess is right," Shiv said, disgust thick in his voice. "She's here for the same reason you are. Have a seat, Lucky. I take it you two need no introduction."

Kori's face flashed fire-engine-red and she averted her gaze as she shook her head. None of what Shiv said made any sense except for the part about them knowing each other.

Kori knew nothing about Rebel and Savage's business. And it would remain that way until the day she died if they had their say. Unless of course she'd stumbled upon something by accident. Still, it was hard to believe she'd betray her new fiancé like this.

Lucky moved around the table and took the empty seat next to Shiv. No way could he stand sitting next to Kori. Being in such proximity to the woman who cut out his heart, smelling her, possibly brushing against her…

Well it was a terrible idea.

Unfortunately, the alternative put him directly across from her and staring into her...bruised face? What the fuck? Anger surged, swift and fierce. He shot up from his chair and ignored the clatter as it tipped and clanked to the ground. With both palms flat on the table, he leaned forward and scowled at Kori. "He do that to you?"

"What?" The bruise almost disappeared, swallowed up by the intense red blush that still suffused her cheeks. A neatly manicured hand covered her cheek. "I'm fine. No big deal. It's nothing for you to worry about." Her gaze darted around the room as the color in her face deepened.

It was then Striker's smirk registered. Christ, he was acting like a jealous moron. They'd be on his ass about that later, for sure. Kori was right. Her wellbeing wasn't any of his damn business. Her life, her choices. He righted the downed chair and returned to it. "Looks like you made the wrong decision, huh?" The little dig felt good until he saw the light in her eyes dim to nothing and she seemed to shrink into the chair.

Shit. He may be angrier at her than he'd ever been with anyone, but that didn't mean she deserved an abusive relationship. No woman deserved that shit. Jester and Striker both frowned at him, adding to the guilt.

"If you're done with the outbursts, Lucky, I'll get right to the point." Shiv tapped ash off the end of his cigar. "Kori claims Rebel and Savage are selling drugs."

She knew? How? How the hell had she found out? He kept his ears open to Shiv, but stared at Kori.

"She claims to have seen the drugs as well as a man possibly killed."

There was a very good chance Lucky's heart stopped beating. "What did he look like?" he whispered.

"What? Oh, um, the man they...uh, well," she grimaced. "It was a little hard to see exactly what he looked like because his face was...bad. But he was thin, unhealthy thin. Brown hair, kinda stringy. And—"

Guilt slammed into him and Lucky held up a hand. "That's enough. It's Robbie." *Jesus, Robbie, why couldn't you just keep your damn mouth shut?*

Shiv slammed a hand on the table. "It is enough. Enough bullshit. Start talking, Lucky. Now."

There was a chance this conversation wouldn't go well for him. Striker and Shiv would be well within their rights to kick his ass for withholding what he discovered for so long. "A little over two months ago I was leaving the clubhouse late and overheard Savage and Rebel discussing drug sales. They've been working with the Grimms down here in AZ. They're fed up with Casper. Apparently, things have been shitty since Snake disappeared, so I guess they'd been at it for a while."

He ran a hand across the back of his neck. The muscles at the base of his skull were tightening by the second and a monster of a headache loomed not far in the distance. "I wanted to gather more information before making a decision on what to do. Then Kori showed up. She was living with Rebel, got engaged to Savage. She was an innocent about to be caught in a colossal clusterfuck, so I held off."

What he didn't say was that he fell ass over tea kettle for her and that was the real reason he didn't want her in the crossfire.

"What the fuck is Rebel thinking?" Jester leaned back in his chair and crossed his massive arms over his even more colossal chest. That was not a man Lucky ever wanted to do battle against.

"Money." Kori answered before Lucky had the chance. "Money and power." She shook her head. "I haven't known him very long, but that much is obvious."

"This why you patched over, Lucky?" Striker asked.

Kori's expression was somber, filled with regret and pain. It just made Lucky's ire flare. How dare she be depressed about his leaving? She'd lost the right to give a shit. "One of the reasons," he said, not shifting his focus from her.

"You ever planning on bringing this to my attention?" Shiv's question was asked around the stogie between his lips.

"Today, if you can believe it. When I first got here we were dealing with all the shit down at the border and with Acer's old man. Plus, I hadn't figured out a way to keep Kori out of it. But I heard from a contact that Robbie was most likely dead. Things are heating up and something needs to be done soon."

"Goddammit. I cannot believe this shit." Shiv crushed the end of his cigar into the metal table. "Anyone else want to shit on this day? Anybody an undercover cop? Maybe my wife's fucking around on me? I have to go out of town. Two days max. Can't be avoided. Sick fucking mother-in-law. I'm calling church for the second I roll back into town. We'll figure this shit out then."

The men in the room nodded and voiced their understanding.

"All right. Everyone get the fuck out. I need to think about all this. Don't leave town, Kori."

"I, uh...I have plane tickets to—"

"Good," Shiv said. "If anyone goes looking, that will throw them off your trail. This is gonna get ugly. Least we owe you for bringing it to our attention is some protection. Plus, you may know details that can help us. But not a word of this to anyone. Especially not any ol' ladies you might get tight with."

She looked like she wanted to argue, but nodded instead. "All right. I'll stick around for a while. And I know how it works. I'll keep my mouth shut."

Fanfuckingtastic. Now he'd have to go to sleep tonight knowing Kori was close by. The sickest part of the whole thing was how much he still wanted her. Even now, with nerves and frustration coursing through him, he was semi hard just because she was in the same room. He stood from the table and followed the others out into the bar area. Time for a drink.

Kori hovered off to the side, staring at her phone, probably searching for a hotel. Good luck with that.

"Hey, Kori." Striker held a beer out to her. "Don't bother looking for a hotel. You won't find one in town, and everything within fifty miles is shit. You're more than welcome to stay with my wife and me."

She'd removed the ponytail and her hair flowed down well past her shoulders. Lucky wouldn't admit it, but he was glad she wouldn't have to stay in any of the crappy no-tell motels out of town. She shifted her eyes in his direction before looking back to Striker. "Well, um, thank you. Your wife won't mind?"

"She won't mind at all. In fact, I'm sure she'll be thrilled. She has a few days off work and I couldn't clear my schedule so I know she'd love some company during the day."

"Okay, ah, I guess…thank you." Kori smiled at him but it didn't reach her eyes. Her glassy eyes appeared ready to spill over any second. The bruise on her face was all the more striking when viewed next to her pale hair. "Sorry, I'm not usually a bumbling idiot. This is all just a little overwhelming."

Lucky had the overpowering urge to yank her into his arms and kiss her until the sorrow and apprehension flowed out of her. And that pissed him off. Made him over the top, irrationally angry. Weeks of loneliness, irritation, betrayal, and resentment, not to mention sexual frustration, threatened to blow the top of his head straight off. And Kori was the perfect target.

"I'm starting to see your pattern, Kori."

Her eyes widened but she remained silent.

"A few weeks with one guy. A few weeks with Savage. You draw a guy in for a while, have your fun, then screw him over good, huh?"

"Hey, Lucky, tone it down, brother. The man fuckin' hit her. You going crazy?" Jester narrowed his eyes and took a step closer to Lucky, his size often a deterrent to poor behavior.

She drew her bottom lip between her teeth and shook her head. "Lucky, maybe we can talk later. Privately."

"Nah, I'd rather do this now. It's too bad for you this time around, though. Striker's married. You'd have easy access staying at his house and all, but he and his ol' lady are pretty damn tight, so it's not really worth your trouble."

Kori gasped. "I would never." She turned to Striker. "Striker, I'm so sorry. We have some personal...issues. I would never—Jesus, Lucky. I would never."

It was as if he was disassociated from his body. His brain heard what an asshole he was being, but that didn't seem to matter to his mouth. Anger flowed through his veins in a deluge of fury. The dam had broken and he was on a roll. Rational thoughts be damned.

He shrugged. "Don't worry. There are plenty of guys here who'd be willing to fuck you. Probably a few who would even ask you to move in with them."

The strangled sound that came from her barely registered as he geared up to spew more bitterness in her direction. "But, you should know—"

"Enough!" Striker yelled. "Lucky, shut your mouth up, right now." He turned to a crying Kori. "Honey, why don't you go out and wait by your car. I won't be five minutes then you can follow me to my house. I'll call my wife, Lila, on the way so she's ready for us."

"Thank you," she whispered before she slunk outside, head down, quiet sniffles the only sound she made.

"Okay," Striker continued when was out of earshot. "I think we all get that you have some kind of ugly history with her, but what the fuck, man? I'm not sure what happened, but public humiliation isn't usually the best way to solve your problems."

Shit. He hadn't lost control of his tempter like that in years. Now that Striker cut through the rage, shame crept in. Kori hadn't deserved that. She'd risked a lot to come here and the contusion on her face spoke of how she hadn't had an easy few weeks. "I'm sorry, brother."

"It's not me you need to apologize to, brother. Get your shit together."

Lucky nodded. That's exactly what he'd do. He put his drink on the bar. Day drinking, finished. Pity party, over. Anger…well, he'd be working on that one.

And now he owed Kori a whopper of an apology.

Perfect. Whenever he was in her presence, he was torn between the desire to fuck her and the desire to scream at her.

Apologizing should be as much fun as a severe case of road rash.

CHAPTER TWENTY-NINE

"You sure you'll be okay here by yourself?" Lila asked as she slung a pristine Coach bag over her shoulder. "I can cancel my appointment and hang with you."

Kori laughed. "For the third time in a half-hour, I'll be fine. I have a lot to think about. Plans to make. The alone time will do me good. And besides, you'll be gone for what? Two hours?" The two of them had hit it off on sight and she felt like she'd known the doctor for years instead of days.

"At the most. Just a cut and color. Then I'm swinging by Emily's to pick her up. The other girls are driving themselves and will be here around two, so get ready to meet the gang. We're a great group of gals if I do say so myself." Lila plucked her water bottle off a console table near her front door and smiled. "I cannot wait to see what you do with that table out in the garage. Striker thinks I'm nuts for buying it. Knock his socks off, girl."

"Well, I'm not sure a refurbished table has the power to do that, but I'll give it my best." During the tour of their house two days prior, Lila had shown her the garage and an old farm table she'd purchased secondhand. The foundation was solid, but the wood needed some serious love in the form of sanding and painting. When Kori mentioned she loved that sort of work, Lila had practically begged her to rehab it. The idea was perfect.

Now she'd have something besides obsessing over Lucky to fill her time.

"Go, go. You'll be late." Kori shooed Lila out of her own house and went to change into work clothes. After settling on cutoff jean shorts and a spaghetti strap tank, she snagged her new phone and headed to the garage. It wasn't the best outfit for sanding and painting, but the temperature was far too high to cover herself fully.

After scrolling through to her favorite playlist, she grabbed the handheld sander and got to work. Peace settled over her as she ran the sander over the weathered wood with rhythmic strokes. Though she'd told Lila the alone time would be used to plan her next move, something she needed to do sooner rather than later, her mind blanked until nothing but the smell of wood and the crooning melody of her country playlist registered.

It had been over a month since she'd had any inner serenity and the momentary reprieve from disturbing thoughts was priceless. Before she knew it, dust covered every inch of exposed skin, her arm and back muscles ached, and an indeterminate amount of time had passed. Best of all, she felt happier than she had in weeks. A little manual labor was better than therapy.

She switched off the sander and joined Carrie Underwood in singing about a nasty tornado. If she wasn't careful, the girls would show up and she'd be a hot, sweaty mess of wood powder. Not the best first impression. Time to head in and get cleaned up.

With a shake of her hips, she sang in a voice that would probably make Carrie Underwood cry with despair. "Shatter every window till it's all—Holy shit!" As she spun, she came face to face with Lucky. His smoldering gaze was low, trained exactly where her shimmying ass had been just seconds ago.

Kori held a hand over her racing heart as though that could somehow calm the rapid beat. Damn he looked good. Jeans fitted over his thick thighs and narrow hips. A black T-shirt under his cut highlighted the impressive contours of his chest.

"Jesus, you scared the life out of me. Uh…what are you doing here, Lucky? Striker isn't here."

Slowly, very slowly, he trailed his eyes up her body, lingering at breast level before landing on her face. Millions of nerve endings on her skin snapped to attention and fizzled as though he'd run his hands over her instead of just his eyes. Wishful thinking. The mind was a powerful thing and she could almost feel his touch. The memory of his hands on her was something that would never fade, something she could conjure up at any time just to torture herself.

"I'm not here for Striker. I know he's at the clubhouse." Lucky prowled forward until he stood just two feet from her.

"Oh, well, is there something you needed?" Nerves began to flutter in her stomach. She linked her fingers behind her back. The action thrust her breasts forward—a fact that clearly didn't escape Lucky's attention—but it maximized her chances of keeping her hands to herself.

He nodded. "I'm here to apologize for the other day. You took a big risk coming here." He snorted. "Hell, you did what I should have done six weeks ago. Anyway, I lost my shit on you and I'm sorry."

She studied him for a second, the sincerity of his words in opposition to the tension in his posture and the rising anger that competed with lust in his eyes. He was still mad at her. Rightfully so. In all reality, the mad would probably never fade. With a heavy sigh, she waved him in. "Let's go inside. It's too damn hot out here."

Whether it was the actual air temperature or Lucky's presence that had sweat rolling down her spine remained to be seen.

A low chuckle reached her ears, as though he caught the double meaning to her words. After they were inside the cool foyer of Lila and Striker's beautiful home, she faced him with a false sense of bravado. "No apology is necessary, Lucky. I deserved everything you said and then some. What I did was— What are you doing?"

He stalked forward, eyes hard, body harder and she backed up until her spine met the wall. Lucky's forward progression didn't stop until he was mere inches from her. One at a time, he slapped a hand on the wall, next to her head, effectively boxing her in. She jolted both times the crack of his palm on the wall broke the silence.

He didn't answer her question, but he didn't have to. The fierce expression on his face said it all. No forgiveness for her. Nor had he forgotten anything.

She swallowed and forced her attention on his stony face. "You're mad. And you have every right to be."

Lucky shook his head. "I'm not mad."

Really? A small pilot light of hope ignited low in her belly. "You're not?"

"No." His voice as hard, impassive. "I'm fucking furious."

Oh shit.

"I had it right all along. For twenty years. Get 'em on their backs, fuck 'em, be done. Countless women. Easy come easy go. No one gave a shit going in; no one felt like shit coming out."

"Lucky," she whispered. It took every ounce of strength she had to keep her arms at her sides. All she wanted in that moment was to grab him and yank him against her. Feel the hardness of his muscles molding into her softness. Use her body to soothe them both. He was so damn close, yet farther than she could hope to reach.

"Then you came along," he continued as though unaware of her murmured plea. "You fucked my mind up, Kori. For the first time in my life, my head was as involved as my dick, and that's saying something because I was on you, and in you constantly. And then, what did you do? Want me to remind you?"

Her eyes filled and she shook her head. If he said it, described just how deeply she'd cut him, she'd lose it.

"No? Well, you know exactly what you fuckin' did. You want to know the worst part?"

Did she? No. Hell no. But she remained silent. He needed to get it out and she needed, even if she didn't want, to hear it. There were consequences to every choice. She chose to go along with Rebel's plan, even if protecting Lucky had been her only thought. Now it was time for the consequences.

"It's this." He closed the gap between them and pressed the steely rod of his erection into her stomach.

Her reaction was instantaneous. Everything in her went soft, as if preparing for his touch, his mouth. Her nipples beaded so fast it was almost painful, and her panties dampened in a rush. God, his weight felt so good against her. So unbelievably good.

"Even after you screwed me over, I want you until I fuckin' ache. Even after having you multiple times a day for weeks I'm harder for you than I've ever been for any woman. Even after you fuckin' gutted me, I'm going to fuck you against this wall until you can't stand."

Yes! Her insides went liquid. Molten at his words. Without warning, his mouth crashed down on hers. The kiss was hard, possessive, rough. He captured her lower lip between his teeth and gave a firm nip before plunging his tongue into her gasping mouth and stealing her air. A strapping thigh worked its way between her legs and wedged against her center. Nothing could have stopped her from grinding against it, riding his leg.

Her head spun and her pussy throbbed with need. This was exactly what she wanted. Wild, unrestrained, consuming, almost…angry. The word pierced through her haze and brought her back down to earth, or almost so. Her body still hummed with an intense desire. "Wait." She spoke around his mouth and gave him a firm push. The word was garbled by his lips, but she got through.

He pulled back and stared down at her, his erection still pulsing against her stomach. "What?" It was more a bark than a question.

"Don't do this."

He scoffed. "You telling me you don't want this? Bullshit. My thigh is fucking wet because you're so damn soaked it's leaking around whatever scrap of panties you have on. And your nipples are practically ripping holes in my shirt. But you want me to stop?" He hadn't backed up even and inch and his chest rose and fell against hers, teasing said nipples with each inhalation.

"No. Yes." She closed her eyes. "I mean, don't do this as a punishment. Rage at me, storm out, never speak to me again, but don't do it this way. I can't—" She shook her head and opened her eyes, meeting his stormy gaze. "I'll break," she whispered.

The breath he blew out seemed to deflate some of the wrath he came at her with. He dropped his forehead to hers. "It's not a punishment. I'm not doing it to get back at you."

"Then why?" She held her breath as she waited for the answer.

"Because I still wake up every morning hard as a stone and reach for you in my bed. Because at least twenty times a day I think of something I want to tell you. Because I smell you in a house you've never stepped a foot in. Because there's only one thing in this world that will make me feel better right now, even if it makes me feel a hundred times worse later on."

There was no way in hell she'd refuse him. He hated her for what she did to him. But there was one thing he still wanted, maybe even needed from her. And she'd give it to him. Willingly. Gladly. Hell, she'd beg for it herself if she had to.

"I've been sanding all morning. I'm filthy."

He nuzzled his nose against her ear. "You think I give a fuck?"

"No?"

"No."

She turned so her lips were less than a breath away from his. "Then fuck me, Lucky. Please fuck me until we both forget. I've needed you like I never thought could be possible these past few weeks."

CHAPTER THIRTY

Something flashed in Lucky's eyes. Something that looked like disbelief, but maybe some of what she said had sunk in, because he captured her mouth in a kiss no longer rife with resentment.

He licked along the seam of her lips and she opened to him at once. There was no thought of denying him, no matter how much deeper the sorrow would be later. She wasn't under any illusion this would fix what she'd broken between them. It was physical, a release. Closure at best. Maybe now she could find the strength to move forward with her life.

"Come back," he whispered, so in tune with her he'd picked up on her momentary drift.

"I'm here." Then she couldn't talk anymore because the heat of his mouth, the softness of his lips and the press of his shaft against her overwhelmed her senses. The searching kiss quickly morphed out of control, growing in strength and potency until it was as intense as it had been a few moments ago. Only this time the hatred wasn't there. This time, it was a need so powerful it trumped all else.

"Lucky." She moaned, tilting her pelvis up. If she were just a few inches taller, her hips would meet his and she could fit herself against him and find some relief.

"I know what you need, baby."

Baby. God, how she'd missed that.

His hands left the wall and slid down her until he found the button on her shorts. With practiced expertise, he flicked them open and shoved the denim down to the ground. Then he ran a fingertip over the saturated lace of her thong.

"Christ, Kori, it's fuckin' pouring out of you, isn't it? I don't know about the rest of you, but this pussy sure has missed me, huh?" Smug satisfaction filled his voice despite the two-sided comment.

"Yes." Had she been in her right mind, the words would have pierced her heart. A reminded of exactly what this encounter was: sex, nothing more. Physical release. But all she could focus on was the clenching of her core, as though it was reminding her how empty she was. Like she needed the tipoff.

Lucky grasped her ass in both palms. With a firm squeeze that had her moaning again, he lifted her. His torso kept her anchored to the wall while he wedged his hips between her legs, spreading her wide. She locked her ankles around his back.

When he rocked forward, stars danced in front of her vision and she groaned. In answer, she ground against him, rubbing her thong covered opening over the fly of his jeans. It wasn't nearly enough. She needed contact. Skin on skin. "Take your pants off, Lucky."

"I'll get there." His voice was low, gravely. He grasped the hem of her shirt and shoved it up, bra and all, over her breasts. "Damn, your tits are a beautiful sight." His head lowered and in the next instant, a strong, warm suction covered her nipple.

She cried out as his teeth raked her nipple. Zings of electric pleasure shot straight from her chest to her clit. Soon she'd be at her limit. She needed him. "Lucky, enough. I don't need the rest, I just want you inside me."

He raised his head and the battle she witnessed in his eyes stilled her words. Happiness warred with misery. Pleasure versus pain. Emotion versus physical pleasure. "*I* need it. I need to touch you, taste you."

"Okay fine, but can you do it while you're fucking me?" She was about five seconds away from begging.

He chuckled. "I suppose that can be arranged." With one hand still clinging to her ass cheek, he used the other to open his jeans and shove them down just far enough to free his dick. To her disappointment, their position prevented her from seeing it, but she immediately felt it as he bumped against her.

Lucky pulled the wet strip of fabric away from her pussy and lined himself up. The head of his cock rested just at her opening. A sense of harmony mixed with Kori's excitement. This was where he belonged. With her, inside her. Their gazes met and he thrust in with one strong stroke.

Kori cried out, loud. Her head fell back against the wall with a thunk, but it didn't faze her. She could feel no pain.

"This what you want, baby? This what you need?"

"Yes," she answered. "This is all I need."

"Damn straight," he said. He drew out with maddening slowness and nudged forward again, inch by exasperating inch. "Tell me it's not like this with him. Tell me I'm the only man who can make you this crazy. I'm the only one who gets to see you out of control and demanding to be fucked."

What? Him who? Jesus, did he mean Savage? There wasn't a chance in hell it could have been like this with Savage, or anyone. But she hadn't had sex with Savage. The few times he'd touched her she wanted to vomit. Lucky didn't know that though. "No, never." It was all she could manage in that moment, with her head spinning and her body screaming for him to move faster, harder.

"Never what?" He stilled, deep inside of her.

She clenched around him and gloried in his labored groan. "Never like this. Ever. Anyone. Please, Lucky, I need more."

"Only me?" He drew out until only the tip remained and she wanted to weep.

"Yes, Lucky. Always you! Only you!" She practically screamed the words at him, unfulfilled lust making her irrational. "Now fuck me before I die."

He growled and powered into her so hard her shoulder blades dug into the wall. Both hands gripped her ass once again and he used the leverage to control her hips, slamming them against each other so fast and so hard the world around her faded into nothing but pleasure.

"That's right, baby. Take it. Take all of me. I'm your fucking man."

"Yes, yes, Lucky." Every muscle in her body tightened as she came so hard her vision blacked for just a second. Lucky wasn't finished with her though, and she squeezed her arms and legs around him as she rode out the rest of the squall. Aftershocks of pleasure zinged through her with each stroke.

With her brain fuzzy from the extraordinary orgasm, all was finally right with the universe.

Lucky's world narrowed with each passing second until nothing existed but the hot as hell clasp of her tight, wet pussy around his cock. He'd nearly shot off when she came, her internal muscles practically strangling his dick, but somehow, he held off. Prolonging the incredible pleasure was his only goal.

But it didn't work for long. How could it with her wrapped around him, moaning and shuddering with his pummeling pace. Minutes after she exploded, he buried himself deep and flew off into the void. Pleasure so intense it was nearly more than he could handle consumed him.

Spent, he sagged against Kori, the only sound that of their near hyperventilation. After a few minutes, the sweat began to cool on his body and his senses returned. The pungent aroma of recent sex mixed with the nose-tickling smell of the wood dust still coating Kori.

An ache in his finger joints alerted him to the fact that his short nails dug into the silky skin of Kori's ass. She'd have marks for sure. He should feel guilty about it, but all he could think about was how hot it would be to pound into her from behind and stare at ten crescent shaped spots over the round globes.

If he wasn't careful, he'd swell back to full capacity in minutes. And Kori had to be sore. Hell, he'd just fucked her like a madman against a hard wall.

She hung limp in his arms. If he stepped back she'd probably slither down the wall into a pile of goo. It was impossible to fight the smugness he felt, so he didn't even bother to try. He knew exactly how to fuck his woman.

His woman.

Damn it.

That's exactly what she wasn't. Technically, she belonged to another man. Sure, she claimed to run from him with bruises on her face, but that was as much as he knew about the situation.

"You're thinking really hard," she whispered.

He was. Too hard. This was simple. They fucked. Now back to their separate corners. "Can I let you down? Will you be able to stand?"

Her chin bumped his shoulder as she nodded. He loosened his grip and she unwound her legs from his back. When her feet were on the ground and he was sure she wouldn't collapse, he stepped back. As he drew away, the purple contusion on her face flashed in his peripheral vision. Without thinking he pressed three kisses along her marred cheek bone then could have kicked himself.

Too tender. Too affectionate. Too telling.

"I'm good. Thanks." Her voice hitched and as he stepped away, he couldn't help but notice the glossy sheen in her eyes. Suddenly the air felt tense, awkward. Hell, he hadn't actually come for that. To apologize? Yes. To fuck them into oblivion? No.

Now what? He stood here, pants around his knees, softening cock dripping with the evidence of the hurricane that tore through the house while she leaned against the wall, thong askew and evidence of their lovemaking dripping down her leg.

Jesus, the idea of a condom hadn't even entered his consciousness. Hopefully she'd stayed on the pill. And hopefully she'd made Savage glove up. Who knew what that nasty motherfucker was walking around with. Ugh, thoughts of Savage and Kori turned his stomach.

If only he could think of something to say, but nothing came to mind.

A tentative knock sounded on Striker's front door. Kori jumped so violently he worried she really might fall.

Lila's uncertain voice filled the foyer. "Um, you guys? Is it okay for us to come in now? Everybody decent?"

Busted.

Kori's eyes flew so wide she looked like a cartoon drawing. A giggle escaped and she slapped a hand over her mouth. It was effective at muffling the sound, but did nothing to hide her shaking shoulders and jiggling tits.

Her amusement was infectious and Lucky laughed right along with her. They'd traded one form of awkward for another and this was much preferable. At least this uncomfortable situation had some humor to it.

"Give us thirty seconds, Stitch," he called using the nickname Lila had earned helping out the club with medical needs. "Pants up, babe." He winked as he tucked himself back into his boxers and righted his jeans.

Kori gasped and scrambled to cover her nudity and smooth her rumpled tank top. Not like it mattered. The women outside knew exactly what they'd heard.

"Okay, I'm good enough. I guess." She shot him a sassy smile.

God, he loved how she didn't freak out at being caught fucking him in his VP's house. And he loved…

Oh, Christ.

He loved her. He fucking loved her.

He also hated her. Could the situation be more fucked?

"Go for a ride with me tomorrow?" Really? Had he just asked that? Apparently, he'd shot a few brain cells out his dick as well as his cum.

Her throat worked up and down as she swallowed. She opened her mouth but no sound came out so she just nodded.

"Okay. I'll be here at two." He wanted to take her in his arms and kiss her like she was his, but he just backed toward the door.

"Come on, Lucky." Lila's whine was clear through the door. "It's hot out here."

A laugh rang out followed by, "I'm not sure it's any cooler in there."

Emily.

He rolled his eyes. Great, now Jester would know exactly what happened here today and that jokester was like a pig in shit when he had something on any of the MC brothers.

He nodded one more time at Kori then turned and gripped the doorknob.

Tomorrow he had a date.

With the woman who smashed his heart to smithereens just weeks ago.

CHAPTER THIRTY-ONE

Kori stared at the inside of the locked bathroom door with a sigh. Time was up. She'd stalled long enough. Four women waited down in Lila's kitchen no doubt gossiping about what a slut she was. Seducing their friend when she was supposedly engaged to another man. A man who hit her. A man who betrayed the club. A man who threatened to kill Lucky.

Not that the girls downstairs knew those last two details. Hopefully the bruise on her face would be enough for them to accept why she'd left Savage. While it would seem an obvious reason to leave for most, sometimes ol' ladies in an MC saw the world differently. In her experience, they put up with an unbelievable amount of disrespect and abuse.

Striker and Lila certainly didn't seem to have that type of relationship and she had a difficult time imagining any of the Crystal Rock men she'd met being abusers, but still...

"Okay, you can do this," she muttered as she opened the door and stepped out into the hallway. After a two-second introduction to a smirking Emily, Kori had escaped to the solitude of Lila's guest bathroom claiming she needed to shower.

Of course, that had set off a round of giggles and questions for her and Lucky about why she needed a shower. The explanation of her being sweaty and dusty only made them laugh harder so she'd given up and fled. Lucky could do the same or fend them off himself.

Halfway down the stairs, Kori heard the clinking of glasses and more giggles. Longing hit her square in the chest. Between caring for her mother and moving to a new state, it had been quite a while since she'd had any time for girlfriends. These women sounded close, like they really enjoyed each other's company.

All laughter halted as she stepped into the kitchen. Three shit-eating grins and one assessing expression trained on her. "Um… hi." She waved a hand in an arc. "I'm Kori."

"Come on in, Kori," Lila said. "Let me introduce you. You met Emily."

Kori's face burned with embarrassment as she nodded at Emily whose eyes sparkled with mirth. God, what Emily must think of her.

"This is Fia. She's Acer's girlfriend," Lila continued seeming oblivious to Kori's discomfort. "I don't think you've met him yet, but you will. He and Lucky are tight." She spoke as though Kori and Lucky were an item of some sort and she'd soon be acquainted with all his buddies.

"Hey, Fia," Kori said. "Nice to meet you."

Fia nodded but didn't smile as readily as the others. Lila rolled her eyes. "Excuse her, she's a little protective of Lucky," she said in a stage whisper. "And this," Lila said, motioning to a long-haired blonde holding a pitcher, "is Marcie. She's pouring the margaritas. We hadn't planned on drinking, what with it only being a little past two, but we figured you could use a few of these."

Marcie snorted and held out a margarita glass, rimmed with salt and full to the brim with neon liquid. "Don't let her fool you, girl. The good doctor was looking for any excuse to break out the margarita mix. The others didn't put up a fight either. They all love it when their men have to come to pick them up because they're a little too silly to drive home. Makes the evening quite fun." She winked as Kori relieved her of the glass.

"Let's head out to the deck and sit for a while." Lila breezed through the door without waiting for an agreement from the rest of the ladies.

Kori tagged along with the group and took a seat at the picnic table in Lila's stunning backyard. They had a huge, sprawling deck that overlooked a large shimmering lake. Beautiful, peaceful, and the perfect place for her newfound friends to grill her.

Marcie wasted no time. "Sooo," she said.

Kori took a sip. Damn, the tart, icy drink hit the spot. Never one to shy from a problem, Kori dove right in. "So, there's no point in playing games. You all know exactly what happened earlier. It's…complicated. And painful." She rubbed a hand over the ache that formed in her chest. "And…and to be honest, I don't know what the hell is going on, or what it means, or if it even means anything. I'm a mess. And Lucky might be a mess too. And now I'm babbling. There you go. Cards on the table."

"You're in love with him." Fia spoke from directly across the table, the untrusting look she'd originally worn replaced with empathy.

"No." The word was out of her mouth much too fast to be believable. She dropped her head to her hands. "I don't know. I'm not—it's just so—well, it's fucked to be quite honest. Even if I do have feelings for Lucky, it doesn't matter anymore." When she looked up, she was surprised to see nothing but compassion on the faces of these women she didn't know.

Ugh, how embarrassing. Here she was, two minutes and three sips into her drink, and she was spewing her emotions all over Lila's deck.

"Look, Kori, I know we just met," Emily piped in from the seat next to Kori. She seemed sweet. Her raven hair was thick and shiny and she had the palest blue eyes Kori had even seen. And she had the cutest little baby bump. "And I know you feel embarrassed about the circumstances, but any of us can see you're tortured by something. It's not easy being with any of these guys. They're rough, possessive, closemouthed—"

"Don't forget they get hit on by club whores all the time." Marcie polished off her drink.

They all chuckled. "Yes." Emily sipped her lemonade. "The constant female attention gets old fast. Anyway, we're a sisterhood as much as they are a brotherhood. So please, if you need to unload, consider us friends."

There was sincerity in her tone and the other women nodded their agreement, even Fia. What would it hurt to share some of her burdens with these women? She'd been alone in carrying them around the past few weeks and the solitude was starting to swallow her whole. She wouldn't share all the details, but she could at least share her pain.

She took another taste, surprised to realize the glass was now empty. A small buzz hit her bloodstream, giving her the liquid courage she needed to share. "Lucky and I were together in Vegas. It was fast, it was intense, it was...pretty close to perfect. And then I blew it. I ended it with him for another man. All that's left now is hatred and resentment."

Lila raised an eyebrow. "Sure didn't seem like he hated you this afternoon."

Sadness swamped her. "Men can sleep with someone they detest." She shrugged. "It's easy for them."

"While I agree with the statement, I didn't get hatred off him today. Anger, sure, sadness too. But not hatred," Emily said.

"I feel like there is a whole lot of that story you left out." Marcie refilled Kori's glass. "You leave Lucky for the man who did that to your face?"

"Savage. Yeah," Kori said, disgust evident to her own ears.

"I've been around here the longest so I know most of the Vegas guys. Gotta say, never been a fan of Savage. Major creeper if you ask me. I hope he's singing soprano these days." Marcie nudged her glass. "Drink. Makes the hard stuff easier to say."

She did as ordered, then set the glass back down. "I was more concerned with getting out of Dodge than getting revenge at the time. Now? Well let's just say if I had five minutes alone with him now, he'd definitely be speaking an octave higher."

Fia smiled and held up her glass. "Now you're talking, girl. Can I ask a question I have no right to ask?"

Kori nodded. Why not. The vault was open now. Besides, it wasn't hard to guess what Fia wanted to know and no doubt all the girls had the same question. "Go ahead."

"You really made it sounds like things were hot and heavy with Lucky. Why did you leave him for someone else?"

I had no choice.

Savage and Rebel threatened to kill him.

I was terrified for his life.

All three sentences were on the tip of her tongue, but she couldn't reveal the real reasons. For one thing, if anyone was going to hear it, Lucky deserved to be the one. And two, she'd promised to keep her mouth shut about club business. Pissing off Shiv and Striker by revealing too much to the ol' ladies right off the bat wouldn't be the wisest idea.

Which all led her back to the question of why she hadn't come clean to Lucky yet. Fear was a huge part of that reason. In theory, the explanation should soften him towards her, make him realize she hadn't wanted to leave him. But what if it didn't? What if the sense of betrayal he'd felt overshadowed the feelings he had for her? What if he realized he was better off without her? Somehow, as ridiculous as it sounded, not knowing was better than hearing him say he didn't want more than sex from her.

She was a hot mess of conflicting emotions.

"I can't talk about all of it. I'll just say that the choice was taken out of my hands. The last thing I ever wanted was to hurt Lucky, and if I had it all to do over again..." Her nose tingled with the threat of tears. She sniffed and blinked, managing to ward them off. "Well, I can't say for sure I'd do anything differently. Sorry, if that's too cryptic to make any sense."

Lila smacked a palm against the table. "I knew it. Something's going on, isn't it? Something within the club itself." She waved a hand in front of her face. "Don't answer that. I know you can't. We all know how this works." Unease creased her forehead.

"Sounds like you may have been trying to protect him from something. Am I right?" Emily piped in. She worried her bottom lip between her teeth.

Kori didn't answer, but held Emily's gaze.

"Thought so." Her voice grew sad. "I can tell you from personal experience that can blow up in your face faster than you ever thought possible."

Marcie reached across the table and squeezed Emily's hand, a sympathetic look on her face. Whatever story Emily had to tell, it sounded like a doozy. Maybe Kori would ask Lila about it later, or maybe Lucky would tell her on their ride tomorrow.

"Just one question. No details, but is it bad?" Lila asked.

"It's bad," Kori answered. Each woman bore a grim expression, lost in their own thoughts for a few seconds. Perhaps it wasn't fair to let their imaginations wander to worst case scenarios, but it was too late to take it all back now.

"Well, shit," Marcie said. "If I had known we were gonna get this morose I'd have made more margaritas."

Emily was the first to giggle, but it spread through the table in seconds. Before she knew it, Kori was belly laughing along with the rest of them.

"Oh my God," Fia said, wiping moisture from her eyes. "I have no idea why we're laughing like crazy people."

"Stress relief," Marcie said. "Okay let's change the subject to something we'd all much rather talk about." She focused on Kori once again. "So tell us, Kori, how was it?"

Her face heated almost before the question was out of Marcie's mouth.

"Oh man! Look at that blush. That good, huh?" Lila asked.

In for a penny, in for a pound. "Uh, no, not that good. Probably ten times better." Kori could barely stand to look at any of them. Here she was with four women she just met, sharing dark secrets and sexual escapades. And damn if she wasn't enjoying herself. There was no real awkwardness. It was as though she'd known them all for years. A sisterhood, just like they'd boasted.

"Damn girl." Emily held up her hand and Kori slapped her five.

Conversation stayed light and easy after that. For the next few hours they drank another pitcher of margaritas, laughed, and tried to forget the impending trouble. When the deafening rumble of motorcycles hit the street, glasses were dropped in the sink and the women ventured outside to greet their men.

Kori remained behind in the kitchen, listening to giggles, teasing about their tipsy states, and the unmistakable sounds of passionate kissing through the open windows.

Her heart squeezed painfully as she took it all in. What she wouldn't give to walk out of the kitchen and find Lucky waiting for her, ready to take her home to bed.

CHAPTER THIRTY-TWO

Lucky sat in the chapel waiting for what could possibly be the most important club meeting of his life and all he could think about was the prior hour's events.

How had things gotten so out of control so fast?

The answer was actually quite easy. He'd been in the same room with Kori for longer than five seconds. Bam. That's all it took. The sight of her in those ass-hugging shorts and that top that molded her breasts in just the perfect way. The smell of her, soap mixed with sweat and the dust from the wood. Her denial that he had anything to apologize for. Weeks of being away from her. Hell, the question should be how did he manage to hold out a whole ten minutes before jumping all over her?

"All right, all right, let's rein it in." Shiv banged a wooden gavel on the table top, an ever-present cigar hanging from his lips.

It took a few minutes, but the room quieted until nothing but the sound of an occasional bottle hitting the table could be heard.

Shiv nodded at Striker who stood and rested both palms on the table. "Okay, boys, I think by now most of you have heard what's going on, or at least chatter about some concerning shit."

Around the room, heads nodded and a low murmur kicked up.

"Is it true Rebel's in the drug game?" Gumby spoke up. Lucky was fast learning he wasn't one to shy away from speaking his mind. Over the past few weeks he'd gotten to know the lanky man fairly well.

"Seems to be the case," Striker answered.

"Shit," Gumby muttered. "What the fuck is he thinking? He's the fuckin' president of the Vegas chapter. He knows what the hell will happen if he's caught."

"He's a greedy bastard." Lucky rested his forearms on the table and leaned forward. "He's actually been at it for a while, making good money and doesn't think he'll be caught."

Striker sat down, his chair scraping on the floor to the tune of nails on a chalkboard. He scratched the day-old stubble on his chin. "Savage is working with him. From what we understand, they've formed some sort of partnership with the Grimm Brothers. Their enterprise is growing, and Rebel is hoping to make enough money to entice the rest of the chapter to join them and expand the business."

"You don't think that will happen, do you?" Jester asked. "There are some good guys in Vegas. Guys that have been around a lot longer than I have. Club loyalty and respect for the bylaws runs deep."

"So does loyalty to their president who's been there as long as anyone in that chapter," Shiv answered. "Yes, I do think there is a risk of at least some of the guys wanting in on their game. Money makes people do crazy shit."

"And the Grimms," Jester said. The room grew silent for a second while everyone watched Jester's jaw tick with strain. "After everything we've been through with them the past few years, that's a betrayal I can't get past." Jester's girlfriend had gone through hell at the hands of the Grimm Brothers MC.

"Tell me about it," muttered Striker whose wife had also been terrorized by the Grimm Brothers a few years back.

"I think we need to pay them a visit in about a week. That will give us enough time to do a little more digging, and really form a solid plan." Shiv snubbed out his cigar in one of the many ashtrays on the table. He always looked slightly lost without something between his fingers. Lucky never took to smoking, but to each his own.

"What do you think, Lucky?" Striker asked. "You know how they operate better than any of us. Is a surprise visit the best way to go? Catch them unaware?"

He took a moment to think about the question from a few angles, then pushed up from his chair and paced the length of the table. He needed to move. Nervous energy was making him restless. "When you say a surprise visit, what exactly are you thinking? Confront Rebel and Savage head on? Show up with force and tear the place apart until we find something? Sneak around and try to find proof in a more covert way?"

Apparently, he'd gone long enough without some tobacco because Shiv puffed on a brand-new cigar. "Somewhere between forcefully tear it up and being stealth. When you left, only Rebel and Savage were involved, right?"

Lucky nodded and reached for his beer. He remained standing, but quit the pacing. Did any of the guys her realize just how hard this meeting was for him? Two months ago, he trusted Rebel and Savage as much as any of the men here trusted Shiv and Striker. And now he was plotting to get them booted from the club, at the very least.

Even though it was the right thing to do for both himself and his club, he felt dirty. He felt like a rat. He felt like a traitor.

"So there could be more now," Shiv said. "I don't want to show up like a pack of wolves until we're certain how many guys might not be on our side. Kori said she saw quite a bit of their product, so she'll be a great resource as we plan. If we can find their shit, we can shut this down easier. Is there anyone you trust up there? Anyone you know for sure wouldn't join in with Rebel and Savage?"

Again, he considered the question. Did he trust Bull implicitly? Fuck no. Rebel's betrayal, followed by Kori's betrayal had taught him a hard lesson about the myth of loyalty. But Bull put himself in danger by coming to Arizona and seeking Lucky out. And he seemed truly appalled by the idea of the club involved in selling drugs.

"Lucky?" Shiv prompted.

"Sorry, pres. Not sure I trust anyone one hundred percent, but there's one guy, Bull. He paid me a visit about a week ago, after he discovered what was going on. I'm about ninety percent certain we can trust him." He sat back down at the table.

"Ninety percent, huh?" Shiv blew out three rings of smoke. "That may be the best we're going to get. Okay. You connect with him, Lucky. Make sure Rebel and Savage are going to be there in a week. He keeps this shit quiet, you hear?"

"Loud and clear."

"I also want to bring Kori in on this. See if she has anything to add that we didn't think of and get precise information on where they're storing the drugs."

Everything in Lucky rebelled against that idea. He wanted Kori as far away from this situation as possible, not jumping right into the mix. But Shiv was right. She knew where the drugs were, she'd been around Rebel and fucking Savage the past month. She was their best source of information.

From one end of the table, Hook cleared his throat. Lucky loved him and his wife Marcie. They were the perfect couple and had been married longer than most of the guys. "Shiv, can I make a suggestion? One you may not like so much?"

"Spit it out, Hook."

"I think we should brief all the ol' ladies on this situation." Shouts of protest came from every angle of the table. Hook held up his hands. "Cool it! Let me finish first. Then we can fight it out. A lot of the wives and ol' ladies know the Vegas guys. They're comfortable with them and view them as our brothers. They need to know contact with members from Vegas may not be safe right now. It's not uncommon for some of them to visit announced or not and we don't know who the good guys are anymore."

"Shit." Striker ran a hand over his disheveled hair. "He's right. If Lila ran into Rebel or Savage or any of the guys, she'd invite them over in a heartbeat, even if I wasn't home. It'd be like any of you stopping by. She wouldn't think twice."

"Aw fuck." Shiv stroked his long beard. "Tomorrow, six in the evening. Striker, get the ladies to make dinner. We'll discuss it then. Ol' ladies and wives only. I don't want to see some girl you've been banging for two days. Only those we can trust to keep this contained. Got it?"

When he appeared satisfied with the response, Shiv stood. "Meeting adjourned."

The mood was somber as the room emptied. No one wanted any part of what was about to happen, but it had to happen. The club was set up the way it was for a reason. Disloyalty wasn't tolerated.

Before he knew it, the only people remaining at the table were himself, Jester, Acer and Striker. One look at Jester's self-satisfied grin and he knew what was coming.

The big man clapped his hands together once and rubbed his palms back and forth, mischief sparking in his eyes. "Hey, Lucky? I got a call from Em earlier. She was outside Lila's house with her. They had plans to meet up with Kori. She was concerned because she heard really strange noises coming from inside the house. Sounded like moans, maybe even a scream or two." He failed miserably at keeping the grin off his face.

Striker's spine straightened. "What the fuck? At my house? Why are you telling him and not me?"

Acer also tensed. Fia was supposed to meet them there as well.

Lucky narrowed his eyes and tried to telepathically communicate with Jester to shut the fuck up. Either the message didn't compute or Jester just didn't give a shit. Probably the latter.

"Well I think everything worked out okay, Striker. Lucky saved the day. Didn't you, Luck?"

He rolled his eyes and flipped Jester the bird.

"Okay, what the hell is going on?" Striker asked.

"Well, what I heard was that Lucky burst in and saved the day. Unfortunately, Kori was so distraught, there was only one thing he could do to help her. Want to tell them what that was, Lucky?"

"No." He practically growled the word. Damn Jester couldn't keep his huge trap shut. Plus, nothing gave the man greater pleasure than ripping on his MC brothers. "I want you to go fuck yourself, though."

"Speaking of fucking..." Jester gave up all pretenses of being serious and spoke around huge chortling laughter.

"Okay, fine. There was nothing wrong in the house. I didn't burst in and save anything. I fucked Kori in Striker's foyer and Emily and Lila heard everything from the front stoop. It just happened. We had no idea they were there. Happy now?" He glared at Jester who practically fell out of his chair with laughter. "Asshole. You need a muzzle."

"Whoa, whoa, whoa," Acer said. "You and Kori?"

"In my house?" Striker's eyes shot darts.

Whoops. Perhaps he should invest in a muzzle for himself as well. He ran a hand through his hair. "Look, it's beyond complicated. And I'm not about to put on a skirt and share my feelings with you ladies. So yes, that's what happened and yes, it's all sorts of fucked up. And that's all I'm gonna say about it."

"Huh, based on what Emily told me, it didn't sound too complicated. Piece A goes into slot B." He motioned with his hands.

"Jester..." Lucky spoke around the other men's laughter.

"In my fucking house," Striker muttered in a low tone as he pulled out his phone.

"What are you doing?" Acer asked.

"Texting Lila to see if she can get us a hotel tonight. I'm thinking we need to bug bomb the place."

The three of them cracked up again and Lucky pushed away from the table. "Fucking children," he said as he stomped from the room.

Hilarious laughter trailed him and he couldn't help but chuckle himself. Despite being the butt of their jokes, it felt damn good to laugh and joke with his brothers again. For a while he'd worried that his club life would never be the same.

Now he just needed to sort out the disaster of his love life.

CHAPTER THIRTY-THREE

The doorbell chimed through the house and Kori hustled toward the front door. Unfortunately, Lila beat her to it, meaning she and Lucky would have to endure even more teasing.

"Kori!" Lila yelled as she turned and realized there was only about two feet separating them. "Oh sorry." She chuckled "Didn't mean to scream in your face."

"No worries. See you later, Lila." She shrugged into a borrowed leather jacket and slipped past Lila out the door to the stoop where Lucky waited. Damn, he looked good in his uniform of jeans and a fitted tee.

So far so good. No ribbing.

"You kids have fun," Lila called out as they walked quickly toward Lucky's bike.

And there it was.

"We won't wait up for you. And I put some condoms in your jacket pocket, Kori. Never can be too safe." Lila laughed as Striker yelled for her to come inside and stop torturing the kids.

"Everyone's a comedian," Lucky muttered then raised his voice. "We'll see you guys in a few hours at the clubhouse."

"You sure you don't need help with dinner stuff, Lila?" Kori asked for what had to be the tenth time that morning.

"No. Go, have fun. Relax. Talk." Lila shot Lucky a severe look then disappeared into the house leaving Kori and Lucky alone.

Suddenly, she felt awkward, unsure of herself and unable to think of anything to say. Even on their first date, they'd had great conversation flow and hardly any tension—unless sexual tension counted. They'd had that in spades.

Now it was all just a jumbled mess of sadness, desire, pain, and uncertainty. To make matters worse, dark glasses hid Lucky's deep blue eyes so she couldn't even see if they were flat and lifeless or filled with emotion. On impulse, she pushed them up so they rested on his head. Emotion for sure, and a deeper blue than usual. But what emotion, she couldn't determine.

Someone had to say something or she might as well just go back in the house.

"We have so much to talk about that I can't even decide where to begin." Lucky said.

Kori's heart sped up. She hadn't expected him to break the silence first. "I know we do. It seems an almost impossible task."

He rubbed a hand over his goatee and she longed to feel the silky fur tickling her skin. "How about we call a truce, shelve the discussion for today, and just go for a ride. I could really use a long ride."

Oh, man that sounded perfect. The part of her that was so afraid he'd still reject the idea of a serious relationship even after knowing the truth was beyond relieved for the brief reprieve. Even it was only a delay of the inevitable conversation. Holding him for hours while feeling the flex and play of his back muscles as he sped through the beautiful desert countryside sounded like heaven.

"Let's do it," she said.

He smiled and her heart seized in her chest. It was a crooked smile. A real smile. Maybe there was still hope.

Lucky drove them far out into the desert. The warmth of the day combined with the vibration of the bike, and the security of Lucky between her legs was hypnotizing. More than once Kori found herself nearly drifting off to sleep.

Lucky

After about an hour and a half Lucky veered off to the side of the road in the middle of nowhere. They spent about thirty minutes stretching their legs, eating a snack, and hydrating. Conversation was kept light, no talk of their ruined relationship or exactly what they were doing spending time together. She couldn't have asked for a more perfect afternoon.

Then, it was time to head to the clubhouse for a meeting she'd been trying not to think about all day. A meeting that had her stomach churning and fear clogging her throat.

Lucky must have sensed a change in her because he prevented her from climbing on behind him with a strong hand around her wrist.

With her throat thick, talking was impossible so she raised an eyebrow in question. He lifted her knuckles to his lips and nipped the middle one. It was followed with a gentle kiss that had her blinking away tears. Good thing she had her own dark sunglasses on.

"Don't worry so much. We'll find a way to make everything right." He released her and she mounted the bike.

The words were meant to comfort, but she wasn't certain what exactly he was referring to. Make what right? The club's issues? Or their relationship?

Those questions and more swirled through her head on the ride until the peace of the afternoon faded to a nervous tension. They arrived about the same time as others were pulling into the clubhouse.

Lucky didn't hold her hand or touch her in any way as they walked inside, and she berated herself for the disappointment that coursed through her. They weren't together. Weren't a couple. Wishing it didn't make it so. She needed to remember that.

The moment they stepped foot inside, Lucky groaned and rubbed his stomach. "Oh, man, it smells amazing in here."

He was right. The women had prepared an Italian feast complete with chicken parmesan, multiple types of pasta and sauces, garlic bread, and a few cakes for dessert. That they'd pulled together such an enticing dinner on short notice was impressive.

Shiv clapped his hands together in rapid succession and the racket lowered to a dull chatter. "Hey, gang. Grab some food, chat for a few minutes, but we're here for a serious reason, so let's get seated and started as quick as possible."

Kori loaded a plate with the mouthwatering food. At some point, she and Lucky had been separated in the rush of hungry bikers to the buffet table. When she didn't spot him after a quick glance around, she grabbed a seat at a long table that had obviously been set up with this dinner in mind. Lila sat next to her and Emily on the other side. Lucky ended up directly across from her.

While she would have preferred to be next to him, she was now able to view his reactions. The bikers and ol' ladies dug into their food and silence descended on the group.

"Okay, I'm going to talk while everyone eats. First of all, thanks to all the ol' ladies who helped put this together with a minute's notice. Amazing as usual. I know you're all a little nervous so I'm not going to keep anyone in suspense." Shiv then went on to explain the reason for calling everyone together.

The women's jaws dropped as he explained Rebel and Savage's recent activities and the potential for more club members to be involved. He warned everyone, but the ladies in particular, to be vigilant and watchful.

"If you see anyone from Vegas around here, let one of us know immediately. Try not to alert them that something is going on, but don't invite anyone to your house. Don't be caught alone with them. We don't have reason to believe anyone would come here looking to cause trouble, but we also don't know who we can trust at this time. A cornered animal will lash out."

Kori felt like there was a flashing neon arrow over her head pointing down at her, directing every eye in the place to her. She was the unknown in this situation, the girl from Vegas who was supposedly engaged to Savage, the brother turned drug dealer. Did they judge her for being with him? Did they question her loyalty? Her innocence? She had to get over her fear and come clean. It was the only way to earn their true respect.

"I know this is not typical of the way we conduct business." Striker took over from next to Shiv. "But we felt it was important for you ladies to be in the loop on this one given the fact that on a normal day none of you would think twice about inviting any of the Vegas brothers into your homes. It goes without saying that nothing you hear tonight leaves this room. Understood?"

A chorus of *yes* rang out from the women.

"I'm going to let Jester fill you in on the plan we have so far." Striker remained standing while Jester rose.

"Hope you don't mind if I eat my cake while I talk." He held a paper plate with chocolatey goodness close to his face. Everyone chuckled and his typical good-humored nature helped loosen a bit of the stiffness in the room. "Next week about ten of us will be heading up to Vegas. It will be a surprise visit so zippa your lippas, ladies. I know it's hard, but you can do it." He chuckled to himself.

"Booo," Marcie called. "You guys gossip way worse than we do and you know it."

The moments of levity were appreciated except for the fact that Kori just wanted this over with as fast as possible. Every minute she sat there, she felt more and more like a windup toy being cranked. At some point the dial would be released and she'd go spinning out of control.

"While we're there, we plan to locate the drugs and deal with the offenders in the appropriate manner. That's all I'll say about that. Kori?" Jester swung his gaze to her.

Even though she knew how nice he was and what a jokester he was on a normal day, being the sole focus of over six-foot-five, at least two-hundred-fifty pounds of intense male was nerve-wracking to say the least.

"Yes?" Her voice sounded small, meek and it pissed her off. She wasn't either of those things, at least not in personality. But if people weren't staring at her before, they sure as hell were now that Jester called her out, and it was just too much. She wanted to crawl under the table and hide until everyone went home.

"We could really use some detailed information about where you saw the drugs, what access is like, the schedules Rebel and Savage have been keeping over the past few weeks. Anything you can tell us that will give us a leg up." Jester relaxed his stance and gentled his voice as he spoke. Perhaps he noticed the deer-in-the-headlights look she no doubt wore. "You okay to stay a bit after the meeting to go over some of that shit?"

Ugh, no. She couldn't stay; she had unbreakable plans to cry herself to sleep. "Of course," she said instead. "I was thinking I should, uh, tag along. You can tell Rebel I came looking for a place to stay and you wanted to return me. Might earn you some brownie points you could use to your advantage."

The clatter of Lucky's fallen chair registered before the sight of the over six-foot male who stood across the table starting at her like she asked to dance naked on the tables. "No fucking way in hell will that be happening."

Jester silenced him with a glower before he addressed her suggestion. The rest of the room remained quiet, but the weight of their heavy stares was palpable. "I appreciate the offer, Kori, but it would be a bit risky. Rebel would immediately suspect that you told us about his drug dealing and we can't risk anything that will tip him off. If he has any chance to get rid of the evidence, he'll take it."

She nodded and pushed her plate away, appetite long gone. It took work to keep her attention trained on Jester rather than Lucky, who still loomed over the table scowling at her. "Okay. What if I go back on my own tomorrow? I can use the week before you arrive to do some surveillance, scout around, and pass information back to you."

Lucky

Lucky slammed his clenched fists down on the table sending paper plates an inch into the air and tipping no less than three full plastic cups. "Are you out of your fucking mind, woman?"

His face was dark with rage and she could practically see smoke swirling up from his ears.

Thankfully, Jester kept his cool. "You think Savage is going to welcome you with open arms? It's too risky, hon."

"Way too fucking risky," Lucky said.

The push-pull from Lucky was getting to her. One day he yelled at her, the next he came to apologize and they ended up going at it like animals. Then he took her on a polite motorcycle ride for hours. Now he was back to yelling at her and apparently, he didn't trust that she wouldn't tip off Rebel and Savage. Why the hell else wouldn't he want her in Vegas? Well screw that. She deserved to see Rebel and Savage taken down.

She placed her own palms on the table with much less force than Lucky and leaned toward him. "Fine, then I want to come with you. I'll stay out of sight until it's all over, but I want to be there. I deserve to be there."

His reach was far greater and he was practically on her side of the table by the time he'd bent as far forward as he could. He was breathing like he'd just run a race. "You deserve to be there? Please, tell us why you deserve to be there?"

Her face was so hot beads of sweat popped out along her brow. She pressed her bodyweight onto her hands to keep them from shaking, but it only translated up her arms until her entire body vibrated with a mix of irritation and humiliation. All around the room wide eyes gaped at the show.

"Listen, Lucky." She somehow managed a strained but calm tone. "I get that you don't think very highly of me right now. And we can talk privately about everything after the meeting. But I'm not looking to tip them off. I'm not looking to screw you guys over." Then a thought hit her, something she should have thought of the moment they unveiled their plan. Shit. It was a thought that could ruin the entire scheme.

Rebel and Savage already knew Lucky was aware of their drug enterprise.

"Jesus Christ, you think I give a shit about any of that?" Lucky pushed back from the table and ran a hand through his hair, making it stick out in various directions. "I don't think you're gonna sell us out, Kori. I don't want you there for your own safety. I'm trying to protect you." Disbelief laced his voice.

Panic clawed at her throat. It didn't matter, none of it mattered. If Lucky showed up there with Striker and Shiv, Rebel would immediately be suspicious. All of a sudden it was too much. The heartache with Lucky, being blackmailed by her own father, seeing a man beaten, and now circling back around to fear for Lucky. "And what the hell do you think I was trying to do when I agreed to marry Savage?" she yelled.

Her hand flew up and covered her mouth as though she could hold in the screamed words that had already escaped.

Lucky grew as still and cold as an ice sculpture.

Oh shit. There went her chance for a personal talk with Lucky.

CHAPTER THIRTY-FOUR

Lucky couldn't breathe. It was as though a tight band wound around his chest constricting further with each passing second. He'd been shocked to realize she assumed he didn't trust her to keep her mouth shut, but it was nothing compared to how stunned her last sentence had left him. "What did you just say?"

Wide-eyed, tears drenching her cheeks, hand still over her mouth, she shook her head. The room was so silent you could almost hear someone blink as every person waited for her next words. "Nothing," she whispered as her hand dropped to her side. "I'm upset. I'm just mouthing off." Her lower lip quivered and her hands trembled. Lucky longed to pull her into his embrace and promise her nothing bad would happen, but he had a feeling it would be a lie. Something very bad was about to happen.

Next to her, Lila gripped Kori's hand and squeezed as though bolstering her and passing along some strength.

Tears continued to course down her cheeks and her shoulders slumped in defeat. She looked broken, beaten down. Then, in a move that filled him with pride, she inhaled, raised her head and looked at him straight on.

"Rebel already knows you're on to him, Lucky."

Gasps sounded around the room. Lucky was as surprised as anyone, but Kori's solemn face told him there was more. A lot more. And the worst was still to come.

"Tell me," he said.

"The morning after I agreed to move in with you, when I went to meet Rebel for lunch, remember?" She was openly crying now, but her voice, though shaky, possessed a core of steel. Lila still cradled her hand and Kori clung to it like lifeline.

Ice slithered through his veins. He remembered that morning well. The day before she ripped his heart out. Fuck. He wasn't going to like what came next. "I remember."

"When I got to the clubhouse, I was told to go meet Rebel in a shed behind the main building."

The shed. What shed? Shit, there was an old storage shed behind the clubhouse. "Jesus, I don't think I've seen that thing used once since I've been in the club. I didn't even know anyone had a key."

"Rebel and Savage were inside. Your friend, Robbie, was tied to a chair and Savage had beaten the crap out of him. It was... awful." She shuddered, lost for a moment in the nightmare of a memory. "He didn't even try to hide the fact that it was him and I immediately knew I was in serious trouble." She paused and drew in a shuttered breath.

There were so many questions on the tip of Lucky's tongue. He was torn between asking her to speak faster and begging her to shut up. To stop the story that no doubt would shatter them both.

"There were stacks of drugs along the left wall. I really know nothing about it, but I assume what they had was worth a lot of money. Rebel told me what they were up to. And how Robbie ran his mouth when they withheld drugs from him. He told me you discovered what they were doing. Gave me two choices: agree to marry Savage or I'd be looking at you in that chair next. They would do to you everything they did to Robbie."

Words were flying from her now like she couldn't stem the flow once the barrier crumbled. She seemed to have forgotten they had an audience. Every word was another slice, another dagger cutting a hole around his heart. He'd failed her in the worst way. She'd been his woman. His number one job was to protect her. In a world like his? There wasn't anything more important. It was a wonder she could stand to look at him.

"He said you'd been thinking of leaving Vegas and my relationship with Savage would be the push you needed, which was what they wanted. He also said you'd never reveal what you knew if I was married to Savage and in any kind of risk. It was a way to control you without having to explain your death or disappearance.

"He didn't give me any time to process, to think. I had to decide right then and there. I knew in my gut Robbie was going to die and all I could see was you in that chair. I made the only choice I could. After that, Rebel had me followed twenty-four hours a day. He even took my phone and keys, and I didn't have your number memorized. Said if he caught me trying to contact you, he'd kill you. I'd hoped to find a way to talk to you after. And then you were gone."

She sank into her chair, sobs coming in great waves of anguish. "I didn't want to d-do it. I didn't w-want to hurt y-you. I never wanted it to end. But they didn't give me t-time. I couldn't think. I had no c-choice. I had no choice."

There was no doubt in Lucky's mind that every word out of Kori's mouth was the truth. That the agonizing decision she'd been forced to make in a split second's time had broken her heart as it had his. Lucky clenched his jaw and locked his knees to keep from running to her. If he touched her, if one millimeter of her silky skin came in contact with his, he'd snatch her out of there and disappear with her, making sure she was far too pleasured to think of anything from the past month.

But he didn't. The magnitude with which he failed her was so great, he didn't deserve to be in her presence, let alone touch her. How on earth had she withstood his touch the other day? How had she let him into her body knowing the misplaced hatred he'd felt. Knowing everything she'd endured over the past few weeks stemmed from his failure to keep her safe.

He shouldn't have waited. He should have come straight to Arizona the moment he'd overheard Rebel and Savage discussing their business. But he'd hesitated, confused in his loyalties, then unwilling to disturb the happiness he'd found with Kori. And in doing that he'd crushed that happiness under the heel of his heavy boot.

One thin thread of his control remained and it was perilously close to snapping. The walls of the room appeared to be moving in on him, his leather cut shrinking around his body. If he didn't get the hell out of there in the next ten seconds he was going to shatter and lose his shit on someone who didn't deserve it.

"Lucky," Shiv said.

He shook his head and backed up, tripping over his downed chair but somehow managing to stay on his feet. "I have to...I can't..." Christ, he couldn't even form a coherent sentence. Kori's dejected gaze met his. "I'm so fucking sorry, baby," he whispered. Then he turned and jogged out the door.

Not only had he destroyed Kori, but he'd unknowingly fucked his club over as well. He couldn't even go to Vegas and be the one to end Rebel's reign and possibly his life. He wouldn't get the satisfaction of feeling the bones in Savage's face crunch under his fists.

Rebel had been on to him all along.

Fuck.

Kori sagged against the back of her chair as Lucky fled the clubhouse. He left. Despite knowing the truth. It was her worst fear confirmed. The room blurred and her stomach rolled. Breathing became near impossible. She bent forward, head between her knees, trying to draw in air.

What a spectacle she'd made of herself in front of his entire club family. Not only had she blubbered and cried, but she'd shared her most shameful secrets. Her failings, her heartbreak.

What was Lucky thinking at that moment? "He hates me," she whispered.

"No honey." Lila's soft, compassionate voice sounded above her and the calming feel of Lila's hand rubbing along the length of her spine helped regulate her breathing. Every time Lila stroked up, Kori inhaled, then blew out the breath on the downward stroke. No wonder people around town raved about her being an amazing emergency room physician. She was a natural comforter.

"He doesn't hate you. Not at all. I'm pretty sure the one he hates right now is himself."

It was hard to speak around the tennis ball sized lump of emotion in her throat. "That's even worse. That's why I didn't say anything after I got here. I can handle his hatred aimed at me, but I don't think I can survive knowing he hates himself over choices I made."

Oh crap, she was still pouring her heart out to a room full of virtual strangers. Face hot, she straightened and glanced around the room, surprised to find it empty except for the four women she'd spent the afternoon with just yesterday. "Where did everybody go?"

"Shiv shooed them all out. You were a bit upset at the time," Fia said, a compassionate smile on her face.

"I think you should go talk to him." Emily's voice was quiet and her light blue eyes reflected past pain.

"He's not going to want to be around me right now."

"Maybe not. But I still think you should go to him. Force the issue, make him see you, talk to you. He's feeling like he failed you."

"What? That's ridiculous. How did he fail me? I'm the one who broke it off with him. I made the choices here." Is that really what had him so upset? She'd known he'd hate the fact that he dragged her into the mess, but failed her? Never.

Marcie sighed. "She's right, Kori. You gotta understand how these guys think. Protecting family, protecting their women is everything to them. And he feels he failed to protect you."

Kori shot to her feet. "Oh my God. I have to find him. Where would he have gone?" She looked around at the women.

"He's at his house." Acer spoke from the bottom of the staircase. "I had a prospect tail him since he was so upset. He rode straight to his house."

"Thank you. Oh God, I don't even know the address."

"I'll text it to you," Fia said, pulling out her phone.

"Perfect, thank you." She grabbed her leather jacket and dug the phone out of her pocket. Lucky's address lit the screen. With a frown, she searched the floor around her chair for her purse. "Oh shit! I don't have my car, or my license, or anything." She must look and sound like an absolute lunatic.

"Here," Fia tossed a set of keys that Kori caught midair. "I'll ride back with Acer and get my car later. Can't help with the lack of license. Just don't speed."

Kori snorted. Don't speed, yeah right. It would be impossible to drive slowly with the insane amount of adrenaline coursing through her veins. Keys in hand, she dashed toward the exit. At the last second, she turned back around. "Thank you, thank you all so much."

"Go, girl!" Marcie yelled and the ladies cheered and yelled encouragement.

Ten minutes later she pulled into Lucky's driveway. They were going to talk and she wasn't leaving until their issues were resolved.

CHAPTER THIRTY-FIVE

Lucky slammed through his front door and kicked his boots off with violent thrusts of his feet. His plan was to stand in a scalding shower hot enough and for long enough to burn away the past few months of his life. Maybe with some penance thrown in there, too, for immediately believing Kori would have left him for Savage.

Next came his pants, cut, shirt, and boxer briefs. Naked he stalked through his kitchen in search of a bottle of bourbon. When he found his prey, he continued toward his room and master bath.

Now, with the crystal-clear vision of hindsight, everything made so much sense. He reached his room and sank down on the edge of the queen-size bed instead of continuing into the bathroom. Welcoming the burn of the bourbon, he let the liquid flow down his throat. Of course, she hadn't left him for Savage.

If he'd take two minutes to see past his own fucking jealously, he'd have known. It was in her actions, wary of the man, uncomfortable in his presence. She wasn't in love with Savage. It wouldn't have mattered how many times Rebel forced the man upon her.

God, she'd sacrificed herself for him. Gave herself to Savage. Slept in Savage's bed, endured his touch...Lucky's stomach heaved.

It would take more than what was left in the bottle to block out the image of his old VP's hands and mouth on Kori's body, but he had to start somewhere. After taking another drink, he rested his forearms on his thighs, head bowed, the almost empty bottle dangling between his knees.

And that's how Kori found him.

Her soft footsteps stopped a few feet away from him and he didn't need to look up to know it was her. Her unique clean and sweet fragrance was burned into his memory. His cock thickened as she stood there silently, her smell permeating farther into the room with each passing second.

Christ, he was an asshole.

"You shouldn't be here right now," he said.

"I think this is exactly where I'm supposed to be," she answered. Her voice was soothing, her own pain obvious, but she held her ground.

He couldn't handle her being here now. Couldn't handle it if she didn't want him. Wouldn't survive if he'd killed his chance with her. "Look, Kori, I know I'm being an even bigger asshole than I've already been, but I just can't do this right now."

"You're going to have to find a way to do this now, because I'm not leaving."

He straightened and lifted the bourbon to his mouth. Out of the corner of his eye, he caught her movements and the bottle froze at his lips. A groan rumbled low in his stomach as he lowered the bottle. "What the hell are you doing?" It was supposed to come out harsh, but it just sounded tortured.

Kori had shed her pants and was pulling her top over her head. What was left was a lacy red bra and panty set that no man could remain soft around. Sure enough, his cock jutted up between his legs, knocking into the bottle of booze.

She didn't answer, but stared at him as she reached behind her back and unclasped the sinful bra. As the straps slid down her arms, exposing her two perfect tits, he couldn't tear his gaze away. Her tight, plump nipples had his full attention.

Heat swamped him and his mouth dried up. He drank some bourbon, not tasting it this time, just to give his mouth enough moisture to form words. "Don't," he whispered as she hooked her thumbs in the side of those itty-bitty panties.

She ignored him once again and shimmied her hips side to side as she worked the delicate material down her legs. After she stepped out of them, she dangled the red lace from one finger. "Wet," she said, a sly grin on her face.

"Christ, Kori." He groaned and his dick twitched. She needed to go. He needed to make her go. If she kept this up, he'd lose the battle and take her. All night long. Until neither of them had enough energy to leave the bed. He was just that selfish.

She sauntered toward him, smooth, silky skin rippling as she walked. Lucky tried to swallow, but the muscles controlling his throat wouldn't respond. When she reached him, she removed the bottle from his hands and set it on the floor. Widening her stance, she continued forward until she straddled him.

Her tits swayed at face level and Lucky ground his teeth together so hard they should have cracked. Kori wasn't having it though. She cupped a breast and brushed the nipple across the seam of his lips. Like a programmed robot, his tongue shot out and swirled around the rigid point.

Kori moaned and eased into his lap, her arms and legs coming around to lock behind his back. Lucky's eyes drifted closed and he lost the battle to remain detached. His arms crossed behind her back, engulfing her into his embrace. Nothing in this world felt as right at Kori in his arms.

She buried her face in the crook of his neck and clung to him with surprising strength. Every available inch of her skin that could be on him was. It was like she couldn't bear to have any part of herself separated from him.

They stayed like that for a while, glued together, absorbing one another. She was right. She was wet, soaked, and her arousal bathed his iron-hard erection where it nestled between her legs.

He kissed her shoulder, her neck, the line of her jaw.

"Baby," she whispered against his ear, so low it was almost a moan.

He slid one hand into her thick hair and pulled her head back until their lips were a breath apart. "I never slept with him," she whispered against his mouth. "He never saw me like this."

A bit of the tightness in his chest eased, replaced by hope. Was it true? Could it possibly be true?

"I can't bear you thinking that I wanted him in any way. I couldn't have done it. The thought of it made me physically ill. Her throat rose and fell with the force of a hard swallow. "I can't say he didn't touch me at all, but it never went too far. It just wasn't possible. I need you to know that."

"You don't have to tell me. I don't have the right to know." But damned if he wasn't glad to hear it. Her words were like food to a starving man.

Savage would have been angry that she avoided his advances. He'd have made her pay. But they didn't need to talk about that now.

"You have every right," she said.

She was so generous, so trusting, so forgiving. He vowed in that moment to earn her full forgiveness and keep her safe from any future harm.

Even if that meant killing her father.

CHAPTER THIRTY-SIX

"Why did you do it?" Lucky whispered against her ear. "Why didn't you tell Rebel and Savage to go fuck themselves and leave me to handle my own shit?"

She drew back and stared at him, unable to keep the shock off her face. "How could I have done that? They took over every aspect of my life. I had no phone, no car, no identification except for the one day I needed it to start work. Someone had eyes on me at all times. I was trapped and escaped the first chance I had."

His expression was serious, troubled, but not angry. It was as though he accepted what happened, but he needed to put a reason behind it to find some peace. She could give him that.

"I know there wasn't anything you could have done. They'd have come after us with everything. You've had weeks to think about all this. I've only had minutes and my mind is trying to find any way I could have kept you safe from this. You were mine. Mine to take care of, mine to protect." His fingertips stroked up and down her back as he spoke.

Echoes of what the girls told her a while ago rang in her ears. *Protecting family, protecting their women is everything to them. And he feels he failed to protect you.*

"Lucky, I'm not some helpless female who needs a big man to protect me."

"That's not what this is about. It's not about some grander ideal. It's about you and me and who I am. You grew up in an MC, you know how fast things can go from shiny to shit. I need to know you're safe and protected and that I'm the one who makes it that way. For me. Not for all cavemen everywhere, just for me."

"I'm not sure I can give you exactly what you want to hear. You want me to tell you if I'm ever in an impossible situation like that again that I'd walk away knowing you could be hurt. Knowing I could be putting you in severe danger." Her voice dropped to a whisper. "I can't make that promise."

His brows drew down and she smoothed a hand over the lines in his forehead. "Why not? Because you feel like you'd be weak?"

"No. It has nothing to do with that, like you said. It's because I love you, Lucky. And that means I can't stand the thought of any kind of harm coming to you."

His blue eyes widened and she rubbed her cheek against the soft hair of his goatee.

"Here's what I can give you. My trust, my devotion, my loyalty. I hear what you are saying about your need to protect me and keep me safe and I will do anything you say in that regard. I'll do what you need me to do so you feel secure. I won't go looking for trouble, I won't put myself in a dangerous situation, and if a worst-case scenario ever happens again, I will do everything in my power to communicate with you and avoid putting myself at risk. But if I feel there's only one option to save your life, I will take it, whether you like it or not."

He studied her in silence and she gave him the time to process her words.

"It's a start," he said with a smirk and she sagged in relief. She playfully bit his shoulder and he laughed. When she looked at him again he was smiling. The crooked smile. The real smile. Her heart soared.

His arms came around her in a tight hold as she snuggled into his chest. "Thank you," he said.

"For what?"

"For being so fucking incredible. For understanding I'm not just a controlling jerk and giving me what I need to feel you're safe. And even though I may spank that ass for it, thank you for caring enough to sacrifice your happiness to save my life. I think you're the most amazing woman I've ever met."

"Lucky..." She wouldn't cry. Now was the time for healing, not crying.

"Do it again, though, and I definitely will tan that ass. You hear me?"

"Yes, sir," she said around a laugh, moving her body in a way that reminded them both of their intimate position.

They fell quiet and the air grew thick with longing and desire once again.

He hadn't repeated the words of love, but for now it was enough. For now, knowing he wanted her as much as she wanted him was more than enough.

But would it be enough if time passed and she fell deeper and deeper?

He'd spoken loving words of forgiveness and admiration. And he wasn't shy about his continued physical desire for her, but despite his claim to understand why she left him, what if she'd killed his ability to love her back?

That was enough talking. If she'd wanted to talk all night she should have kept her clothes on and her pussy away from his dick. Lucky couldn't keep his mouth off her any longer. Tightening his hand in her hair until he had full control over her head, he took her mouth. The kiss was deliciously slow and controlled, but hard and devouring.

She had no choice but to accept what he gave her and that's exactly how he wanted it. He needed to show her he had her, he'd take care of her, give her the pleasure her body was begging for, and keep her safe.

She moaned into his mouth and consumed him in return. His heart swelled at her easy acceptance of him, of his dominance, of his need. Their bodies craved each other, but this was so much more. This was the hope that they still had a chance.

He tugged on her hair and pulled her head back, exposing her throat when she started to rock her hips along his throbbing length. With his lips, tongue, and teeth, he attacked her bared neck.

"Please, Lucky."

"What do you need, baby?" He nipped along her collar bone and she shuddered, the action grinding her against him. His eyes nearly crossed. It wouldn't be long before he had to end the game and fuck her.

"More of your mouth. Suck me." She sounded breathless, needy.

"Fuck yeah," he said as he pulled her head back further, arching her back and giving him access to her tits.

When his mouth closed over one pointed tip, he sucked hard and she cried out in abandon. He was completely enraptured with the picture she made. Head back, mouth open, lips swollen from his kiss.

They'd had rough, fast, hard, and frenzied.

And they'd had slow, gentle, tender.

This was somewhere in between. His lips were hard and controlling on her mouth, her neck, her breast, but there was a tenderness, too. The pace was slow, almost lazy, but the intent deep, dark, and desperate. He owned her in this moment. Kori was caught somewhere between a blinding need for release and a slow build up to ecstasy.

He switched to her other breast and the need for him to fuck her grew unbearable. "Lucky," she cried out. "More, more."

Juices dripped from her, coating his shaft and driving them both insane as she slid along his length.

"Enough!" He released her breast and her hair at the same time and she almost fell back. "I need inside you." The commanding rasp of his voice sent shivers down her spine to her clit.

Strong fingers gripped her hips and lifted her a few inches off his lap. Enough to line up the head of his cock with her weeping pussy. Their eyes locked and they both groaned as he drew her fully back into his lap.

She could barely breathe. Fully impaled on his length, she was so full, so stretched, so…in love.

"You are so fucking hot, angel."

She smiled. "I love when you call me that."

"Good, because I'm going to say it a lot."

She had the urge to move, to lose control and let her body take over, but Lucky held her captive so all she could do was grind down on him. With her internal muscles, she clenched him again and again while rocking her hips back and forth and grinding her clit into the base of his pubic bone.

She loved the feeling of Lucky slamming into her over and over as he drove her toward the finish line, but this was intoxicating as well. There was an extreme closeness and intimacy to their position. Their bodies were fully entwined, eyes locked, breath mingling.

"That's it, baby," he said. "Make yourself feel good. Work that little clit on me and squeeze my cock with that sweet pussy."

His words were as effective as a physical stroke in driving her higher. Heat radiated from both of them. It was a wonder they didn't set the room ablaze.

Lucky banded one arm around her lower back, anchoring her torso with his while the other hand stroked up her body and tangled in her hair once again. "Eyes on me," he growled as he claimed her mouth in a kiss that made the room whirl.

The closer she got to coming, the harder it was to keep her eyes opened, but she kept her gaze on his while he devoured her mouth and stroked into her with tiny thrusts of his hips.

She began to tremble in his arms.

Lucky broke the kiss. "Give it to me, baby."

It was all she needed to fly off the face of the earth. She buried her face against his neck and held him with everything she had. Her arms, her legs, her internal muscles, all clamped around him as though afraid he'd disappear after the raging waters calmed.

"Fuck!" He followed her, holding her just as tight while riding out his own storm. They stayed entwined, bodies cooling, muscles with the occasional quiver until she'd almost drifted off. Inside her body, he softened until he nearly slid out. They were wet and sticky, but she didn't care. All that mattered was being back in his arms.

"Come on, woman," he said as he lay back on the bed, taking her with him. "Let's get some sleep. We can both use it."

She allowed herself to be drawn into the warmth and safety of his strong embrace. For the first time in weeks, she felt relaxed, protected, and sheltered. She'd do everything in her power to keep the sensation forever.

CHAPTER THIRTY-SEVEN

A week later, Kori sat astride Lucky's bike waiting for him while he finalized some last-minute details with the club. The group of ten bikers plus her were due to roll out in the next few minutes.

Much of the preceding week had been spent going over details of Savage and Rebel's lives with Jester, Striker, and Lucky. They'd grilled her mercilessly and for hours, day after day, on exactly where the drugs were, what the inside of the shed looked like, how often Rebel seemed to go in there. Some questions she answered with confidence and certainty, while others she could barely speak to.

Her brain swirled with memories and at some point, began to play tricks on her. Doubt seeped into her mind. Had she seen four or five stacks of drugs? Had Rebel or Savage mentioned where they came from? So much of the remembrances from that day were emotional, traumatic, gut-wrenching reactions that clouded her ability to recall anything with logic and objectivity.

The men had seemed satisfied, though, and praised her continually for her recall of detail and willingness to help. Lucky had remained quiet during her questioning, having undergone a similar interrogation himself with regards to his investigation. Every now and again the weight of his stare would become tangible and she'd glance over to find his hot gaze full of respect, pride, and white-hot lust.

Each night—and most mornings—Lucky made the mentally grueling pace of the week's activities worth it with hours and hours of physical pleasure so great her body still hummed hours later. He was insatiable, and their sex was even hotter and more intense than it had been prior to her leaving Vegas. Something which, at the time, she hadn't thought it possible.

He was a vocal lover, whispering filthy words and desires in her ear that had her drenched for him before he'd even laid a hand on her. Once he did get to touching her, the fireworks were spectacular. Then he'd always follow up with the most tender and caring words she'd ever heard. He thought she was amazing, brave, strong. He admired her courage, her willingness to help his family in any way possible. He thought she was beautiful, smart, compassionate.

But still, he didn't say the three words she longed to hear and her heart was beginning to lose hope. How long could she stay with a man she loved with her whole being if he couldn't return the sentiment? Was physical desire and a deep admiration enough? Or would the unrequited love eventually eat away at her soul?

"Ready to roll, angel?"

Kori jumped. She'd been so lost in her own world, she hadn't noticed Lucky approach.

"You okay, baby?" he asked with a frown.

Baby. Angel. He was back to using the endearment and nickname almost exclusively and she wasn't sure which she liked more. Most of the other guys had picked up the handle and now referred to her as angel, but it didn't pack nearly the punch as when Lucky did. "I'm great. And yes, ready to go."

The frown stayed in place and was now accompanied by muscular arms crossed over his chest and a raised eyebrow. Damn the perceptive man.

She rolled her eyes. "Okay, I'm a little on edge. Just nerves. I'll be fine once we get going." Apparently, the smile she gave him wasn't as convincing as she thought it was.

He stepped forward and cupped her face between his large hands. "You know I'm not going to let him get near you, right? Nothing is going to happen to you."

The others milled around, loading their bikes, kissing their ol' ladies goodbye, reviewing last minute plan specifics. But all of that faded into the background as she concentrated on Lucky.

"I'm not worried about me." Seriously, did he not see how important he and his club had become to her over the past few weeks? "I'm worried about Striker and Jester and the others. Did you know Jester's girlfriend is pregnant? What if something happens to him? What would she do?" She'd tried so hard to hide her stress from Lucky, but with one tender touch, her walls came crumbling down.

"Oh, baby, I wish I'd known you were this anxious." He captured her mouth in a soft, but thorough kiss. "I love that you care so much for my brothers and their women, but everyone will be fine."

There it was. Love. But not directed at her. At least he knew the word.

"What do you think this whole week has been about? The hours of questioning and developing plans A through F? That was about being prepared. Keeping everyone's ass safe and making sure we all travel home together and whole. Nothing is going to happen. You hear me?" His voice was strong, sure, confident and it went a long way toward assuaging her fears.

"I hear you. Thank you, Lucky." She nuzzled her face into his hand.

"Don't keep that shit from me, angel. No need to stress on your own. You got me for that, okay?"

She nodded. Did she have him? Really have him? His actions sure said yes. Still, she was insecure.

"Okay, so you and I are going to a hotel on the outskirts of Vegas where we'll sit around bored out of our minds while the others have all the fun. Once everyone is rounded up and it's safer than safe, I'll take you to see Rebel. You can say your piece, then your sexy ass is out of there."

She couldn't help but chuckle. "I know, Lucky. We've been over this four hundred and seventy-two times in the past twenty-four hours. I just want to look Rebel in the eye and have him know he didn't defeat me. I want him to know he destroyed any chance at having a daughter." She snorted. "He probably won't give a shit, but maybe there's a small part of him that cares about me in some way. He's my only remaining blood relative and he turned out to be a ruthless jerk. I just need some closure. I have no desire to stick around and see what you all decide to do with him. There are a few things I'd like to say to Savage as well."

Despite all evidence to the contrary, a small part of her held a fierce hope that his soul could be redeemed. A part of her that so desperately clung to the idea of having a family. Losing her mother, finding a new father and now finding out he wasn't the type of man she hoped he'd be was a lot of emotional trauma in such a short period of time.

Lucky grunted. "I'm sure there are. For the record, I hate the idea of you being anywhere near either of them. Even if I understand it."

With a smile, Kori wrapped her hands around Lucky's biceps —or as much around the impressive muscles as she could get— and drew him to her. She teased the seam of his lips with her tongue, but apparently, he wasn't in a playing mood as he opened his mouth and basically inhaled her.

"Hey!" Jester yelled across the parking lot. "Unless you two are gonna get nekkid and give us a real damn show, stop sucking face and let's roll out!"

Lucky kept his mouth on his woman but moved one hand off her face and held his middle finger up in Jester's general direction. When he finally pulled back, Kori's face was flushed with a deep pink blush he assumed wasn't strictly from embarrassment. Since her eyes were lust-glazed, chances were good.

"Go time, baby," he said as he flicked a finger down her nose.

She nodded and reached for her helmet, securing it with a brave smile that hid her anxiety. God, he fucking loved this woman.

Yes, loved her. It was a fierce and consuming feeling he hadn't experienced before and knew deep in his gut he never would again. Yet, when she'd uttered the three words to him, he remained silent.

And she hadn't said it again. It made sense. Putting that out in the universe only to not have it returned had to be a kick in the balls. Or lady balls in her case, because she had them in spades.

He wanted to say the words. They'd been on the tip of his tongue countless times this week as he watched her endure hours of questioning by the club leadership. Sure, they weren't trying to intimidate her or treat her like any kind of suspect, but they were intense and the strain of being the focus of that intensity had shown.

Each time he came, which had been many this week, he'd had to grit his teeth with jaw-cracking force to keep from bellowing out his love for her. He just couldn't put voice to it. Not yet. Not while there was another man out there who thought he had rights to her. There wasn't any fear that Kori wanted Savage, but Savage wanted her and thought he had a claim on her. Lucky planned to make it crystal-fucking-clear that he was dead wrong.

He wanted to come to her with all of this behind them. Then he could tell her and he'd tell her ten times a day to make up for any insecurity he'd caused her this week. He just needed her to hang in there a little longer and she'd get the words she yearned for. And so would he, because he couldn't fucking wait for her to say it again.

The ride to Vegas was uneventful and they reached the outskirts in the usual under three-hour trip time. Lucky revved his engine and waved at his brothers as he took the exit for the hotel he and Kori would be stashed at until it they were sure it was safe to be seen. If either of them were spotted before Striker and Shiv put their plan into action, someone would tip off Rebel and blow the whole thing to hell.

Still, it slayed him to be left out of the action and he planned to make the most out of doling out a righteous punishment once he received the all clear from Acer as was the plan. For now, at least he got to kill the time with his woman.

He checked them in with cash, under a false Mr. and Mrs. Name. The motel was somewhere on the spectrum between piece of shit and mediocre. Fancy Vegas resorts tended to raise an eyebrow at cash transactions, so a motel it was.

Kori was quiet as he let her into the room. She dropped her overnight bag next to the door and stuck her hands in her back pockets. Dark circles ringed her eyes and she swayed a bit.

"Tired, baby?" he asked.

"Actually, I am. I was good until the last twenty minutes of the trip and now I feel like my eyelids weigh eighty pounds."

"So lie down. Take a nap. We've got time to kill." He moved to her and pushed the leather jacket off her shoulders, revealing the creamy skin her Harley tank top exposed. He couldn't resist a quick lick along her collar bone, but he should have because his cock surged to attention the second her flavor burst on his tongue.

"Hmm," she said, letting her head fall back and giving him access to her neck. "Seems like you have something besides sleep in mind."

With a chuckle, he sucked the skin of her neck between his teeth. "That is on my mind every second of every day, baby." Reluctantly, he stepped back. "But I do want you to sleep. If we're lucky we'll have time to play a bit when you wake up." He turned her and gave her a nudge toward the bed.

"You're no fun," she said, pout evident in her voice.

"I'll ask you to reevaluate your opinion on that later when I'm balls deep in you with my fingers on your clit." Jesus, he needed to stop the sexy talk or her nap would never happen.

A visible tremor ran through her. Dirty talk did it to her every time.

"What are you going to do while I take a nap?" she asked over her shoulder as she kicked off her riding boots.

"Hold you." Like he'd miss an opportunity to have her in his arms.

"That's what I was hoping you'd say." She rested back on the bed and scooted to the far side, rolling over until she faced the wall.

Lucky toed his own boots off, shed his cut and shucked out of his jeans. Then he crawled into the bed and curled his body around her much smaller one. The sigh of contentment Kori emitted made his chest ache in an unfamiliar way.

Within minutes she was fast asleep, the even rise and fall of her chest synching with his own breathing. Lucky closed his eyes and let the fatigue wash over him. For someone who had once been averse to any female sleeping in his bed, he sure as hell loved the feel of Kori tucked in tight against him.

To be honest, he couldn't even remember the appeal of hopping from bed to bed. Not when he'd found perfection and had access to earth-shattering pleasure whenever he wanted.

CHAPTER THIRTY-EIGHT

Rebel scooted his hips to the edge of his leather chair, leaned back against the headrest and folded his hands beneath his head. The new club whore who knelt between his knees got to work extracting his dick from his pants and stroking him.

She'd been coming to parties for the last two weeks. Young, maybe twenty-two with huge tits, a tight ass, and from what he heard, a mouth that sucked better than a Dyson. A good blowie was just what he needed to take his mind off all the shit he was dealing with.

Fucking Kori had been gone about two weeks now, and Savage was growing more pissed by the day. A printed receipt for plane tickets to Florida had been discovered in her dresser drawer. So, he'd sent two prospects to Florida to look for her, but they'd been unsuccessful so far.

Savage couldn't be spared at the moment even if he was the one who wanted to drag Kori back by the hair and remind her that the club owned her. They had an enormous shipment coming in tomorrow. A shipment that would shoot them to the top of food chain in Vegas's drug trade.

It was time to bring in some additional club members. Their operation was growing faster than they could keep up with and the money was rolling in. That was the second source of stress keeping Rebel up at nights. Who should he ask into his inner circle? Which of his men would jump on board the fast-moving money train? There were some who he was almost certain would drool over the potential earnings and join up no questions asked.

Others, like Bull, would be a harder sell. Who gave a fuck? If they couldn't get behind their president they could get the fuck out of his club. He was prepared and more than willing to lose members to protect what he and Savage had busted their asses to build over the past year.

"Um…" A confused voice sounded from between his legs.

The whore still knelt between his legs, her pouty painted lips turned down in a frown and his flaccid dick resting in her hand. Her green eyes were wary, nervous.

Fucking stress messing with his damn hard-on. "Well, work the fuck harder," he growled at the girl, whatever her name was. He fisted a hank of her curly dark hair and shoved her face in his crotch. "Put it in your fucking mouth. You need written instructions, bitch?"

She squeaked but did as he asked, closing her mouth around his soft cock. With a hand still guiding her head, Rebel closed his eyes and thought about all the money that would be rolling in over the next few weeks.

He was lord of the fucking manor around the club and would soon have the green to match his status. Not surprisingly, his cock filled at the thought of the money. Worked every time. What could he say? Money and power turned him on.

He held the girl's head still as his erection grew, filling her mouth to her throat. She gagged and tried to pull back but he forced her to stay in place and adjust.

When he finally released her head, she snapped up and coughed like she'd been choking. Watery eyes that held a hint of fear stared up at him and he grew even harder. That's what he liked to see. A woman who knew he was in control, master of the fucking house, and not afraid to let her know it.

"It ain't gonna suck it self, girlie. Get back to work."

She returned to her task and Rebel's eyes drifted closed as pleasure washed over him. Looks like the guys were right. She was damn skilled at sucking cock.

A forceful banging on his office door had her yelping and releasing him again.

"What?" he barked. "This better be fuckin' good."

"Zip it up, Pres," Savage called through the door. "Shiv and some of his boys just rolled into the yard."

Rebel's blood ran cold. Just what he fucking needed. Those boy scouts invading his space a day before the biggest deal of his life. "Goddammit." He stood up so fast, the girl on the floor sprawled back on her ass. "Get the hell out of my office."

She scurried across the floor and scrambled to her feet, slipping out the door without a word. A million things ran through Rebel's head in that moment, not the least of which was fear. And he didn't do fucking fear. Others feared him.

Was it coincidence? Shiv showing up just as he was about to receive an enormous shipment? Or had Lucky tipped them off? No, he wouldn't dare. Kori had had such a firm grip on his balls, no way in hell would he have put her at risk.

Rebel strode down the hallway toward the bar area, making sure to instill enough swagger in his gait to appear unconcerned by his unexpected guests. Shiv and Striker sat at the bar joking with his prospect, a bottle between them.

"Hey, Shiv, Striker! To what do we owe the pleasure of a visit from the mother chapter's president and VP?" He slapped Striker on the back and squeezed Shiv's shoulder. "Get me a glass, prospect."

Shiv tensed. It was so fast and so slight there was a chance Rebel imagined it. Shiv recovered quickly, standing and giving Rebel a back-slapping hug. "Hey, brother. Guys were itching to take a road trip and the ol' ladies were itching for some girl time. You know, drinking wine, putting goop on their faces, all that shit. We haven't been up here in ages so we figured it would be the perfect time."

His voice was friendly and the explanation made perfect sense, but Rebel had been around long enough to learn shit wasn't always as it seemed. Something about Shiv's expression twisted Rebel's stomach into a complicated knot.

"Savage around?" Striker asked.

Good question. He'd been the one to warn Rebel of their chapter brothers' arrival, but now he appeared to be in the wind. Lucky bastard. "Not sure what he's up to, actually. I ain't seen him around yet today." He shrugged. "Lucky with you? Be good to see him again."

"Nah," Striker answered. "Sure, he's a club veteran, but he's only been with our chapter a few weeks. Gotta prove himself a little before he gets to have fun. You know how it is."

Some of the knot unraveled and Rebel was able to take a breath. No way Lucky would have stayed back and missed out on the action if they were here to fuck with Rebel's drug business. Maybe it really was a coincidence. "Wish you guys had warned us ahead of time so we could have prepared for a visit."

Something flashed in Striker's eyes and Rebel knew in that instant this was no fucking coincidence. *Motherfucker.* His insides seethed but he kept on the mask of a man who didn't have a care in the fucking world.

"Hey, look," Shiv said. "We ain't here to fuck with your day." He waved a hand in Rebel's direction. "Do your thing. We'll hang, drink, my guys will flirt with your ladies. Later, we'll catch up."

As much as he dreaded leaving the Arizona chapter guys unsupervised in his clubhouse, he needed eyes on Savage and fast. Then he needed to make sure there was no way any of them could discover the two hundred thousand dollars' worth of heroin they had stashed in the shed. They may know too much, but without proof they really knew shit.

"Sounds good," he said, and tossed back his drink. "Know a great place for us to cause a little trouble tonight."

"Perfect," Striker said.

Rebel nodded and speed walked back down the hallway. He bypassed his office and jogged out the back door and straight to the shed. A van had been backed up to the entrance, the rear doubled doors wide open.

With a violent jerk, he wrenched the shed door open and almost dropped to his knees in relief when Savage greeted him. The business end of Savage's pistol loomed two inches from his head but he couldn't have given any less shits.

"Fuck! Sorry, Pres." Savage holstered his weapon.

"Forget it. Just move as much as you can. They're inside getting fucked up. We can slip all of this out of here easy."

"They know?" Savage held an armful of heroin packages.

Bile rose in Rebel's throat. "Suspect something, I think."

"Fuck."

Silence descended as they loaded the van in record time. Three or four more trips should do it. With his arms full, Rebel used his back to open the door to the outside. He spun around to deposit the packages in the van and stopped dead in his tracks.

Jester stood, blocking the open van. The asshole was so wide, with his hands on his hips and legs in a shoulder width stance, he spanned the entire rear of the van. Striker stood to the side of him, pistol trained on Rebel.

Fuck, fuck, fuck. He couldn't even reach his damn weapon.

"It's over, Rebel," Striker said. He motioned with his gun for Rebel to unload his arms. "Spin around," he ordered after the packages hit the ground.

No fucking way was he going to turn around and wait to receive a bullet in the back of his head. Striker could just shoot him in the face like a fucking man. He stared the two men down like their discovery of his actions didn't bother him in the least.

Jester rolled his eyes and held up a set of plastic handcuffs. "No one's gonna kill you…yet. Turn the fuck around."

Just as Rebel began to turn, Savage burst outside gun drawn. He dove for Striker before the other VP had a chance to react, and pistol whipped him clear across the face.

"Fuck," cried Striker as his cheek split open and blood poured down his face. Savage swept his foot behind Striker's legs and he crumpled to the ground. With a laugh, Savage sprinted toward the clubhouse.

Rebel slammed against the side of the shed as Jester's mammoth body rammed into him. Jester roughly jerked Rebel's hands behind his back and secured the handcuffs. He then kicked Rebel's feet out from under him.

His entire body crashed to the ground. Fuck, that hurt. Jester bound his feet as well then slapped a piece of duct tape over his mouth before turning to Striker. "You okay, VP?"

He tuned out Striker's grunts of pain as Jester prodded his face and helped him to stand, letting his brain spin with a plan. They'd all be fucking dead soon.

Every last one of those do-gooder Arizona assholes. No one fucked with him. He was one week and one shipment away from owning Vegas.

He'd kill them all.

CHAPTER THIRTY-NINE

Lucky awoke to a warm woman cuddled in his arms and the sexiest ass he'd ever known slowly squirming against his cock. Damn, this woman was perfect for him.

He slipped a hand under her shirt and over the sleep-warmed skin of her soft stomach. Up he went until the lush weight of a breast filled his palm. He cupped it, thumbing the nipple.

"Oh," she said, a false innocence in her voice. "Sorry, did I wake you? I didn't mean to."

"Mmm." He licked the shell of her ear. "Didn't mean to rub that gorgeous ass all over my cock?"

She giggled. "Nah, I definitely meant to do that." She gasped as he raked his teeth across her jawline.

"You want me, angel?" He pinched her nipple between his thumb and forefinger which caused her back to arch pressing her ass further into his hard-on and her breast more fully into his hand.

"God, yes," she said on a moan.

"What do you want?"

"Anything."

He stilled. His fantasies about Kori knew no bounds and if she gave him carte blanche, he'd take it and run. He released her breast and trailed his hand back down her torso and around to her ass. After a caressing squeeze to one cheek, he ran his finger along the seam of her ass. "Anything?"

"Yes, Lucky. Anything. You can have anything, do anything."

He groaned. "Christ, baby." The writhing had to stop or he was going to shoot all over her back and owe her big time. "This is not the time or the place, but that ass will be mine. Soon."

"It's already yours, Lucky. Everything is yours."

Jesus, she was blowing his mind today. Time to show her just how much. He rolled her to her back settled on top of her. Her legs parted at once, cradling him with the warm, wet heat between her thighs. "For now..." he said as he lowered his mouth to her.

Lucky's phone blared out a text message alert from the table next to their bed. Great fuckin' timing.

"Lucky? Aren't you gonna get that?" Kori asked as she ran her hands up and down his spine.

"Nah. They can wait. Actually, I kinda like the idea of Rebel and Savage waiting on ice while I ravage you."

"Lucky," she swatted his arm as his phone chimed again. "Check it."

With a sigh, he rolled off of her. "Yes, ma'am." He snatched up the phone and swiped it open to a text from Acer.

911. Shit hit fan.

Need assist.

"Fuck!" He shot out of the bed and wrestled into his jeans.

"What's wrong?" Kori sat straight up, the sheet covering her nudity. Her eyes were wide with fear and she clutched the sheet like a lifeline.

"Not sure. Acer said shit went bad and they need help. I can be there in five minutes." While he spoke, he shoved his feet into his boots and reached for his keys.

"I'm coming too." Kori jumped out of bed no longer attempting to cover herself.

"No fucking way."

"Lucky, be reasonable. You may need my help." Her hands were on her hips, a mutinous expression on her face. If it were any other time, Lucky would have laughed at the naked warrior ready to jump into battle with him.

"No, baby. Not just no. Fuck no. You aren't getting anywhere near that clubhouse without a guarantee that you'll be one hundred percent safe. Once I have that I'll come back for you. You'll get to confront your father. I promise."

"But—"

He shook his head. "No buts. I can't do what I need to do if I'm worrying about you. It will be a distraction I can't afford. You don't want to risk anyone getting hurt because I'm not on my game, do you?"

It was the low road, putting responsibility on her, and her narrowed eyes let him know she thought so too, but she relented. That was all that mattered. Besides, it was true. He'd be ineffective if he had to worry about her. If she stayed here he could do what he needed to do, secure in her safety.

"Fine. But you call me the very second you can. Okay?"

He tugged her close and kissed her. "Okay, angel. Don't leave this room. For anything. Understood?"

"Yes!" She shoved him away. "Go! You're wasting time."

He kissed her one more time then dashed out the door leaving her standing stark naked in the center of a sleazy motel room. When this was all over he was taking her to a five-star resort and they'd drown in delicious food, drink, and each other for a week.

Lucky paid no attention to speed limits as he raced toward the clubhouse. He made it in four minutes. The street outside was quiet, but at least twenty bikes were lined up in front of the building indicating the problem must be inside.

There wasn't a soul he could call for backup. Everyone he would have normally called was already inside and it would take far too long for anyone else to ride up from Crystal Rock. "Fuck it," he muttered as he shoved the entrance door open.

"Holy shit!" The scene that greeted him was insane. There had to be fifteen to twenty pissed off bikers in the clubhouse with guns pointed in every direction he looked. Once he had a second to get his bearings, he realized the men were mostly lined up opposite each other. Vegas on one side, Arizona on the other with weapons pointing across the aisle.

Savage stood in the center, his gun trained on Bull who also stood in the empty space but appeared to be trying to talk some sense into the Vegas crew. His arms were up in a position of surrender and his eyes were glued to Savage's trigger finger.

Intent on the volatile standoff, no one seemed to realize Lucky had entered the building.

"Bullshit," someone called out. It sounded like Vee. "No fucking way are they selling drugs. You assholes wasted your time coming up here." Mutters of agreement came from the rest of the Vegas side of the room.

"Look," Bull said. "I know it sounds crazy, but I swear on my Harley that it's the goddamned truth."

"Shut the fuck up," said Savage. He lunged toward Bull, raising his weapon so it was centered between the other man's eyes. If Savage discharged his gun, all hell would break loose and a blood bath would ensue in the middle of the damn clubhouse.

Time to do something before the inside of the clubhouse rivaled the streets of Afghanistan. He raised his hands much in the same manner as Bull. "It's true."

Every head in the room swiveled in his direction. Relief was written on the faces of his Arizona brothers, while no less than five men from Vegas—men he would have given his life for—trained their guns on him. Savage's face twisted into a sinister smile. All he was missing was the long black mustache to twist while he cackled like the evil villain he was.

Lucky's knuckles tingled with the urge to ram into Savage's smug face. The arrogant bastard thought he was home free. Thought no one would believe Lucky. Little did he know Lucky wasn't leaving until Savage was unconscious at the very best, in a body bag preferably.

"Thank God," Bull murmured.

"What the fuck is going on?" This time he was sure it was Vee who'd spoken. Apparently, he was the self-appointed spokesman for the Vegas crew.

With his hands sill raised, Lucky took slow, sure steps until he was in the chasm between the two groups. "Rebel and Savage have been pushing drugs here in Vegas for months. Their two-man enterprise is growing and very lucrative. It's a kick in the nuts to the club on a number of levels. First, it's against the bylaws. And second, they are raking in the dough for themselves. Not the good of the club."

The faces of his Vegas brothers began to change from irritated disbelief to shock. Lucky had been well respected within the chapter. They'd believe him where Bull may not have gotten through.

"How do you know all this?" Vee asked.

"I overheard a conversation. Did some investigating. I was ready to talk to Striker and Shiv about it when Kori showed up and put a wrench in my plans."

Vee nodded. "You didn't want her hurt."

"Yeah, well turns out it backfired. They blackmailed her into agreeing to marry Savage to keep me alive. They've had thousands of dollars of product right under your noses in the shed out back."

"Fuck," someone muttered. "I didn't think that damn thing even opened. Where's Rebel now?"

"Jester has him and the drugs out back in a van until we can deal with him," Acer said.

"Now you all have a choice. Savage and Rebel are looking to up their game. Looking for help. Tempting, all that potential for money. But think about this. What's the foundation of this club based on? The belly of our beast? Loyalty, brotherhood, club before all. Rebel and Savage spat in the face of all that we stand for. You really want to join up with two selfish assholes like that?"

Slowly, weapons on the Vegas side lowered, directing toward the ground instead of the visitors. Acer, Hook, and the gang from Arizona shifted their weapons toward Savage.

The click of Savage's round loading in the chamber echoed through the confused silence. "This is between me and Lucky. Has nothing to do with any drugs. His panties are just in a wad because Kori left him for me."

Lucky tipped his head to the side and couldn't have suppressed his grin for a million bucks. "Really? You sure about that? Where do you think she's been the last couple weeks? Whose bed you do you think she's been in?"

Savage's face turned a deep dark red. A split second of worry blasted through Lucky. There was a very good chance Savage would actually shoot him. Might be worth it for the satisfaction of knocking him off his high horse. "She's been in Florida," he ground out between clenched teeth.

"Sure," Lucky said, that satisfaction growing by the second. "That's where's she's been."

"Everyone get the fuck out." After barking the order, Savage tossed his gun to the ground, out of reach.

Yes. One on one. Him and Savage. No weapons. No holds barred. Lucky was no stranger to hand to hand combat. He excelled in the Marine Corps Mixed Martial Arts Program, receiving a second-degree black belt faster than anyone in his battalion. Since then he'd trained in various martial arts and even won a few bucks fighting at various times.

Every pair of eyes in the room flicked to Lucky as if looking for guidance. He nodded. "Go ahead. Leave us."

One by one the guys shuffled out of the clubhouse. Acer remained behind, his mouth drawn tight in a look of disapproval. "I'm not leaving, Lucky. I don't trust him for shit."

"Aww," Savage said. "You worried I'm gonna hurt your friend, Acer?" Savage's tone was full of mocking.

Lucky met Acer's gaze and his friend nodded before backing out of the clubhouse. He'd stick by, close to the door if needed, but also give Lucky the freedom to kick the shit out of Savage.

Alone with a man whose death he'd had been plotting for weeks, Lucky shrugged out of his cut and threw it on the bar. No need to bloody it up. And while he was confident in his ability to tear Savage apart, he wasn't fool enough to believe it'd be easy or he'd walk away unscathed. Every bruise would be well worth it.

The pulse of Lucky's blood in his veins picked up speed as adrenalin flooded his system. His fight or flight instinct kicked in with no thoughts of fleeing until Savage was in a heap on the ground.

"So the bitch crawled back you, huh? Savage asked with a smirk. "Gonna be rough for you when she's back in my bed." He raised an eyebrow and licked his lips. "Her pussy still taste as good as I remember?"

Lucky's nostrils flared as anger surged. He flexed his fingers and rolled his head along his shoulders. Savage was clearly taunting him into throwing the first punch. He wouldn't give the man the satisfaction of knowing how deep under Lucky's skin his comments pierced.

"Damn, it is good, isn't it? Mmm. And fuck she was tight." Savage smiled and grabbed his crotch.

She never slept with him. Lucky repeated the mantra again and again.

"I'm thinking I must have gone a little too easy on her though. This time around, she'll damn well know where she belongs. Sounds like she needs a rougher hand."

Fuck it. Savage wanted to goad Lucky in to making the first move then he damn well deserved to be the first one to have his face smashed in.

Lucky flew across the distance between them, cocking his fist on the way. When the crushing pain of his knuckles landing on

Lucky

Savage's smug, grinning face registered, Lucky welcomed the hurt. He cherished it, craved it.

Let the games begin.

CHAPTER FORTY

Alone in the less than luxurious motel room, Kori hopped in the shower—a quick rinse to rid herself of the road. Then she brushed her teeth, combed her hair, and redressed.

Nervous energy fluttered in her stomach as she sat on the edge of the bed. Her foot wouldn't stay still and bounced like the ground was laden with hot coals. She glanced at her phone.

All right. She did pretty well. Held it together like a champ for the fourteen minutes since Lucky left in a rush to investigate Acer's cryptic and concerning text.

Good enough.

She sprang off the bed, stuffed her room key, identification, and some cash in her pocket, grabbed her phone, and darted out the door. Three minutes later she climbed into an Uber and sped off toward the clubhouse.

Maybe she needed to rethink being an ol' lady, because it seemed she was shit at taking orders. Particularly the kind where she was told to stay away and out of her man's business. Lucky would be pissed, but that was just too damn bad for him. She wasn't the type of woman who could sit by and knit while the man she loved battled danger without backup.

And she did love him.

Another thing that was just too damn bad for him.

The six-minute drive felt more like an hour and somehow in that short time, she managed to think of every worst-case

248

scenario possible. By the time the driver braked in front of the clubhouse, she was a jittery mess of extreme anxiety, convinced she'd find a clubhouse full of dead bikers.

"Thank you," she managed to get out to the driver despite the arid quality of her mouth.

Men, both Vegas and Arizona, lingered in the parking lot, the tension so thick it was practically a fog around them. Acer hovered by the entrance to the clubhouse, arms folded across his chest, his head inclined toward the door.

Where the hell was Lucky?

A loud crash sounded from the clubhouse and Kori's heart skipped multiple beats. Every head in the lot swiveled and stared at Acer. He frowned, but kept up his position as sentry.

Her legs felt disconnected, separated from her brain as they propelled her forward despite the screaming in her mind that this was a horrible idea. Something was wrong. Lucky should be out here. If she walked in that clubhouse and found him injured —or worse—she wouldn't be held accountable for her actions.

"Kori! What the hell are you doing here?" Acer was the first to spot her and he vacated his post, tromping across the lot.

Yikes. He was one pissed off biker, and Lucky's anger was guaranteed to be ten times more intense. Whatever. He could rail at her for hours as long as he was safe and unharmed.

"W-where's Lucky?" She held her breath waiting for the answer.

"Kori…" Acer stopped her forward progression with a firm hand on each shoulder. "You need to go back to the motel. Now."

Everyone stared at her, but after the show she put on at the meeting the week before, she was becoming accustomed to being a spectacle.

She shook her head. "Not happening. Where the hell is he?" Another crash broadcasted from the clubhouse and she met Acer's sympathetic gaze. "Is he in there?" she whispered.

The door to the clubhouse flew open and Savage stumbled out looking like someone from a cheap slasher movie. No, not just someone. The lunatic-eyed murderer. Blood flowed from his nose and somewhere on his head, raining down his body and soaking his torn shirt. He still moved well, as though he suffered nothing more than a papercut.

"Oh my God." All rational thought fled her mind. Self-preservation flew out the window. Thoughts of safety and her personal wellbeing, gone. She shoved Acer with all her might and darted around him charging for Savage.

"Kori, no!" Acer yelled from behind her, but his words glided in one ear and straight out the other.

"What the hell did you do to him?" Kori screamed as she rushed toward Savage. Her palm connected with his face before her brain had time to warn her of the danger in attacking such a lethal and furious man.

He was on her so fast, she never saw the assault coming. Pain exploded on the left side of her face as his fist collided with her cheek. The punched rattled her brain and stars danced in front of her vision. Unable to remain upright after being unbalanced by what felt like a Mack truck, Kori dropped like a stone on the unforgiving ground.

Disoriented, she tried to scramble away, but Savage was too big and too fast. His booted foot connected with her side and she screamed in agony. The next thing she knew, a crushing weight pressed down on her chest. Finally, her vision cleared and she looked into the face of a murderous Savage straddling her chest and impairing her ability to breathe.

She screamed, grappled, and slapped him with everything she had left, but she was no match for his strength. The bare skin of her upper back and shoulders felt like it was being ripped from her body as she struggled between a two-hundred-pound man and the scorching asphalt.

It all happened in the blink of an eye. The entire encounter couldn't have lasted more than five seconds. Savage managed to connect one more face-smashing blow before he was violently yanked from her body. His boot snuck in one more rib shot while three huge men dragged him away. "You're fucking dead, bitch," he screamed. "I own you. I'm gonna fuck you then kill you while Lucky watches."

Acer grasped her under the arms and pulled her back at the same time his brothers yanked Savage away. Her ribs screamed in protest, her head pounded like a heavy metal drummer had set up camp, and the abraded skin of her back scraped across the hot ground drawing a cry of distress from her.

While Lucky watches.

Lucky had to be alive to watch anything. A small seed of hope developed.

"Sweetie, we're going to call an ambulance. Can you sit up so I can look at your back, or is it too painful to move?" Acer asked.

Just as she opened her mouth to answer, the clubhouse entrance opened again. Lucky erupted through the door like a Hollywood stunt man, a wild look in his eyes. Blood dripped from his nose and lip and a purple ring was swelling around one eye, but he appeared to be in better shape than Savage.

He spotted her sprawled on the ground, her head resting against Acer's thighs and everything in him hardened. His eyes went flat, his posture grew rigid and he turned toward the men restraining Savage.

It was then she noticed the pistol dangling from Lucky's right hand. This was it. Savage was a dead man. Kori's stomach rolled over. "Lucky!" she cried. "Help me sit up," she ordered Acer. Teeth gritted against the pain in her side and back, she muscled her way to a sitting position with Acer's help. The world wobbled in front of her, but pushed through the pain and remained upright.

When Lucky turned, she shook her head. "Don't kill him. Not over me. He's not worth the energy to pull the trigger."

His face was impassive. Did her words register? Was he too far gone into his rage to heed her advice? It wouldn't be his first kill; he'd been a sniper for Christ's sake. But that was different. That was for a purpose, to serve his country, defend freedoms. This would be straight up revenge, outside, in broad daylight. Sure, they were on the No Prisoners' compound, but that didn't guarantee immunity.

He nodded once then turned back to Savage who started laughing like a hyena when Kori asked Lucky to spare his life. Lucky hit Savage's face in an open palmed slap that knocked the laughter out of him. Then he leaned in and said something Kori couldn't hear.

Savage however didn't miss a word and his bloody face paled. He ceased struggling and finally lost some of the overconfident swagger he always employed. It was as though the gravity of his situation just sunk in.

"Bring him around back and toss him in the van with Rebel. We'll deal with them both in a few minutes," Acer told the men holding Savage.

Good. Maybe it was wrong and a bit sadistic, but she preferred him to suffer a little rather than escape with a quick death.

Now that she'd laid eyes on Lucky, knew he was okay, everything that happened in the previous five minutes bubbled up inside of her and the emotional trauma came pouring out of her eyes.

Lucky spun around and started in her direction. Savage was hauled around the side of the clubhouse. Whatever his fate, Kori could wait until later to learn it. What she needed right now was Lucky. To touch him, kiss him, hold him. To cement with her mind and body that he was alive and planned to stay that way.

"Angel," he whispered as he knelt next to her. He cupped her face between his battered hands and pressed a gentle kiss to her lips.

She wanted nothing more than to throw her arms around him and sob in his strong grip until there was nothing left inside her.

But her ribs hurt so bad breathing was becoming a challenge. Instead, she settled for nuzzling her face into his palm.

"We need to get you to the hospital," Lucky said as he rested his forehead against hers.

She shook her head, rocking it against his. "No. I'm okay."

"Your back is ripped to shreds. It needs to be cleaned and bandaged." When she didn't answer right away, he brushed his nose against hers. "Please," he whispered.

The soft plea was her undoing. She'd endangered her life, walked straight into danger, ignored his orders. Anger, yelling, perhaps even the silent treatment was what she expected from him. Not the sad, devastation that shone from his eyes. There was nothing she'd deny him in that moment. "Okay. But you need to go too."

"Baby, I'm not leaving your side for a second. Maybe not ever."

Despite everything that happened, happiness bloomed inside her. She was a fool for doubting Lucky's feelings and worrying over the three little words he'd yet to say. They were just words. He showed her everyday just how very important she was to him.

"I meant you need to go checked out too."

"Well if I'm going to be there anyway…" He shrugged.

Lucky and Acer helped her to her feet as the blaring siren of an ambulance entered the lot. No way was she going through the humiliation of being scooped off the ground by paramedics. Despite how hard she tried to suppress any outward show of pain, a small gasp escaped as she rose. The rib pain was truly excruciating.

"Random attack," Lucky muttered as he slid an arm across her lower back and helped her hobble toward the ambulance.

"What?"

"We were attacked by an unknown assailant, right outside the clubhouse," he said.

Oh, right. Jesus, she hadn't even thought of the need for a cover story. There was a high chance the paramedics would alert the police after questioning them, if they weren't on their way already. "Got it."

She peered over her shoulder and found no sign of Savage. Most of the other guys retreated to the clubhouse and there was no evidence of the violence that went down just moments before.

Unfortunately, it still wasn't over.

Rebel had been MIA since she arrived. Acer said something about him being in a van out back. Would they get out before the cops came?

The real question was, what did they plan to do with Rebel and Savage now?

CHAPTER FORTY-ONE

"All right, sir, the nurse will be in with your discharge papers in the next few minutes." The fresh-faced intern slung his stethoscope around his neck and held out a hand to Lucky.

Sir. Jesus, after the ruckus he caused demanding to be in the same curtained off room as Kori, it was a surprise the physician didn't tell him to fuck off and good luck with his battered face.

Lucky caught Kori's eye as he grasped the doctor's outstretched hand. Her bottom lip was between her teeth as though warding off giggles and her gaze was unfocused from the pain medication. Stubborn woman had tried to be stoic, but didn't stand a chance at hiding the severity of the pain from him.

"Sorry for all the trouble I caused," he said to the doc. He didn't do apologies, but he had been a bit over the top when they first brought him in. Worry for Kori mixed with a healthy dose of anger that she hadn't stayed in the motel room found an easy target in the medical staff. Now that she was more comfortable and he had a chance to cool down, he felt bad for being such a dick.

"No worries, man," the doctor answered. He winked at Kori, earning himself another scowl from Lucky. "I'd act the same way if she were mine."

Lucky frowned. Was this asshole hitting on his woman? He was just about to take back his apology and blast the young doctor when Kori jumped in.

"Thank you, Doctor Coleman. We appreciate everything you've done."

"My pleasure. You two should be out of here in fifteen minutes tops." The doc tossed her a smile then left the room.

The hospital really had gone out of their way to accommodate them. While they weren't willing to break policy and keep him and Kori in the same cubicle, they had given them adjoining rooms and kept the center divider open so it became one big room with two separate plinths. While Lucky regretted not being able to touch her while they examined and cleaned her wounds, he supposed he should be grateful they allowed him to be a witness.

The moment the curtain swished closed, Lucky was off the plinth and across the room. He wasted no time gathering Kori into his arms and pressing soft kisses to her face. She sagged against him, a hitch in her breath the only indication that this was anything more than a hug between lovers.

"How you feeling, angel? And don't give me that fine bullshit. How are you really feeling?" He was careful to keep his hands low on her back. The burning hot asphalt had done quite a number on the skin over her shoulder blades. She'd required extensive and delicate cleaning to care for the road-rash type abrasions and second degree burns that covered her upper back. She also had a fractured rib and quite the colorful array of bruising, including on her beautiful face.

When his work was finished, the physician had rattled off ten minutes' worth of aftercare instructions and bandaging techniques. Lucky had paid close attention, but planned to hand the responsibility off to Lila as soon as they got back to Arizona. Best to leave it to a professional. He wasn't taking any chances that the wounds would become infected.

"Well," she said with a sigh as she drew back and gave him a soft smile. "I'm sore all over, but whatever it was they gave me for the pain really seems to have helped. I'm not too excited about how I'll feel when it wears off."

He swallowed, hard. Part of him itched to be back at the clubhouse doling out punishment to Rebel and Savage. If Kori hadn't needed medical attention, there wouldn't have been a chance in hell he'd have gone to the emergency room. As he suspected, all he had was a busted-up face, mangled knuckles, and a mild knock to the head. He was divided in his desire to be with Kori and his need for revenge. Hearing her admit to being in pain made it all that much harder to resist charging out of the hospital and wrapping his hands around Savage's throat until the man's eyes rolled back in death.

Then he'd move on to Rebel…

"How about you?" she asked in a soothing voice. With one fingertip, she traced the purple swelling under his right eye. Her touch was soft, exploratory. He'd give his left nut to be alone with her and have them both uninjured. There was only one thing that would truly calm the raging waters inside of him and that would have to wait until Kori was feeling better. Looked like he'd have to settle for a little vengeance for now.

"Been worse, baby. Much worse. Don't give it a second of your thought."

She snorted and rolled her eyes. "Tough guy."

"Damn straight." He winked and kissed her. "Where's that damn nurse?"

"Hey, what did you say to Savage? At the end. When I asked you not to…you know."

Kori was quick, not much got by her. She was smart enough to recognize an admission of murderous intentions wasn't a smart move in a bustling city hospital.

"I just let him know how things were now. How his reign was over. No drugs, no money, no club, no friends. Just enemies. Enemies who weren't the type to forgive or forget." He held her gaze, not about to apologize for his vicious statement.

"I want to see him, Lucky."

No point in pretending he didn't understand. She meant Rebel, not Savage. His stomach clenched as his body literally rejected the idea.

"It was part of the deal."

He arched an eyebrow. "The deal? Oh, you mean the deal where you were supposed to wait in the motel room until it was safe for you to come to the clubhouse? That deal?"

A red flush stole across her face. "You're mad."

"Fucking pissed is more like it. But I'm way more worried about you being hurt, so you're off the hook for now. Later though?" He cocked his head and slid his hands down until he cupped her ass. "Let's just say we may revisit the topic when you're feeling better." He gave her cheeks a squeeze then backed away as the nurse entered the room.

Five minutes later, armed with pain medication and a bag full of ointment for Kori's back, they walked out into the hot Vegas sun. Acer waited, resting against the side of a black mustang convertible. Lucky had no idea whose car it was, but he was grateful for it. Kori was in no shape to be on the back of a bike.

"Ready to rock and roll?" Acer asked.

Lucky nodded. "Get us the fuck out of here. I hate hospitals."

"Are we going to see him?" Kori asked.

Lucky lifted their joined hands to his mouth and kissed her knuckles. He studied her for a second. The sight of the lumpy bandages under the scrub top they'd given her after cutting away her shredded tank top made him want to wrap her up and hide her away.

But this was her father they were talking about. A man she never knew existed until a few months ago. A man who'd given her hope for a family then ripped it away in the most ruthless way possible. A man who almost got her killed.

She deserved to confront him, to say whatever was on her mind and to see him pay for his crimes. No, she'd never know exactly what the club planned for him, but she'd at least have some closure. So, while it made him want to tear apart the clubhouse with his bare hands, it wasn't about him, and he'd take her to see her father.

His heart broke a little for her and the loss of her family. But he understood it, having no blood family of his own. This was the first time in his life he was putting a woman's needs before his own and he was good with it. Better than good. Seeing to her needs felt right.

"Yeah, angel, we're going to see him." He glanced at Acer who nodded and moved around to the driver's side of the mustang.

"Thank you," Kori said when Acer was out of earshot. "I know you don't want to do this so I want you to know how much it means to me."

He kissed her, absorbing her surprising strength and sweet flavor. "I just want you to be safe, happy, unafraid. Whatever I have to do to make that happen, I'll do." He kissed her again. Keeping away from her was becoming impossible. They needed to hurry this along so he could take her back to the motel and show her just how grateful he was that Savage hadn't harmed her further. He'd have to be creative due to her injuries, but he loved a challenge and a little natural painkilling chemical in the form of multiple orgasms would do wonders for Kori.

"You two want to break it up any time soon? My woman is a few hours away. It's cruel to get me all riled up like this." Acer rapped his knuckles against the top of the car then disappeared inside.

A giggle snuck out of Kori. "Thank you." She snaked her arms around his waist and squeezed tight, too tight. It had to be straining the abused skin of her back. "I love you," she whispered against his chest.

The answering words burned the tip of his tongue in their struggle to break free, but still he held it back. Maybe it made him an asshole, keeping her in suspense this way, disappointing her. Soon, he'd say it soon. Right after he looked Savage in the eye and told the man who Kori really belonged to.

CHAPTER FORTY-TWO

The muted colors of the vast desert flew by in a blur as Acer navigated them...somewhere. They'd been driving on a two-lane highway into the nothingness for a good thirty minutes. Hopefully it wouldn't be long before they arrived at their destination. The back of her seat pressed against her ruined skin, creating a gnawing pain she wouldn't be able to tolerate for much longer.

She'd tried to sit toward the edge of the seat, but every time they hit a pothole on the poorly maintained road, she'd fall against the backrest. The sharp jolt of discomfort had been so shocking, she'd inadvertently cried out. The resulting panic in Lucky's eyes kept her from trying that position again.

"You sure you don't want to lie down? You can try to lie on your stomach with your head in my lap."

Acer barked out a laugh and Kori giggled as well. The moment of levity felt great, but didn't do anything to wipe the scowl off Lucky's face.

"What the hell's so funny?"

"Dude, she was just discharged from the hospital a half hour ago. Maybe you could give her another twenty minutes or so before you start demanding she shove her face in your lap?"

Kori's giggles turned into a full blown laugh. She couldn't help it. The look on Lucky's face was priceless. It was clear, a blowjob was the furthest thing from his mind at the moment.

Okay, maybe it was never that far from his mind, but he certainly hadn't been requesting one.

"That's not what I meant, dipshit." Lucky smacked the back of Acer's head. The car swerved into the oncoming lane before Acer had it back under control.

"Hey! Don't you think we've had enough drama for one day? You looking to roll the car as well?"

"No. I'm trying to offer my injured woman a way to relax in this rattletrap while you hit every fucking bump in the road. That okay by you? And for the record, I'm telling Fia what an insensitive prick you're being toward an injured woman."

Acer's eyes flashed in the rearview mirror. "You wouldn't."

"Fuck yeah I would."

"Oh, ow! Stop!" Kori clutched her left side as the muscles around her ribs spasmed and tightened. "Don't make me laugh anymore, please."

"See what you did, asshole? Take a deep breath, angel. Ignore this moron. He's just the driver," Lucky said as he ran a hand over her hair.

Both men shut up, allowing Kori time to take a few deep breaths to calm her protesting ribs. "I'm good, I'm good. Whew, you two always like this?"

"Pretty much." Acer said. "All right kids. We're here."

The shenanigans of the past few minutes were the perfect diversion. She hadn't even been aware that the car had rolled to a stop. Lucky stepped out and came around to her side. He helped her rise from the low car and guided her around a smattering of low shrubs until they reached a sandy clearing.

It was a bewildering sight. Six or seven bikers in leather, chains, and heavy boots stood in the sand. Now that she was here, her stomach and her courage took a nose dive. Was she really ready to face her father? Part of her wanted to forget the whole thing, dive back into the car and let the men do what they were going to do. But then she'd never know. Never know if

Rebel really did care about her and was just driven off his path by greed or if he was truly an evil man.

"How you feeling, honey?" Striker's voice startled her from her musings. Geez, his face looked worse than hers. A white bandage stood out against the gross purple swelling of his cheek. A splatter pattern of dried blood coated his T-shirt. Lila was going to freak when she found out he didn't get medical treatment.

"I'm holding up, thank you." The polite answer was all she could manage. Her focus was already on the two men bound by duct tape and kneeling about fifteen feet apart on the sandy ground. Each man's cut lay on the ground in front of them.

Unease snaked through Kori. They were pretty far out into the desert, not a soul in sight besides the group of bikers. No cops, no residences, not even a lone coyote to witness what was to come. It was the perfect place for a grave. Or two.

Swallowing her fear, she ignored everyone and walked the distance toward where her father was, Lucky hot on her heels. He was on his knees in the sand, hands and feet bound by the tape. A strip of tape covered his mouth as well. Sweat ran in rivers down the sides of his face, and a deep V of moisture was visible on the front of his shirt.

He looked old, vulnerable, defeated. Nothing remained of the man who'd threatened her a few weeks ago. The powerful and dangerous MC president had been reduced to nothing more than an old man. Her hands shook so she placed them in her pockets.

"I'd like to speak with him," she said to Lucky. "Can the tape be removed from his mouth?"

"You bet, babe." Lucky walked up to Rebel and ripped the tape off the man's mouth in one swipe. Kori winced and her father grunted, but showed no other signs of pain.

She worked hard to keep her face neutral, impassive, calm. But inside, a jumble of emotions crashed together like bumper cars in a rink. The most concerning and baffling of which was compassion. Why should she feel anything toward this man but hatred? Yet seeing him on the ground like an animal tugged at her heart strings.

Despite everything that happened, he was still her father. Her blood. Someone she'd hoped would fill the hole in her heart her mother's passing had left. Instead, he'd carved out a chunk of her heart and stomped on it. Still, his blood flowed through her veins.

She inhaled a fortifying breath and looked Rebel straight in the eyes. "Are you sorry for any of it?"

"I'm your father. You going to let them kill me and dump my body out here in the desert like trash?" His voice was even harsher than usual, but his non-answer answered her question.

Her nose tingled with impending tears as she realized this was it. This was the last conversation she'd have with her father. Maybe the last conversation he'd have in his life.

She glanced around at the group of angry bikers pretending to give her some semblance of privacy. They all hovered just feet away though and couldn't possibly miss the conversation. "I'm not sure I'd have the power to stop their plans even if I wanted to. But you ignored my question. Are you sorry for any of it?"

"I'm sorry for two things." He sounded as though he'd been snacking on the sand around him. "I'm sorry I let him live." He cocked his head in Lucky's direction. "And I'm sorry I believed your bitch of a mother when she told me she was on birth control."

It was a comment meant to hurt, to pierce her heart, and it hit the mark. Kori used every ounce of concentration to keep from crying. She would not give this man the satisfaction of hurting her one last time. She could cry in Lucky's arms for hours later.

She took another look at the man kneeling in the sand and hardened her heart. All she saw then was a desperate man lashing out, trying to take out as many people as he could on his way down. Any compassion she'd been experiencing evaporated into the parched desert air.

This was exactly what she needed. A few minutes to ensure he was really the monster she'd come to know. Now she could sleep at night without the guilt of knowing she had a hand in harming a man with the potential for good. There wasn't anything good in this man.

She stepped forward and retrieved the sand coated duct tape. With two hands, she stretched it taut and smashed it over Rebel's mouth. "It was much better this way," she whispered. After one last disgusted look at her father, she met Lucky's gaze and gave him a single nod. The she turned her back on the man who'd given her life and walked straight toward the Mustang, head held high. Except for Lucky, the men's attention was on the two bikers in the sand. No one noticed the trembling in her lips or the stray tear that slipped down her cheek.

The engine was still running and she slid into the cool interior. From the position and angle of the car, she couldn't see what the men were doing to Rebel and Savage. It didn't matter. Though no one came right out and said it, the result was obvious. Neither man would walk out of here today. She understood. She just didn't need to see it happen.

Kori jumped when the driver's side door opened and Lucky dropped into the seat.

"What are you doing here? Is it over already?"

He shook his head, put the car in drive and peeled out, throwing up a cloud of dust in their wake.

What was he doing? She'd thought for sure he'd be the one to end at least one of the betrayer's lives. "Don't you want to stay?"

He still didn't speak, so Kori stopped asking questions. Maybe he just needed time to process. Maybe he planned to take her back to the hotel then return to his brothers. Questions danced through her brain, but they could wait. Lucky seemed to need quiet.

After five minutes of retracing Acer's route, Lucky pulled the car to the side of the road and came to a dead stop. He left the engine idling but stepped out and walked around the car. Kori tried not to let her nerves flare, but she failed miserably. What was going through his mind?

Lucky opened her door and pulled her out of the car. He maneuvered her around the open door and backed her up until her ass rested against the hood of the car. What was wrong with him? Her heart pounded so hard in her chest she grew lightheaded. "Lucky, what's wr—"

He cut her off with an unrestrained kiss that knocked the stability right out of her. Her knees buckled and she sagged against him, helpless to do anything but surrender to his ravaging mouth.

Before her head had a chance to stop spinning, Lucky broke away. With her face cradled between his large hands, he stared down at her with an intensity that made her shiver. "I love you, Kori," he said before he kissed her again, brief this time. "I love the fuck out of you."

Kori's insides melted into a puddle of mushy love. The three words she'd been dying to hear sounded even sweeter than she'd dreamed. "What? You do? You're telling me now?"

"It's over, you're free. He has no claim on you, real or imaginary."

"Is he...did you..."

Lucky kissed her cheeks, her nose, her eyes and she sighed with pleasure. "No. I had a quick chat with him. Man to scumbag. About where you belonged, who you belonged to, and where he belonged. I needed him to know he'd lost. Know he never had you, never would have you. It didn't feel right saying it until then. I'm sorry if I made you doubt us."

She put her hand over his mouth. "None of that matters. Just say it again."

He spoke behind her palm, making the sound extra muffled and unintelligible. When she pulled her hand away he winked and she laughed.

"I love you, Kori," he said, all teasing gone.

"I love you too, Lucky." Her heart was full, the hole left by death and betrayal now packed full of love for Lucky.

"Please come back to Arizona with me. For good. Forever. I know you may think your family is gone, but you have a family. A rough, messy, slightly vulgar family, but a family that will always have your back. Me, my brothers, their women. We may not be your blood, but we are family." His voice wavered as though he were nervous and unsure of her answer.

Those words were exactly what she needed to hear. They were a bandage for her wounded soul. "Where else would I go?" she asked as she pulled him down for another passionate kiss, this one full of the love they'd just professed.

EPILOGUE

Lucky leaned back in the unyielding vinyl chair and watched the women oohing and ahhing over the tiny person sleeping next to the bed. The two women were a study in contrast at the moment, one with raven-black hair, tired eyes, and that new-mother glow someone had once told him about.

The other was his own personal angel with her radiant hair flowing around her shoulders and her eyes alight with life and happiness. What the two women had in common besides love for a rough and uncouth biker was that soft, dreamy look all women got when in the presence of a new baby.

"May I hold him?" Kori asked. She'd been begging all morning to come and pay the new parents a visit. Lucky managed to hold her off for a little while, but she'd been far too excited to be denied access to her friend's new family.

"Of course," Emily said. "It's been about ten minutes since he last ate, so he'll probably be awake in a second for another meal anyway."

Both women chuckled. Lucky didn't really get the joke, but he enjoyed the sound of their amusement nonetheless.

Something happened the moment Kori snuggled that baby in her arms. She was a natural, settling little Jackson into her embrace like she was born to. It hit Lucky like a punch to the gut. This could be him, them. At any time. They had every available opportunity ahead of them.

"Pretty powerful shit, ain't it?" Jester asked.

Lucky's friend stood in the doorway, a takeout bag in his hand. "Hey, brother. Congratulations," Lucky said as he stood and slapped Jester on the back. He nudged the bag Jester held. "We could have picked something up for you so you didn't have to leave."

"I kicked him out," Emily said on a laugh. "His hovering was driving me nuts."

"Yeah I could see that. He is kind of a big brute."

The baby chose that moment to let out an ear-piercing wail.

"Ahh, told you he'd be hungry in a minute." Emily extended her arms for her new son.

Before handing the baby over to his mother, Kori flashed Lucky a radiant smile. "We'll get out of here and give you guys some privacy. He's absolutely perfect, Em." She pressed a kiss to the baby's fuzzy head then dropped a peck on Emily's cheek as well.

"This kid wants to eat fifty times a day." Jester accepted a hug from Kori as well. "Smart boy. He knows where the good stuff is. We're starting him off right." He winked at his girlfriend, whose face was now bright red.

Lucky laughed and blew Emily a kiss. "Take care of yourself, momma," he said. "Be good to her, Jester." He shook his brother's hand then slung an arm around Kori's shoulders as they left the new parents.

"Oh my God! Isn't he the cutest?" Kori said as soon as the room door closed behind them. "I just want to squeeze his chubby cheeks." She squealed and did a little shimmying dance under Lucky's arm.

He laughed and tugged her close. Had he ever seen her so elated? Babies were like crack for some women. As they stepped into the bright sun, he slipped on his sunglasses and steered Kori toward his motorcycle. "You want that?" he asked when there reached the bike.

She turned into his embrace and squeezed him around the waist. "Want what?" Her eyes widened.

He inclined his head.

"A baby? Do I want a baby?" Her mouth flapped open and closed a few times. "Well…I guess…I mean…yes. Someday I do. What about you?" She pushed his sunglasses from the bridge of his nose to the top of his head.

"Never really thought about it before, to be honest." He slid his hands into the back pockets of her ass-hugging jeans and pulled her close. "You looked good holding that baby." It was a cop out as an answer, but admitting out loud that watching Kori hold that baby stirred some unknown longing deep inside of him was scary as hell.

She took pity on him, though her smile said she saw straight through him. "Well, I'm still pretty young. No rush for me. You on the other hand, well, you're getting up there in years. A baby might be too much for an old man like you to handle." Her eyes sparkled with mischief and she bit her bottom lip ineffectively suppressing a smirk.

"You calling me old?" He held her still and rocked his ever-present erection against her denim-covered core. She gasped and the teasing in her eyes heated to desire.

"If the shoe fits," she said, her voice dropping an octave and taking on a smoky quality.

"I'll show you what fits." He nipped at her lower lip. "And while I'm at it, I'll show you exactly what this old man can handle."

She giggled as his lips descended to hers. As usual, the kiss turned hungry in a matter of seconds. They clung to each other, uncaring of the fact they were in public, in broad daylight losing themselves in each other.

"Shit," he said as he came to his senses. Another few minutes and the unsuspecting hospital visitors would be getting quite the show. "Hop on, angel. I'll have you home and under me in five minutes tops."

Eyes dazed, she swayed on her feet, his words taking a few seconds to penetrate the lusty fog she appeared to be in. "Oh, right…bike."

He chuckled as she scrambled on and settled in behind him. After securing his helmet, he grasped her hands and pulled them even tighter around his body. Plastered together, they zoomed out of the parking lot and toward the home they'd made together over the past months.

Not every moment had been roses and sunshine. Despite Kori's initial claims that she was fine with her father's fate, it took her some time to come to terms with losing both parents so close together.

Lucky stuck to her like glue and helped her through the rough patches. As a result of all they'd endured, they were strong, solid. An unbreakable bond had forged between them. Never had he imagined life with a woman could be so good. They were comfortable together, like two puzzle pieces that fit with perfect precision.

Yet the intense desire hadn't faded. Not one bit. Even now, his dick was hard as a stone and straining to get inside the woman he loved.

They'd made it through the darkness and came out shiny and new. Lucky wouldn't have it any other way.

Thank you so much for spending some time in the No Prisoners' world. If you enjoyed the book please feel free to leave a review on Amazon or Goodreads.

Join Lilly's mailing list for a **FREE** No Prisoners short story.

www.lillyatlas.com

Keep reading for a preview of **SNAKE**, the next book in the No Prisoners series.

Books in the No Prisoners Series
Hook: A No Prisoners Novella
Striker
Jester
Acer
Lucky
Snake

Trident Ink
Escapades

Hell's Handlers MC
Zach

Lilly Atlas

Maverick
Jigsaw
Copper

SNAKE PREVIEW

"He still alive?" The pissed-off voice cut through Snake's hazy confusion.

"Yeah, bastard makes a wheezy, gurgling noise every so often. I'm surprised he survived the long trip. The big man worked him over good. His face is unrecognizable," a second voice, as well-known as the first, yet not identifiable, said.

"That was Jester," the first man said. The high pitch, almost whiny quality of his voice was familiar, but just on the edges of recognition. In fact, both voices seemed close yet not quite in Snake's reality. Like they were coming from a television. There, but not real.

Pain was there in real time, however. That was for damn sure. But even the hurt was difficult to place. It seemed to come from every pore in his body. But that wasn't possible, was it?

"What's the plan here, Casper?" A third man, also a familiar voice, spoke up.

How did he know these men? Maybe he should say something. Ask for help. With the level of pain, he was experiencing, something was obviously wrong. Snake moved his mouth to speak, but the only noise that came out was a garbled mess of unintelligible sounds.

And then the pain localized.

Holy shit, his face throbbed like it had been pounded repeatedly with a sledgehammer. Inside his mouth, his tongue filled the entire cavity like an air-filled balloon, making speaking near impossible. He drew in a breath, but the air met resistance before it ever reached his lungs, stopped by a throat that felt swollen shut.

Snake's brain registered these things like a laundry list of items, and it recognized that he should probably be in panic mode, but that was as far as it went. Everything else was fuzzy and he couldn't get himself together enough to make sense of his reality.

"Toss him down the ravine. I'll fire a couple slugs in him. See how overgrown it is down there? No way in hell anyone will ever find the body."

It was the higher voice that spoke. Casper, another had called him. God, that name...it was dancing on the edges of Snake's diminishing consciousness. So memorable...

"You got it, boss."

Strong, rough hands landed on his body, jerking him forward and then he was airborne. The weightless flight couldn't have lasted more than five seconds, then came a crushing jolt and the insane sensation of the world spinning out of control.

Laughter sounded from a distance. "Shit, brother. Look at him roll down that ditch like a fuckin' sack of potatoes. You probably don't need to waste any bullets, Casper. No way he survived that. It's what? Thirty feet. And with all those rocks and branches. Something musta smashed in his skull."

"Yeah, well, Snake's a slimy bastard. I want to be one hundred percent sure. Can't have him slithering back into our lives six months down the road," Casper replied.

After what seemed like an eternity, Snake's broken body slammed against something hard and the rolling stopped. His head was still spinning out of control, but at least the physical movement stopped.

He tried to move, but there was a disconnect between his body and his brain. None of his muscles obeyed commands and all he could do was lie there, a giant, unmoving target.

A pinpointed, hot, burning pain bloomed in his thigh, followed by another in his shoulder. Had to be bullets.

Odd.

He'd been shot before and it had hurt a lot more than it did now. His brain must be pretty fucked up not to be registering the pain of two bullets. Of course, the rest of his body was one giant ball of agony. Maybe there was a limit to how much pain the flesh could experience. Maybe after the body hit the pain ceiling, it no longer registered.

He thought he'd known pain before, but it was nothing compared to this full body excruciating sensation. Bullets, a knife wound or two, betrayal. A man didn't live his kind of life without pain.

His kind of life...

Casper.

It was right there. If he could just reach out and grab the fuzzy memories.

"Nice fucking knowing you, Pres."

The words were called out about three seconds before a final hot flash of pain entered his side. Gut shot. The fatal blow.

Pres...

Casper...

As the darkness behind his closed eyes grew even blacker, realization dawned.

President. Of the Grimm Brothers Motorcycle Club. In Sandy Springs, Arizona.

Casper. His long time right-hand man. Close and trusted friend.

Reality faded into the distance, taking some of the pain with it. Would there be peace in death? Not for him. Not going out this way. There were men who had to pay whether now or in the afterlife.

Men like Casper.

His loyal vice president.

A murderous traitor.

About the Author

Lilly Atlas is a contemporary romance author. She's a proud Navy wife and mother of two spunky girls. Every time Lilly downloads a new eBook she expects her Kindle App to tell her it's exhausted and overworked, and to beg for some rest. Thankfully that hasn't happened yet so she can often be found absorbed in a good book.